False Alarm

False Alarm

HEATHER DROHAN

A ZYZZYVA First Book

CREATIVE ARTS BOOK COMPANY
BERKELEY, CA
2000

Cover design: Ingalls + Associates, San Francisco
Cover painting: Timothy Rene Lynn, *Middle of the Road,* 1999,
courtesy: Olga Dollar Gallery, San Francisco.
Author photo: Bob Adler

For information contact:
Creative Arts Book Company
833 Bancroft Way
Berkeley, CA 94710

ISBN 088739-3195
Library of Congress Catalog Number 99-69455

Printed in the United States of America

Acknowledgements

Many thanks to Leslie Crawford, who read and listened from the beginning; Susan Novell Eberts, who has always encouraged me; Julian Guthrie, my friend since 5th grade, who went all out; Belinda Hanson, a great friend and the funniest person I know; my brothers, Stanford and Steven Stallings, for Beta and bathroom fires.

And special thanks to: Gail and Bob Drohan, Gray Drohan, Tom Drohan, Graham Hewson, Donald Hill, Nina LaFleur, Lee Ann La France, Alberta Lloyd, Jerry Martinson, Caroline Paul, Will Rose, Dennis and Leeanne Stallings, and Rob Thomas.

An early version of this novel appeared as my first story in print, a story in *ZYZZYVA* Fall '98. I am grateful for a grant from the Creative Work Fund of the Haas Foundations, which supported my collaboration on this project with *ZYZZYVA*'s editor, Howard Junker, to whom I am grateful for his insight and encouragement.

False Alarm

*K*ate slowed down as she passed the Mission District firehouse. She idled at the stop sign while she sipped a Mountain Dew. Two firefighters wearing tight pants and taut blue T-shirts were hosing down a hook-and-ladder truck in the driveway. Half-naked men with hoses. The snapshot was as suggestive as a Calvin Klein ad. What was Sandy thinking? How could her husband, who'd just made junior partner at his law firm and still had student loans to pay off, want to become a firefighter? If he just wanted to drop out and "dabble"—hang out in coffee shops, occasionally defending the falsely accused—fine. That she could understand. But growing up to be a 35-year-old fireman? Wanting to live with the boys for five straight Rice-a-Roni nights a week, then to drop back into their lives—meanwhile relying on Kate's paycheck?

Kate had toyed with several theories. One was his fascination with fire, and anything related to fire, including chopping wood, which he did in his Home Depot metal shed in the back yard. The fires he assembled in their fireplace were put together with a pride left over from his Sea Scout days on Puget Sound. He lit the fires with a large butane torch, careful never to let their son, Gus, see him do it—like a dog hiding a bone. And when the embers burned down, glowing, he squirted them with kerosene!

The larger of the firefighters squirted his buddy with the hose. Their shouts ramped Kate's headache—floaters did laps around her brain. Maybe she had a concussion: that morning at the Mission Street BART station, someone had hit her in the head with something that felt like a rock out of a sling-shot. She had been waiting at the Mission Street BART station. She'd fallen, skinning her hands and ripping the knees of her nylons on the sidewalk.

Kate suspected a blond Hispanic woman, curvy in hot pants

and stilettos, who had taunted Kate before disappearing behind a Good Humor truck.

"Hey, Red!" she had called.

Kate's hair wasn't really red. It was auburn, and she'd always hated that name.

"Yeah, you with the skin shoes. Looks like you got hit."

The woman—or whomever—had ripped off Kate's purse.

Kate glanced in the rear-view mirror. Her hair was still damp; the bump on her head had lifted it into a tease. She needed aspirin. She was a wreck with no purse, without her notes from last night's SportsCenter, her son's match-box cars, her daughter's favorite bink, and her night guard she was supposed to take to her dentist that day. Kate was a nighttime grinder, and she'd ground a hole through her current night guard. Their dog had chewed the last one, nosing the plastic case off her nightstand, then cracking it open like a clam. Now the dentist would have to make new plates, stretching her mouth with a metal plug, while she chatted her up about what Michael Jordan was really like.

The other fireman retaliated, dumping a bucket of water over the bigger one's head.

Or was it more the hero-thing? At their holiday party last year (dinner for eight at eight), Sandy had lit a fire in the fireplace and smoke had filled the room as Kate passed the salmon mousse. Unbeknownst to Sandy, pigeons had made a nest in the chimney— that's what he told the guests as he evacuated them to the front porch. Firefighting combined heroism and pyromania, that was it. Kate also couldn't help thinking of the homosexual undertone— men sleeping in the same room, the long ride down the fire pole, the well-groomed Dalmatians, the well-groomed mustaches. But she knew these were all excuses. She feared that he wanted to get away from her.

*T*he turquoise paint was chipping off the Edwardian flat where Pinto lived. As Kate went up the short flight of concrete steps, U2 music blasted from inside. She rang the bell for #8. No one came, and 15 seconds later she rang it again. Then she knocked.

She could leave his paycheck and go, but that wouldn't solve her problem: getting him to the lab. So far all the attempts by the boys in the office had failed and her boss, Kingsley Gartmore, had been very specific: "No more foul-ups."

The door was ajar and Kate pushed it open gently. "Hello?" she called, stepping into the foyer. A crucifix and a cheap seascape hung on the walls in the entryway. The carpets were worn and stained, but the furniture was expensive red leather. Everything in the apartment looked oddly humongous—the overstuffed L-shaped couch, the monolithic lamps, the monster-truck speakers. Clouds of steam tumbled out of an open door. The U2 song ended, but someone was still singing along. A shower door clinked. She turned to go—some other time.

"Who the hell are you?"

Kate stopped in the doorway. Little needles tapped along her arms. This job was too hard, she thought. Maybe she could become a firefighter, too.

"I rang—the door was open," she said. She didn't turn around. She heard the rustling of fabric. She pictured Pinto, large as his furniture, struggling to pull on a robe.

"What kinda sorry excuse is that?" he said. "You think you can just walk into a person's private home, just like that?"

"Sorry." She could smell the new leather through his perfumed soaps.

"Betcha no one just walks into your house," he said. "You don't know what that feels like—do you, girly girl?"

Kate stared at the COME AGAIN diner sign on the back of the door and swallowed. Christ's hands on the porcelain crucifix were congealed with bright blood.

Pinto cleared his throat. "I could call the cops," he said. "They'd haul your little ass to jail."

Kate, uncomfortably aware that he was staring at her ass, turned around. She was almost eye level with the top of the maroon towel that was wrapped around his waist. She inched her eyes up to his handsome sharp face; his ears stuck out beyond his wet hair. A diamond-studded crucifix stood out amongst the half-dozen gold chains around his neck, sparkling through a mat of black chest hair. She'd seen him around the office, but they'd never been introduced.

"I have your paycheck," Kate said.

Pinto's mood improved immediately. "Hey, you're that girl from the sports firm," he said, flashing the silver in his teeth. His stomach muscles flinched when he spoke.

"Right," she said. "We've talked on the phone." She stomped her feet on his thin carpet, trying to regain the circulation.

"Nice shoes," he said.

Kate remembered that her cocktail-party shoes, a half inch higher than her other pumps, were supposed to impress him. He undid the towel and shimmied his front side. "Have a seat," he said. "At least let me get some clothes on."

Kate turned quickly, but not before she glimpsed his hulking bare ass.

"You should really be more careful," he called from the bathroom. "I could of shot you by accident."

"Sorry about that," she called sweetly, wondering how many people he'd shot by accident.

The drug test needed to be a surprise. She needed to get him into her car and to the lab at Van Ness and Sutter without a struggle. And do it well before her breasts became so engorged she'd have to plug the pump into the car's cigarette lighter. There was no law against pumping while driving (which she'd done on more than one occasion), but in her opinion it was far more dangerous than open containers (which she'd been meaning to try). It now occurred to her that her babysitter, Consuelo Riviera, was without her own car that day, and Sandy was at a meeting in the East Bay. She would have to pick up the dog at Raul's Pet Palace by four o'clock—Raul had been very specific. Stirling Moss had never been groomed at Raul's, but he was sensitive about having his toenails clipped and the Mission Pet Hospital hadn't been able to hold him down. So in desperation—to avoid the house being completely taken over by late summer fleas—she had checked him into the Palace across town.

On top of that anxiety, she felt a pang of guilt for not attending the book club hosted last night by one of the mothers from Gus's nursery school. She wasn't doing a good job socializing with the other mothers, and she'd been the only mother who had not brought worker-bee cupcakes for the Friday before the Labor Day weekend, and she hadn't remembered to send Gus with a show-and-tell item last Thursday. It had upset Kate more than Gus, but still. I'll go crazy for Halloween, she vowed. She would bring a pumpkin goody bag for each of the 26 children. She would sew Gus a Spiderman costume. Sewing was devotion, she thought. Sewing was mother-of-the-year.

Kate sank into the leather couch, making a whoosh. She played with her wedding ring, a nervous habit. She tried pulling it over the knuckle, as she often did to test if she was still as thin as she was when she got married five years ago. Today she had to tug to get it over the knuckle, chafing her skin. Impossible, she thought, wrenching it back on. She'd lost the baby weight by working out relentlessly—she'd jogged up to Twin Peaks with Camille, her eleven-month-old daughter, in the jogging stroller, subscribed to "fruit before noon," and avoided salt and caffeine (she cheated on the caffeine). What did it take? How hard did she have to work?

Kate looked around the room for any evidence of drug use, but there wasn't even a beer can or an ash tray.

On the glass coffee table were a half-eaten bowl of Fruity Pebbles, six remote-control devices as complex as her HP 12-C reverse-entry financial calculator, and a Game Boy. These guys were as smart as they wanted to be, she thought. Pinto was the bodyguard for Georgie "Porgie" Porshay, the 49ers' flamboyant tight end, and the reason he needed a drug test was because Georgie's mother (!) had insisted that Pinto looked "a tad beady-eyed," one day when he'd picked up Georgie for the airport, barefoot (and intending to drive barefoot), with a bottle of Corona wedged between his thighs.

"O.K., Miss Kate," Pinto said, emerging from the bathroom dressed in black slacks and sports jacket. He looked purposeful, and Kate wondered what he planned to do that day to earn his 100K annual salary. You can start by peeing in a cup, she thought, popping to her feet—the leather had spring!

"Now, how 'bout that paycheck?" he said.

"It's in the car," Kate said. She still had no plan. Did she intend to lift up the hatchback and push him into the Taurus wagon when he wasn't looking?

"I'll escort you," Pinto said, making a dramatic sweep of his arm. He was at the front door in three steps.

Kate jammed her hand into her pocket, squeezing her car keys, taking comfort in the jagged edges. "May I ask you a favor?"

Pinto put up his huge hand, his face back to the who-the-hell-are-you expression. "Not you, too," he said. "I get it. Your boss, Think-tank Gartmore, and his goon, Munger, couldn't get me, so they send bait. If they think Pinto's gonna chase some short skirt to the lab-or-at-ory, they've been out-foxed again. Just look at yourself."

Kate stared at her sandals. They were metallic colored—too flashy for a business suit in the middle of the day.

"I thought a smart girl like you was above that."

Well yes, Kate thought, she'd walked into his apartment wearing her vamp shoes, but it still made her angry: if J.P., the marketing director of her firm, had arrived unannounced—even if he'd been shirtless, wielding his overdeveloped pecs (breasts, Kate liked to think of them)—he wouldn't have been scolded. No, she thought, he would have been shot.

"I'm sorry," she said, but the corners of her mouth curled up—the thought of J.P. shot in the ass in one of his Armani suits.

"You're always sorry," Pinto said. "Looks to me like you're cracking up."

"I'll go get your paycheck." She turned, swallowing giggles. She hurried to the front door. It was illegal to withhold a paycheck—she'd have to think of something else.

"Wait a minute, *mi amor*," he said. "I like a woman who laughs easy. I got nothing to hide."

Pinto sat next to Kate in the passenger seat with his knees almost up to his chest. It was three o'clock as they passed the corner where she'd been hit. It could have been downtown Guadalajara. Everything was for sale, but all the signs were in Spanish. You could buy firecrackers at the corner *groceria* and a social security number at the *farmacia,* if you knew how to ask.

Kate was getting nervous about the wrath of Raul if she didn't pick up Stirling by four o'clock. "Mind if we pick up my dog on the way?" she asked Pinto.

"What kinda dog you got?"

"He's a Gordon setter," Kate said. "Like an Irish setter, but black and tan."

"Not so dumb as the Irish, I hope?"

Kate considered her bird dog's latest bumble: Sandy, who liked to envision Stirling Moss in a Norman Rockwell pheasant hunt, would never be persuaded that the dog wasn't brilliant; last weekend, they'd entered him in a Gordon setter field trial in a wooded area outside Sacramento. They let him loose amongst the long frozen grass and skeletons of fruit trees to "test his instincts"—but Stirling was disqualified—he ignored the birds and quickly mounted a female dog. There's your proof that the elevator doesn't go all the way up, Kate thought. But Sandy insisted that the dog was having sinus trouble. Nothing that a $2,000 operation and daily sinus tablets (Kate fed him the tablets in fingerfuls of cream cheese) wouldn't cure. The dog was also taking a new medication, Clomicalm, for anxiety; Kate needed an Excel spreadsheet to administer it (also in fingerfuls of cream cheese). The half-tablet was to be increased by a quarter tablet every other week, until an "equilibrium" was reached, whatever that was.

They idled at a stop light. It was a flea market on the sidewalk; the amateurs were out—blue-haired women snapping pictures, teenage boys in cut-off jeans sucking on cans of Budweiser. It smelled of hot tar, cotton candy, and greasy Chinese food. At a hot dog cart—*Peros Calientes!*—Kate noticed a woman in hot pants and roller blades eating a hot dog. Over her arm she wore a black Coach purse with a gold buckle.

Kate stopped the car. "That's her—that's my purse!"

Pinto jerked his head. "Her? No way, that's Kim Novak. She's a fun girl."

"I'm pulling over," Kate said. *Kim Novak?* "Like the movie star?"

"I'll handle this." Pinto jumped from the car before Kate could object. First, her purse gone, now her chance at "no more foul-ups" gone. The news that Kim Novak was a "fun girl" particularly annoyed her.

The light turned green and Kate pulled over into a bus zone. She watched Pinto approach the woman; her lips curled into a purple smile of recognition. They chatted, him touching her on the arm, her looking over at Kate and waving. Then she skated away with Kate's purse, weaving through the crush of humanity.

Pinto climbed back in the car. "She says that's her purse."

"Don't you think a Coach purse is a little conservative for her?" Kate asked, pulling back into traffic. "She looks like a stripper with a lunch pail."

"I dunno, I just took her to dinner once."

"Trust me, she's into zippers," Kate said, then, "You dated her?"

"Maybe it was a concert—I might be confusing her with Batwoman."

"You dated Batwoman?"

Pinto was rummaging in the side pockets. "Got any food in here?"

"Try the glove box," Kate said. There was no time to deal with her purse now. If traffic was this bad to Market Street, they were going to be late for Raul.

Pinto opened the glove box and pulled out a jar of Skippy peanut butter and a box of Ritz crackers. Emergency snacks for the children, Kate called them, but really the kids weren't that crazy about peanut butter and she was the one who ate it by the tablespoon.

"So, are you an athlete, too?" Kate asked. "You've got the longest legs."

"I'm a businessman," he said, digging a Ritz into the peanut butter. The jar was getting low and he could barely fit his hand inside. "Why is it," he went on, "if you're over six-five, everybody thinks you play ball. Makes me feel cheap, you looking at my legs like that. What if I say to you—you got nice legs, you must be a body-builder?"

Kate tugged at the hem of her skirt so it covered more of her thighs.

"You know your knee's bleeding, don't you?" Pinto said, handing her a Kleenex from a box on the dashboard.

"Fuck," Kate said, grabbing the tissue and pressing it over her knee. She had to quit swearing. Jennifer Popkins, the office bookkeeper, carved hatch marks for cuss words by the name of each employee in her top desk drawer. So far, Kate was winning.

Pinto was looking at her legs. "How much you squat?" he asked.

"I don't squat."

"See how it feels?" He slapped his knee. "You know, we don't see too many ladies in this business. Betcha meet a lot of big boys."

"I'm more like the office wife," she said, turning onto Fillmore Street. "I don't get out much."

Pinto whistled, but his whistle sounded more like the sucking sound a straw makes at the bottom of a McDonald's Coke—peanut butter was stuck to the roof of his mouth. Kate wondered if peanut butter had some quality that masked marijuana and other drugs in urine. That thought made her breathe hard. She was not in the business of deciphering the effects of peanut butter in urine. If they wanted an expert, they should have brought in Vice.

"They should let you out more," Pinto said, his hand deep in the Skippy jar. "I don't understand a word of what Mr. Gartmore says. And that get-up he wears"—Pinto whistled, but it was only a peep—"brown socks with a navy suit."

"They bury me." She honked at a jaywalking dowager with a miniature schnauzer in a jewelled collar. She was angry that she was feeling angry again, and she couldn't feel her fingertips. She was numb around the mouth. "I'm doing laundry while they're all out hustling new clients—like Pedro Araguz."

"Old Pedro's tired of the jock-sniffers."

"You know him?" A silver Jag pulled out of the spot directly in front of Raul's. Maybe her luck was changing.

"Sure—he stops by for a pick-up game now and then. You should call him up."

Kate recalled the latest spread in *Sports Illustrated* about the famous wide receiver. Pedro Araguz, a legend at 33, turning up his straight nose (a nose so elegant and Argentine) at a mob of college girls.

"Me? Call him?" Kate backed into the parking spot with uncharacteristic ease. Such slick parallel parking, she hoped, was not lost on Pinto.

Pinto brushed crumbs from his shirt into his cupped hand. "Why, sure—call him," he said, "he likes a girl with balls. Tell him I said we should get together at my place for a six-pack. I'll even spring for the Coronas—usually he brings 'em—he can afford it."

"He likes a girl with balls."

Pinto patted her on the back. "Let me give you his number,"

he said. He found a pen in her glove box and wrote his number on the box of Ritz crackers.

Kate looked over his shoulder—415 area code. Pedro lived right in San Francisco. Finally, her nose to the grindstone, scrubbing the minutae with a toothbrush, she had stumbled onto a lead.

She turned off the engine. "Does Pedro have a bodyguard?"

"*O si, como no!* Pedro don't need it," he said. "He's my friend. Friends do things for friends."

She'd insulted him. He worked the meddlesome details, just as she did. She was, really, Kingsley's bodyguard—keeping him in his protected world, hoping for just one ovation of her own.

Raul pressed an intercom button. "Margarite, Stirling Moss's mommy is here." He turned to Kate. "Your pet is awful."

Raul went on, eyeing Kate's hair, "He needs his claws snipped and another comb-out, but it's going to take us two days, and certainly thrice the price." He glanced up at Pinto, who then turned to examine a fur-tonic display.

Kate pulled her fingers through the tangles in her hair and felt the goose egg where she'd been hit. She didn't dare ask what that price would be. Exhausted from the ordeal of getting the appointment and driving across town and determined to stop the fleas from nipping at her ankles while she slept, she didn't care. "When can I pick him up tomorrow?"

"Mrs. McCabe," Raul said, pushing up the fashionable wire frames that had fallen onto his nose. "This is a salon, not a hotel. Please bring him back tomorrow during business hours—that's ten to four."

Pinto poked Kate in the shoulder with his finger. "No self-respecting dog would show his face in a place like this," he said as twin toy poodles with red bows under their chins trotted out of the back. Raul, greeting another mommy with a sad-faced chow, pretended not to hear.

Then Stirling Moss—all 90 pounds of him—sprang out of the back, straining the leash held by a white-jacketed attendant.

"Sit!" Raul snapped, and Stirling halted to attention.

A mustached gentleman with a well-behaved Rottweiler in

tow held the door open for them.

Pinto coughed. "Betcha that one wears clip-ons," he said as they left the Palace. The chow's mommy, who was testing a pet deodorizer on her wrist, turned crimson underneath her polka-dotted hair scarf.

*K*ate pushed through the revolving door first. On the other side of the glass, Pinto shoved his big hands into the front pockets of his slouch pants and squinted at the nurse behind the reception desk. Kate waved her arm at him. *Come on!* She hadn't gotten him this far to have him back out now. It was cold—the icy air-conditioning crawled down her shirt—but she wiggled out of her suit jacket stubbornly and draped it over her arm.

Pinto pouted his lip and slammed the revolving door with his shoulder like a three-hundred-pounder hitting the blocking sled. He emerged even paler than he'd looked through the glass. Kate took his arm gently. "This'll be quick," she whispered.

He scowled and ran a hand through his shaggy black hair. "*Sí, como no,* Miss Kate."

The clinic's vast lobby was neon white. An antiseptic smell hung on the air-conditioning. The only sounds were the hum of the fluorescent lights and the crackle of the plastic wrap that the tight-lipped nurse was peeling off her sandwich.

Kate was uncomfortable in clinics. The week she started high school, her freshly divorced mother had gone to work at Planned Parenthood to counsel pregnant teens. Kate visited her there after school, and her mother, while spinning urine in a noisy machine, would mouth the names of the girls who were pregnant: Sara Perkins, Kate's former babysitter—she'd run from the lobby upon seeing Kate's mother; Hillary Michaels, in Kate's homeroom at Lewis & Clark High School; and Violet Tremain, from Kate's old Campfire Girl troop—she claimed to be pregnant by Mr. Reed, the Spanish II student-teacher.

Kate's mother assumed that Kate was having sex, and she left bowls of colored condoms around the house like party balloons. Kate had been a little put off by the flip charts of the female anatomy that her mother kept in the kitchen, where she practiced her lectures to Kate and her girlfriends, pointing out the cervix and the Fallopian tubes with the salad tongs.

Pinto finished signing the clipboard and pulled a bag of Corn Nuts from his pants. He tossed a handful into his mouth. The crunching that followed caused the nurse to look up from her ham sandwich. "He can't do that in here," she said, her mouth full of food. She pushed back a strand of dark hair that had escaped from her hair bun. Bits of lettuce and mayonnaise were stuck between her manicured fingers.

"Shhh," Kate said to Pinto as she handed the nurse the requisition form. The nurse pushed her sandwich aside and time-stamped the form. She continued to stamp it, violently, as if whacking moles.

The nurse attached Pinto's paperwork to another clipboard, then slapped a bell on the counter. An enormous man with a shaved head burst through the swinging doors. Lifting the clipboard off the counter, he asked, expressionless, "Hi, I'm Jim, which of you is Pinto?"

Pinto raised his index finger.

"Both of you follow me," Jim said, twirling his stethoscope.

They followed him through the swinging doors. Jim shuffled along with his head down, his tennis shoes squeaking on the linoleum. Patients wearing bandages on their arms floated by, balancing tiny cups out in front of them. Jim stopped at the water cooler and yanked a Dixie Cup from the dispenser. "We're outta sterile cups," he said, handing it to Pinto. "But this is about the same thing."

Jim pointed to a closed door. "There's the men's restroom," he said. It was the type of restroom found in nursing homes and institutions. The door looked like the self-closing variety that you couldn't open to escape quickly—the type you couldn't slam.

"We have a men's restroom and a women's restroom," Jim went on like a flight attendant on his safety spiel. "The women's restroom is not your concern. Do not touch anything, especially if it's marked 'danger'—that's *peligro*," he said, louder.

"First, you need to urinate in the can, then you wipe yourself off with this, cuz we don't know where it's been." He handed Pinto a packaged alcohol swab from the pocket of his lab coat. "Then urinate in the cup. Do *not* fill it up all the way." He turned to Kate and held the clipboard up to her eye level. "You need to watch him complete this procedure and initial here that he followed the rules." He pointed to the "witness" box on the form.

Kate glanced back at the men's bathroom—the **MEN** in all caps with a droopy **E**—then at the blurred fine print on the clipboard. "Oh, noooo," she said. "I got him here—that's your job."

"I don't do that," Jim said. "The witness is required to watch or the results will be read as invalid."

"The nurse, then," Kate said, looking over her shoulder toward the swinging doors.

Pinto laughed, cutting the sealed air. The fluorescent light sparked his shiny teeth. "They shouldn't have sent you, Miss Kate." She could barely understand him through his hysteria. He wiped at his eyes with his fingers.

Jim flipped to the last page of the clipboard. "Who's KM?"

This time Kate held up her finger.

"I see you initialled that you read and understood the rules. Rules are rules. It's a policy, the way it is when Sears has a policy. You're either the witness or you come back later with another witness and start over."

Kate looked at the slick floor. If Pinto failed the drug test and Georgie Porgie's mother fired him and Georgie fired Sports Financial...his revenue would be deducted from Kate's client-revenue-basis, if and when they let her in the Get-That-Man! race.

She had been their last chance. The *closer*, she liked to think. With Kingsley incapable and J.P. having "washed his hands" of Pinto, she was sent in to clean up. But even when Kingsley gave her a client-contact (or a client-contact once removed), he was still having her clean the company toilets.

"All right—let's do it," Kate said, lifting the clipboard out of Jim's hand. She yanked open the restroom door. "After you," she said to Pinto.

Pinto was still giggling; his huge shoulders bounced as he strolled in.

Kate pressed her back up against the far wall as Pinto unzipped and prepared to piss in the Dixie Cup. She cleared her throat and tapped the clipboard. "You skipped the first two steps," she said. "Pee and wipe." As a mother of young children, this felt natural; it was the way she cut everyone's meat into bite-sized pieces.

Pinto shook his head, ripping open the alcohol swab. "You're tough," he said, glancing back at her over his shoulder and grinning. "Aren't you going to come over and get a better look?"

"You're on the honor system." She didn't imagine him as the type to pack apple juice, but she had a responsibility. She watched the sturdy stream of pee flow into the urinal and echo off the walls; she held her head at the perfect angle, the way a movie camera filmed sex scenes while hiding the body parts.

"Why'd the old lady fire the last guy?" Pinto asked.

"Smoking pot."

"Wow, they'll fire you for anything." He was still peeing.

"Wait! Stop!" Kate said, lunging for him, then stopping herself and backing up to the wall. "You won't have enough for the cup."

"Oh," Pinto said, dribbling, then dripping. Then nothing.

Kate waited.

"I don't think I can go any more," he said, still straddled over the urinal, shaking off with jerks of his elbow. "We'll have to wait. Unless you want to go for me." He held out the cup.

Kate stumbled and her feet slid out in front of her and her butt hit the linoleum. "Tell me I didn't do all this for nothing," she said, as Pinto zipped up and reached out to help her. Kate waved him away. "It's going to be positive, isn't it?"

Pinto pulled out the package of Corn Nuts and poured the remainder into his mouth. "Have faith, *mi amor*."

Kate pulled herself up, shoes pinching her toes, resolved to stay for the duration. Something in the way he looked at her and crushed the empty bag of Corn Nuts in his hand told her he would pass. Everyone wanted him to pass—Georgie, Kingsley, J.P., and, really, Mrs. Porshay—but in a darker place in herself Kate knew that she'd been an *enabler*.

*K*ingsley Gartmore loved football. He wanted to play, but the boys, even at Princeton, were too big, and he didn't have the killer instinct—so he joined the swim team instead. But he found the mechanics of football fascinating: the fact that players could legally assault each other on the field meant they needed help in a lot of other areas.

He had a master's in economics and a natural way with investing. He'd never worked for a big firm; instead he'd set up out in the boondocks, in Clear Lake, California, and managed to get a handful of clients and even a few broken-down athletes. He worked out of a small cabin in the middle of some farmland where sheep grazed outside his window. He rarely met the clients until his wife got bored and found them a place three hours south in San Francisco.

A week before the market crashed in October '87, Kingsley observed some quality in Chairman Greenspan's voice—and moved all of his clients into cash. The clients bitched and moaned, but only until they noticed the miracle that had come their way. Then the broken-down athletes, who would have been a lot more broken-down, told athlete friends who weren't so broken-down, and one referral led to another.

Kingsley did one thing very well. It wasn't managing people, so he hired a lieutenant whom he'd watched win $55,000 on *Jeopardy*.

When Kingsley made hiring decisions, he didn't consider résumés; he might hire an ex-ballplayer to man the reception desk using the same criteria that he used to select stocks: fundamentals. Past performance was no indication. Deacon Durkin, the *Jeopardy* winner, struck him as fundamentally sound. He thought that anyone who could compile an encyclopedia of useless information and catalog it in their head and still be able to carry on a normal conversation, must have a lot on the ball.

Deacon, who did have a lot on the ball, hired J.P. Nevin to sell.

Kingsley had met Kate on a fuel dock when he was in Anchorage for a fishing trip: she was auditing one of the canneries.

At first Kate had turned down the offer—she was looking for a firm with a track record of promoting women—but then Kingsley had met her for lunch wearing a threadbare suit too tight in the shoulders, a Hawaiian tie, and a Bic pen clipped to his breast pocket. When the waiter had brought a tray of orange rolls, Kingsley knocked them all to the floor, and Kate had felt that he needed her.

By that time Deacon had already hired Peter the Red, a sales guy who had played college baseball. Then the screwballs snowballed and the Dow went higher, the clients' memories got shorter, and the office pranks got stranger. When Kingsley opened his office door on April Fools' Day, 1998, he was besieged by barn animals and Peter the Red squealing in his office down the hall.

By then, it was four-to-one, boys-to-girl, and the boys were a fraternity who talked the talk and wore their ambition—and their old high school letters, if they had them—on their sleeves. Kate knew that the good news was that she was a woman, and the bad news was that she was a woman. They wouldn't be hiring any more women; they regarded her as curious, tiptoeing around her as if she were guided by the phases of the moon; they looked confused when she wore pants or pulled a lipstick out of her purse; sometimes she caught them inspecting the Kleenex box on her desk as if it were from Venus.

"There," Kate said, slapping the lab results on Kingsley's giant green desk. Various baseball paperweights secured stacks of papers around his feet, which were propped up on the desk.

Kingsley recoiled from the sound. He rubbed his gaunt face— Skull, they called him. J.P. sat on the sofa thumbing through *Auto Week,* while Deacon squatted in the corner, fiddling with the dials on an old TV. There were two old sets in Kingsley's office: he used one for sight, and one for sound.

"He passed!" Kate said, slipping into a guest chair. And so did I, she thought. "And I've got some big news." She couldn't wait to tell them she'd gotten a line on Pedro Araguz.

The drop of Deacon's mouth as he tuned in the six o'clock news told her that this was the wrong time to bring home her report card. Her timing was notoriously bad. There was the time in high school when her mother hit a dateless plateau; Kate saw a strange car in the driveway and flung open her mother's bedroom door: "So mom, who's the guy—"

Kingsley lifted the edge of the folder with an Ichabod Crane finger. "If we all only had such goals," he said, shaking his head, tsk tsk tsk. Kate knew that he meant Pinto's goal: clean urine (which really wasn't Pinto's goal at all), but somehow it made her feel small. Her goal had been getting Pinto to pee in a cup, while Kingsley's goal was investing the zillions that poured into the firm, and J.P.'s goal was bringing in the zillions. It was all very clear.

Kate looked at the coffee cup full of Diet Pepsi on the desk, a fat bulb-shaped bat, bigger than the bulbous-nosed player who held it, and she wanted to let them run the place without her. Let's see them print from their laptops, she thought, a task so perplexing to them that it seemed to get her the most applause, no matter what else she accomplished. Her tasks kept piling on, and when Kate complained—"I can't do it all"—they flattered her, sending her e-mail high fives. They liked the crisp way she stapled the weekly reports and brought life back to their frozen computer screens. They couldn't live without her, and Kate, needing to be needed, had a hard time saying no.

Kingsley's feet were in front of Kate's face. Although both shoes were of the tasselled variety and equally scuffed and worn, one was black and one was clearly navy blue. Her job assignment from the last meeting had been to spruce him up. There wasn't going to be a *My Fair Lady* situation here, Kate knew. They'd set her up to fail.

"Well, fine, Kate," Kingsley said, slamming the folder shut.

"Fine?" Kate said. "I've got Pinto's piss on my hands, and you say fine." She stormed to the door. She would go home to her kids, to Sandy assembling Gus's fire-truck puzzle in the living room, and to Stirling Moss, who needed her most of all.

"We're having a PR problem," Kingsley called to her.

Kate paused at the door. "We're always having a PR problem," she said. Still, she was interested, and peeked over her shoulder at the sight television: Peter the Red was shoving Randy Nester, the Bay Area megalo-agent, and two 3-Com Park officials in heavy yellow raincoats pulled him away.

They played it in slow motion. They played it backwards. Then, the worst part: "Kingsley Gartmore is a prince of a guy!" the now beet-faced Peter the Red shouted. "He's the best! Don't forget that!" Deacon turned the sight set off, but the sound set still had Peter yelling, "Kingsley Gartmore is a prince of a—" He turned that off, too.

Kate, realizing that this was unusually bad, began to feel sorry for Kingsley. She stepped back into his office and sank into the ratty green couch that, according to Kingsley economics, had intrinsic value because Joe Montana had slept on it during college. "The game must have been a little slow today," she said.

From across the coffee table Deacon gave her a little wave. "You look lovely," he said, winking. "Always nice to see you in navy."

Kate crossed her legs at her bloody knee and smiled. His mother told him he was cute once, she thought, and he believed it.

Kingsley slapped his forehead with his open hand. "How can I divorce myself from this?"

Randy Nester worked across the Golden Gate in an office with satellite TV and bullet-proof glass. In addition to negotiating contracts for his clients, he managed their money, a dual role that Sports Financial considered a conflict of interest at best, if not flat-out illegal. A snake, Kingsley called him, slithering around in the gray areas of securities laws.

Deacon shined his tortoise-shell glasses on his pants leg. "We need to fire him, and fast," he said. "People might think you wanted the plug."

"Not like this," Kingsley said. "We need to practice delayed gratification."

Kate thought Kingsley was one of the few who did practice delayed gratification, waiting—at least 48 hours—before deciding to purchase office equipment costing over $200. The office artwork was limited to photographs of him hanging with the firm's best clients. He looked oddly out of place, like Bogey in a Pepsi commercial; his ghostly face appeared pasted under the athletes' cavernous armpits. And then there were the photographs contributed by his wife, an accomplished amateur, black-and-whites of aging athletes, octogenarians riding hang gliders.

J.P. dropped the *Auto Week* into his lap. "I think he's gotta go," he said. "Nester's gonna be all over this."

Kingsley hefted the bulbous-nosed cup to his mouth, then crunched the ice unpleasantly. He'd never stand up to J.P. It was still his firm—he was the 100% shareholder—but J.P. could call him names and hang out in sports bars during the day and fly first class and watch three hotel movies at night and drink from the mini-bar all because he brought in clients. J.P. hung with the athletes on dusty back porches in their home towns, shooting groundhogs in the brush with heirloom shotguns. His relationships with them were mother-daughter: he was the mediator of family disputes, social planner, confessor, and stand-in best man (if the best man got too drunk at the bachelor party). He could explain away a market correction and describe how a bond worked, in layman's terms, and scold them about their cellular phone bills.

"Hold on," Kate said. She had a soft spot for Peter and knew that his baseball players were the bread and butter of the firm. "Let's talk to him and recommend counseling for his temper. He doesn't have a non-compete. He's going to walk with our baseball players."

Kingsley had made his mark being a bottom-line guy and, when presented with a situation that had financial repercussions, brought out his HP 12-C like a soap-on-a-rope. Though he didn't need the 12-C—he could do long division in his head—he practiced trust with verification.

Kingsley crunched the HP buttons while he smoothed his comb-over with the palm of his hand. "Let's first see what he has to say," he said, slipping the HP back in his breast pocket, tenderly, as if tucking it in for a nap. "I'll put a call in to the labor lawyers, then I'll leak it to the press that we have him in therapy. But he can't blow his stack anymore—never. Find him a shrink, Kate."

"I think he's way past couch-time," J.P. said, who was always looking for an excuse to fire someone. "I can call up his guys and ask if they saw him on the news. Once they know what a nut-case he is, they'll stay with us."

"You're wrong and we'll be poor come bonus time," Kate said. The Super Bowl bonus was on everyone's mind. Kingsley planned to pay double last year's total bonuses to the man who brought in the most client-revenue by Super Bowl Sunday. Kate assumed she wasn't included.

"So what's your big news?" Deacon asked her.

Kate saw that the tie he wore today had a volleyball theme, tasteful at first glance, $140 at Neiman-Marcus, but if you looked closely at the paisleys, they were really blond Kewpie dolls in bikinis.

She shrugged. "The pissing contest was all," she said. She knew that she shouldn't say "piss" or "pissing," not until she could pee her name in the snow on the firm's annual ski trip, anyway.

O n her way back to her desk, Kate passed Peter's office. His desk was tidy: nothing was in the trays—in or out—the blotter was crumb-free. He was clean and neat, Kate thought, bordering on compulsive. She was clean but not neat, while Sandy was neat but not clean. When he was a bachelor, Sandy kept the coffee cups in his cupboard at forty-five degrees, but they had dried puddles of coffee at the bottom, because who put anything in them but coffee? Clean but not neat was the essence of herself; she had enjoyed the pantyhose confusion of her drawers, until she had had children and became neither clean or neat, which started out at home where she allowed the children to eat spilled Fruity Pebbles off the floor and now extended to her office where she recklessly ate poppy-seed bagels over her keyboard.

Photographs of Peter with his Sun-Devil teammates, taken a dozen years earlier, hung on the walls. On his filing cabinet he had lined up a dozen bottles of supplements: Vitamins A, C, and E, garlic tablets, copper, soy, licorice root, Omega 3 & 6, iron, zinc drops, and a slippery bottle of flaxseed oil. He was obsessed with avoiding free radicals.

Kate flipped open his Lincoln High School yearbook, 1973 Badgers. A paper clip marked the page with Peter's senior portrait. At 18, he had had a full head of strawberry-blond hair. His eyes looked small behind puffy cheeks; he seemed to have a completely different set of tiny teeth. Under his name it read "Sweet talker."

The American Medical Reference sat on top of his monitor. Kate slid into his chair and flipped it open to the index. Numbness. She was surprised it had ten listings. She told herself that that wasn't unusual. Many things caused numbness, although right then she could only think of aneurysms and blood clots. Tingling. There were only three listings, but still three!

She turned to the pages listed under numbness and read about several neurological diseases. Her legs were getting more numb as she read. She squeezed her toes to keep the tingling from shooting up her calves. She cross-referenced tingling to numbness and found multiple sclerosis. Just the night before, she'd seen a commercial for MS—you didn't know when it would strike. The young woman in the commercial couldn't pick up her baby, because her arms were too numb! Kate read on. *The disease strikes young adults ages 28 to 40*—she was right in there at 31. *Numbness, tingling, and other unusual sensations.* Her fingertips had felt wet that afternoon, while waiting for Pinto to pee. *Affects eyesight.* And what about those floaters doing laps around her brain? She'd seen them even before she was hit on the head—she'd convinced herself that they were flakes of mascara sitting on her contact lenses. *Frequent urination.* The sound of running water always did it for her; when she stood by the fountain in the office lobby she'd barely make it to the bathroom upstairs. She pictured herself in a wheelchair. She needed to call Sandy, no, the doctor. *No cure, but early intervention....* She found her family doctor's listing in a phone book under Peter's desk.

"Dr. Epman," he answered. She couldn't believe it. It was six o'clock, and she'd expected to have to leave a message.

"As long as you don't wake up numb and go to bed numb, I don't worry about numbness," he said.

"You don't think I need to come in?"

"Not unless you're numb all day." He tended to be abrupt, as if he had things to do that were more serious.

"Thank you, doctor," Kate said, much more cheerfully than she felt. She hadn't gotten to the part about tingling, but it was such a silly word. What was *tingling* anyway? It almost sounded sexual. "You've made me feel better," she said.

"Always glad to help," he said, then clicked off.

Kate pulled the box of Ritz crackers out of her new purse, an old burlap book bag with no pockets (now who would steal that!) and set it on her desk. *4156778299* Pinto had written with no dashes. Trendy, Kate thought, but not surprising. Once, Georgie Porshay had sent her a tailor's name from the Tall Man's Store and had written out the phone numbers in longhand: four one five eight.... Why he took the time to do that, and wouldn't take the time to sign his tax return, she would never understand.

Kate picked up the phone. But she waited too long to dial,

and the operator came on. She hung up and stared at the phone number again. Pedro's phone number was a gift. How many salespeople were lucky enough to get Pedro Araguz's private number? She looked around Peter's office, then swiveled in his chair. This was where he called clients, she thought, which somehow put her at ease. She would assume Peter the Red's m.o.: don't think, don't answer unasked questions, never get embarrassed. Her book *I Hate Selling* highly recommended phone selling. Less can go wrong. *Remember, the client can't see you! Are you still wearing polyester suits?*

Kate picked up the phone again. *Maintain a powerful physiology.* Kate threw her shoulders back. *Make snap decisions. Practice making snap decisions. Don't dally in front of a menu. Glance at it, then order the special.*

Kate thought that the snap-decision part was going to be hard for her; she agonized about wearing open-toed shoes at the office and never made the right decision about bringing an umbrella. She didn't know what she would say, but did Peter ever prepare for a cold call? And this call wasn't cold—they had a mutual friend (would she refer to Pinto as her friend?)—this call was lukewarm.

Three rings. Kate held her breath.

"Yo," a sleepy voice said.

You have his total attention.

"Oh no, I hope I didn't wake you," Kate said. Kingsley, Deacon, and J.P. marched past the open door. She waved her fingertips at them, smiling.

"Laura?" he said with a slight accent, one difficult to place. Kate thought of Buenos Aires—though she had never been there—violent, seductive, at the dark mouth of the Rio de la Plata with its jagged rivers and castles jetting out over slums, eating cake with enclaves of fair-haired Germans. But of course his accent was Spanish, though Castilian Spanish—stubborn bullfighters and naked beaches. "I thought you were here," he said.

The office front door slammed shut. "No," Kate said, breathing. "It's Kate—"

"Damn, I must have fallen asleep." Silence. He was trying to place the name, then, "Kate?"

He can't see you!

"I'm sorry, this is Kate McCabe. We have a mutual friend,

Pinto—," For the life of her, she couldn't remember Pinto's last name. He was always just Pinto. Pinto needs money, PINTO=ASSHOLE on a Post-It from Kingsley on her computer monitor. She was usually good with names and had tricks for remembering them. As a cocktail waitress in college she'd been a whiz at remembering which drink went with which customer. A gin fizz went to the man with an Afro who looked as if he had a bad hangover. Surely, Pinto's last name had been on the drug-testing form that she'd signed—declaring under oath, for permanent record, and copied to Mrs. Porshay—that she'd observed Pinto pee into a Dixie cup. But she couldn't remember ever seeing his last name. Was Pinto like Madonna?

Pedro's laugh crackled with sleep. "How's ole Pinto doing?"

"Very well," Kate said, unclenching her hands. Better now, she thought. Pedro was nice. Rare for superstars. She hated to tell him: she was just someone else who wanted something from him.

"So how do you know Pinto?"

"We share a client."

Pedro sighed. "What are you selling, Kate?"

He wasn't hanging up, Kate thought. Pedro's tired of the jock-sniffers, Pinto had said. Pedro sounded as if he was lying on his back, stretching. She needed to keep him awake.

"I'm not really selling," Kate started, though of course she was. She wouldn't think of the pain and suffering of rejection. She needed to "test their personal chemistry." *Are you comfortable with the prospect?*

Kate went on, "Pinto just thought that I—we—were doing a good job managing his investments and he thought you might need a hand." Of course Pinto didn't think this, Pinto probably thought they were in the business of testing urine. Was it impossible to sell without lying?

"Pinto—investments?" Pedro giggled. "Maybe under his mattress. Really, what is it that you do?"

"Well, we—"

"Not we," he said. "You."

"Oh." Kate felt her face turning red. *He can't see you!* "I review the portfolios, keep the clients happy."

"How happy do you make them?"

Don't be afraid to sell yourself, Kate thought. *People buy other people*. She sat up straight in the chair. "I've been managing investments for five years. I'm a CPA and—"

"A CPA?" he asked. "How old are you?" It sounded as if he were walking around the house, opening the refrigerator.

Kate hesitated. Nowhere in her reading did it say anything about the prospect asking personal questions. "Twenty-nine," she lied. Why she found it necessary to lie about two years, she couldn't say. It was something that her mother would do. Her mother had lied about her own age, and Kate's age, since Kate had been in junior high.

"Poor girl," Pedro said. *"Pobrecita."* He sounded genuinely sorry. "You must have studied all your life."

"Yes," Kate said, shaky. It was so true. She thought of the nights she'd studied in the stacks at Suzzallo Library at the University of Washington. Even Saturday nights, while frat parties on the other side of sprawling Red Square cranked Billy Idol, the floors sticky with condoms and rum punch. Kate could never raise that kind of hell. Sneaking a cup of coffee into Suzzallo past the library policeman had been her big thrill. Now she was studying for the CFA, memorizing earnings per share and hedging formulas on the Stairmaster, doing regressions in the line at Safeway and on BART, holding on with one hand. When Kingsley had suggested that a Chartered Financial Analyst would be more impressive than a Certified Public Accountant, she'd told him that their clients wouldn't know a CFA from their batting average. He'd come back with his speech about bells and whistles: If the competition shows up at the dance in fox stoles with gardenias in their hair, then, dammit, so will we. If we're going to dance, we have to play the game. (Always the game!) Now Kate didn't want to be a wallflower, did she? So Kate had signed up for the exams, believing that at some point she would be good enough. But she felt like a child who'd climbed too high on a roof, the other children cheering her on—now she couldn't get down.

"So Pinto's place," Pedro said. "How about tomorrow night at six?"

"We can talk about your investments."

"We can talk about anything you want to talk about," he said and hung up.

Kate stood, woozy, the floaters in front of her eyes playing

Combat Flight Simulator. She jammed the box of Ritz crackers into her new purse, which wasn't really a purse at all.

Peter could hear Kate on the phone. He took the back way to his office, through the kitchen, so he didn't have to talk to her. He didn't want her to see his throbbing hand soaking blood through the gauze bandage. The plucky coplet at the 2nd precinct had wrapped his hand. "Easy, sister," he'd told her, the pain like metal gouged into flesh. He liked to see a woman in uniform, though he was betting she had a desk job and a boob job, too. Not like Angela, his 24-year-old girlfriend—hers were real— realtits.com—he knew the difference, he used to live in L.A. Angela had kicked him out as soon as he'd opened the front door that evening—she'd seen the six o'clock news.

As soon as Kate left, he planned to fold out the Joe Montana couch and settle down for the night—yesterday he thought he saw a few cartons of Chinese food in the fridge. He'd be the early bird at the office—not for the first time.

As he passed Kingsley's office, he heard Kate hang up the phone. He wondered if she'd understand that he'd done it for Kingsley and the good of the firm. Skull was too gentle to defend himself—Peter could still see Nester's red mouth, the words yo-yoing out—whatdashethink, he's Billy Graham? Peter knew how to deal with sneaky agents and pampered superstars, and when the Wizard of Oz needed his help, he was there. The guy had saved him a time or two.

Peter was on the road most of the time, on the company dime, so if it wasn't for the frequent layovers in Vegas, he'd be a rich man. But he often found excuses to go to Vegas—some college kid who threw like a gun needed more quality time at the all-you-can-eat buffets. And Kingsley bought into it every time. It had gotten so that nobody kept tabs on where he went, as long as the clients kept coming in. But the loan was a different story. Last week Kingsley had loaned him $10,000. Now it was gone, and he hadn't paid his rent. Sometimes he thought that his bay view was the reason that Angela stayed with him. Kingsley hadn't asked him why he needed the money—it wasn't like him to pry—but Peter knew that there'd been some credit inquiries at the office and when

Kate saw the employee receivable on the balance sheet, she'd be on him like a rash.

The octagonal fish tank on Kingsley's bookshelf caught Peter's eye. The water was murky; the poor Chilean piranha, Beta, couldn't see out. His pet could poison itself in its own waste! He didn't want Kingsley to arrive at work to a floater. His job was to protect him from those things.

Peter grabbed the tank and hauled it to the kitchen. Piranhas weren't as vicious as everyone thought. He would simply pour the fish into a vase—a therapeutic waterfall—while he scrubbed the tank. For such a dumpy office it had an old but fancy sink with a spray nozzle, so it wouldn't be tough. It was the least he could do while using Skull's couch.

As he poured the water into the vase, the fish whizzed past— a blue streak—bouncing past the vase and sliding down the garbage disposal.

Peter could hear the fish down there, the flapping gills like shallow breaths. Of course, he needed to reach in. The bandage might protect him from the razor-sharp teeth, but the blood might turn the tranquil maneater into a killer. But, alas, he remembered, his hands were too big for a standard disposal, and he was saved from having to save.

"Kate!" he yelled.

The scuffle of her shoes on the thinning carpet. Her slender bluish wrists, the long white fingers. She was looking at his bloody hand; she had twisted her copper hair into a messy bun and secured it with a #2 pencil. "What are you doing?" she asked, a loose streak of hair hanging in her eyes.

"It's Beta," he said, pointing his bloody hand, "down the chute."

He could feel her pull toward the dying creature, her heart go out. She did it without thinking. Her hand was down there, her arm gone to almost the freckled elbow, her forehead furrowed into jagged lines.

Beta was in her white hand, twisting and flapping. She plunged him into the vase and watched him dive to the bottom.

She turned to face him. "What were you doing?"

"You know that's a piranha, don'tcha?" he asked.

Her lips parted to speak, her gray eyes wide. It was the look she'd given him when Blake Johnson, a marketing guy who'd taken Peter's client out for a bucket of fries, never came back to work after the Christmas party. The security guard told Kate he'd seen Blake leaving the building holding his bloody face. Kate never told anyone what she suspected. Maybe he could trust her. She might not flip the switch when his hand was in the disposal.

"Honestly, I was gonna warn you," Peter said, "you jumped in too fast."

"Peter," she said, wiping her damp hands on her skirt, "we need to talk."

That evening in bed, Kate and Sandy watched Peter on the eleven o'clock news, while Kate nursed Camille. The newscaster referred to it as a "stadium fight provoked by Peter Munger of Sports Financial." At six o'clock, they'd been calling it a disagreement—a human-interest story. Now it was hard news.

"Did they arrest him?" Sandy asked, zapping the television with the remote. He flipped back and forth from Channel 2 to ESPN. It made Kate crazy, this lack of commitment, this continual search for something better.

"No—I'll be meeting with him tomorrow," Kate said, shifting Camille, who was sleepy and easy, to the other breast. She feared Peter had advanced in his dysfunction.

They had agreed on *no sports in the bedroom* a few weeks back. When she'd made her demand—"you never really look at me when the game's on"—he'd hugged her with his great arms, smelling faintly of beer, and said he was sorry, that he only followed sports to unwind, that it was like her reading the *Enquirer* in the grocery line. That night he hadn't turned on *Monday Night Football*, but lay next to her and read her phrases he liked out of *A Moveable Feast*. "Sometimes death scares him more than others," he'd said. This was not really a conversation, she'd decided.

"You won't believe who I'm meeting with tomorrow," Kate said, laying Camille down between them. Normally, for something this big—and exactly what Sandy had hoped for—she would page him or shriek on his voice mail. But she'd waited—for him to come home from his client dinner, take off his tie, then his shirt and his pants, and the moment for shrieking had passed. What was she hiding?

She felt him staring at her, his Italian Mafioso junkyard-dog look.

"Who?" He grabbed the Heineken off his nightstand and took a swig.

Kate swore the stubble on his face grew before her eyes. She preferred his face smooth; she liked the contrast with his chest hair that he hid underneath his crisp button-down shirts like a prison tattoo. He hid things. Even though he teased her—about her compulsive exercising and list-making (she'd jot down accomplishments just to cross them off and even vacuum chest hair out of bed!), he wasn't as easy-going as he appeared. It has nothing to do with Pedro Araguz, she told herself. It's something else.

"It's Pedro Araguz," she said.

"Nice going!" Sandy said, toasting her with his Heineken bottle. "Is he yours?"

"It was just a fluke."

"I knew you'd do it," he said, fluffing his pillow. "I knew you'd win. You're a star. My star!" He wanted her to be successful, and he was proud of her, but in the way a father was proud: Kate accomplishes more in a day than I do in three, he'd say, his eyes watering.

"No guarantees he'll give us any money," Kate said. She didn't like the pressure, Sandy ramping up plans for the big move to the fire station.

"You're on a roll, hun," he said, pulling his laptop onto the bed. The laptop beeped and came alive, scrolling blurry commands. "Bring in Pedro and you'll be in with the guys. I'm sure there're lots of these athletes who would love talking to a girl like you. If you could only get more of them to ask what you do, you could give them your card."

"I've never had a man ask what I do." Until today. "That'd be like asking for directions."

A lot had happened that day—Pinto and Peter and her conversation with Dr. Epman, but—like most evenings—she would only touch on the highlights, the ones that couldn't go untold. "Your mother called. And we're going to bounce checks. Our child has ringworm." Bullet-point style. No time to chat about a piranha named Beta that had almost taken off her finger. Sometimes she wondered what was going on with him that he was too exhausted to tell her about. (Or was exhaustion even it?) She longed for a good night's sleep, but Camille would be up in a few hours and there would be patting and rocking, up-and-down, up-and-down all night long.

"Do you ever feel tingly all over?" Kate asked, rubbing her numb arms. It would make her feel better if her condition happened to normal people, and she thought of Sandy as supremely normal. He was her control group.

"When my arm falls asleep."

"It's not like that." She wouldn't mention talking to Dr. Epman. Sandy only went to doctors for things like kidney stones.

"You're just stressed out. Quit breastfeeding."

Kate pulled her knees up to her chest. "There must be a reason that the American Pediatric Society recommends at least one year."

"I thought you said they were a bunch of bottle-fed old men."

"The breast milk might make her smarter."

Sandy rolled his eyes, typing commands. "And tofu might prevent cancer. That doesn't mean I'm going to eat it."

Camille sighed. Would Kate ever sleep that peacefully again? "I'm quitting tomorrow," Kate said, propping herself up on her elbow. When she lay on her stomach, she was balancing on top of aching water balloons.

"Good," Sandy said, his fingers flying over the keyboard. "Does that mean I can touch them again?" Since she'd been breastfeeding—for eleven months—she didn't like him touching her breasts—the breasts got enough handling; they were oversized and awkward and didn't feel like her breasts; they were an extension of her electric pump, functional as a mini-van.

"They'll shrink, you know," Kate said, squeezing her right breast through her cotton nightgown. "I won't be *Baywatch* anymore."

"I don't care. They're just on loan anyway." He dialed up the modem. Camille stirred, flinging an arm into Kate's face.

Kate sat up and stared at herself in the armoire mirror. She didn't look too tired, she thought. Her skin was pale, but a pretty blue pale with very few freckles—unusual for a redhead. Her cheekbones and the ribs in her chest were pronounced, but she had cleavage that held up her gray cotton nightgown while the spaghetti straps fell down on her shoulders. A man on the BART train had whispered to her yesterday that her shoulders were exquisite. Swimmers' shoulders, he'd said. A perfect T. But had he really been talking about her shoulders?

Kate turned to her side in the mirror. The breasts were really quite exceptional, she decided. Poor girl. *Pobrecita*. She was having no fun. Really, no fun at all.

She would stick out the nursing for the next few months. It was definitely better for Camille. "I might get fat if I quit," Kate said, lying down again. "I won't be able to eat Big Macs. Nursing uses about one—maybe one and a half—Big Macs a day."

"For gawdsakes, you've never even eaten a Big Mac. And you'll never get fat. It's not your nature."

Maybe she would just get fat. Skip her Wednesday workout— low-fat, instead of non-fat lattes—she could really let herself go. Then she realized that she would never give herself permission to get fat, and that made her sad.

Kate drifted asleep for a moment, but Sandy's relentless clicking on the keyboard was worse than her own grinding. She covered her head with the pillow. "When you move to the firehouse," she said, "I'm afraid we'll never have sex again."

"I'll have Tuesday nights off."

Kate tossed the pillow aside and sat up on her elbows. "You'll be too tired from fighting fires at night."

Sandy alt-tabbed to his e-mail. "Then we'll do it in the afternoon."

"I work in the afternoons."

"Not Friday afternoon. Consuelo can watch the kids."

"It'll never happen. There are the dishes. There's day-time TV."

"We'll have to be creative then. Remember when we used to do it on the kitchen floor?" He made a fist and jabbed his elbow into his hip, grunting as if remembering some lewd sexual act that Kate couldn't place.

"That must have been before we had Gus," Kate said, "or before Gus started feeding himself in the kitchen."

Sandy hunkered down over the keyboard again, the typing

gaining momentum. "I'm sure the firehouse has conjugal visits."

Kate pictured herself sneaking into the firehouse where a dozen men snored and groaned, their viscous breathing plastered on the windows. Sneaking into the fraternity sleeping porch was the type of thing that college girls did, Kate thought. "I need to have normal sex at the normal time of day. I need a normal relationship."

"Nothing's changed," he said, patting her on a shoulder blade. "I promise we'll work out a schedule later. Let me finish paying these bills." Kate had noticed that he'd become obsessed with the Internet, buying CDs and paying their bills electronically late into the night as he watched the PIP screen of the various games.

Kate rolled to her side of the bed and curled into a ball. She could just picture this schedule—the grid in the same Excel workbook as Stirling's Clomicalm—where they would attempt to shoe-horn sex into their marriage. It seemed obvious that now would be a good time to do it; they could banish the laptop and push Camille to the other side of the bed. Kate might even take off her nightgown; she would insist that he remove his white athletic socks. The last few times they'd had sex almost fully clothed, and this troubled her (wearing socks during sex especially troubled her). It might be one of the last opportunities for sex without a schedule, Kate thought. For naked sex. But that would be too easy. She shut her eyes to the click, click, click of the keyboard and wished for sleep.

*H*er feet were numb when she fell asleep, and numb when she woke up, and while she was getting ready for work. Was this what the doctor meant by "numb all day"?

On the way to work Kate called Dr. Epman's nurse and made an appointment. It had certainly been 24 hours that she'd been numb, although not in the same places, and she needed to know the precise reason. She didn't like loose ends; she was unhappy in gray areas. Deep down, she was a numbers-cruncher. Stress was a mutating, amoeba-like creature that she couldn't get her arms around. She couldn't say, I am numb, therefore I'm stressed. Stress was no answer. Calling it stress was a chicken-or-the-egg routine; stress caused illness and illness caused stress. When an employee went out on sick leave, everyone would nod knowingly—quit the stress—but it was advice as murky as don't go swimming after a big meal.

"*I*t could be MS," Kate told Dr. Epman as she lay on his examination table wearing a tissue-paper gown. "I'm in the right age group and I sometimes get this wet sensation on my fingertips and then tingling all over." She ran her hands up and down her body, rustling the tissue paper.

He pinched her big toe. "You feel that?"

"Sure. Is that good?"

He neither agreed nor disagreed. It was his policy to make no comments while the patient was vulnerable, dressed in the tissue-paper gown. He had bushy silver eyebrows and wore a tight cap with a miner's headlight. He kept samples of medications in his jacket and wore a holster of instruments around his waist. Just when she thought he was through, he pulled out a knee hammer.

"Ouch! Was that supposed to hurt?"

Dr. Epman floated his index finger over her nose. "O.K. Squeeze my finger as hard as you can."

Kate squeezed.

"O.K., stop!" he said, shaking out his finger. "We're through here. Get dressed and I'll see you in my office."

Kate threw on her blouse, then pulled up her skirt. The nylons took the most time and she managed to wriggle them on without running them. As it was, she had a pack-a-day habit.

She stepped into the hall and threw open his door.

Startled, he looked up from his desk, still wearing his headlamp. He checked his watch. "Forty-five seconds," he said. "That's got to be a record."

She stepped inside and shut the door behind her. He was making a joke. That was a good sign. But his bedside manner involved tapping his foot while she spoke: the meter was always running.

"Have a seat, Mrs. McCabe," he said. Amongst his framed certificates were framed posters from the *Star Wars* trilogy.

He tapped his pen on her chart. "Nothing is wrong with you."

Surely something had to be wrong with her. Not everyone was running around numb. There had to be an answer. "What about my symptoms? What about MS?"

"MS is a dramatic, but rare disease. Numbness is a symptom, but MS also shows other symptoms that you don't have."

Kate leaned forward in her chair.

"And I'm not going to tell you what those are," he said, flipping the pages of her chart. "People as conscientious as you shouldn't be self-diagnosing."

"Then what do I do about it?"

"Just give it some time," he said, madly writing notes on her chart. She wondered how many times you could write "normal, normal, normal."

"Try something for me," he said, still writing. "Take several quick breaths."

Kate sucked in her breath.

"Faster—pant."

Say that again with a straight face, Kate thought.

But he was serious, the shape of his frown mirroring his mustache, the mining light like a prison strobe on her face.

Kate panted. She wondered if they were playing that childhood game—he would grab her from behind and she'd hold her breath for the burst of stars.

"How's the numbness now?"

"Not better," she said. She wasn't sure it was worse, but she was dizzy.

He pulled open his top drawer and handed her a small brown bag.

"A lunch sack?"

"I want you to breathe into the bag to restore the oxygen/carbon-dioxide balance," he said.

Kate sealed the bag over her mouth and breathed for what seemed like five minutes.

"Better?"

"I'm not sure." Kate set the bag on his desk.

He flipped his hand. "Ahh, it'll probably go away eventually."

"What if it doesn't?" Kate asked, cracking her knuckles.

"Have you tried relaxation tapes?"

"They stress me out," Kate said, recalling how she used to

fast-forward through the relaxation section of her Kathy Smith pregnancy exercise video.

"You can try Dr. Fuller." He jotted the name on a card and handed it to Kate. "She's a psychiatrist. She's helped a lot of my patients."

"A psychiatrist?" Kate wondered why not a psychologist. A psychiatrist could prescribe drugs and commit people. Was it that Dr. Epman only knew other medical doctors, or did he think she needed the heavy? She wasn't going to ask him. He'd pushed the light up onto his head, so even when he studied her chart, it blinded her. Shrinks were for the Peter the Reds, which reminded her that she needed to find him one. She was sane. She got an A in being sane.

"Your symptoms are probably psychosomatic. People who hyperventilate are under stress; they tend to be obsessive and excessively body-conscious. Has your stress level increased recently? Having any problems at home?"

"I've got a toddler in my bed."

Dr. Epman pulled a prescription pad from the top drawer of his desk. He was writing slowly, like a traffic cop, taking his time wrecking her day.

"Try this," he said, handing her the prescription.

Kate couldn't read his writing.

"Valium." He reached in his jacket pocket and tossed her some samples. "Works great for toddlers."

Kate stared at the red-foiled pills on the desk.

"Just keep it to one a day."

"You don't have to worry about me," Kate said, tucking the pills into her jacket pocket. "I was the girl at high school kegs pouring her beer out in a plant." She held up the pills. "These won't solve anything," she said. "They're like a Band-Aid."

"Sometimes you need a Band-Aid."

I just couldn't believe he'd talk about Skull that way," said Peter the Red.

Kate was sitting in his office with the door closed. She had her notebook open and pen poised, planning to broach the subject of the shrink. Peter had lined up 20 supplement pills and begun the ritual of popping a pill, then gulping water from a plastic cup. Pop, gulp, pop, gulp.

"Loyalty is always appreciated," Kate said. She was wearing her employer hat. "But you just can't get physical with our competitors." She swiveled in his guest chair. His office was always freezing, but movement helped. "Or anyone, actually," she went on. "You can't touch people in general. Studies have found that people aren't receptive to prolonged touches—and by that I mean four seconds. It always comes back to you, you be can sure of that. And what you did was assault." His contentious behavior had escalated. Last week, when Kate told him that his inability to get along with the staff was a serious problem, the next day there was a jar of chocolate kisses on everyone's desk.

"He didn't press charges." Peter raked his thinning hair with his hand. "Vitamin A overdose," he said, examining the strands of reddish hair that had come loose in his hand. Kate had never seen him in jeans and a sweatshirt. He'd played third base for the Sun Devils and still had the slouch and the scowl and the gold jewelry, but now, as VP of Marketing, he tried to overcompensate by wearing three-piece suits with French cuffs and silk pocket hankies. He wore tuxedos to tailgate parties.

"He got so much free publicity out of this," she said, turning to look away from him wiping the loose hair off his hands, "he didn't need to press charges; it made him look like a hero."

"I just haven't been myself lately," Peter said. "I've got this brain virus."

Here we go, Kate thought, nodding sympathetically.

"The cycle started when my doctor gave me tetracycline for zits when I was a kid. All the meds know, but never talk about tetracycline—it makes you depressed and shrivels your organs. Then they put fillings in my mouth which have mercury. The mercury reacts with saliva and creates tetracycline. So it's like I've been taking tetracycline for 30 years. Look, the nerve damage has scalloped my tongue." He stuck out his tongue.

It did look scalloped, Kate thought. Maybe there was something to the nerve damage. But, a brain virus?

"Peter, let's talk more about self-improvement," Kate said, crossing her legs to appear less threatening. The crossed-leg position, she'd learned from her executive training courses, was submissive. During interviews and almost all situations, the experts recommended sitting like a man, feet square on the ground, fingertips pressed together to take up more physical space.

"It's not too late for you, Kate," Peter said. "Your body type's perfect for this—lots of lean-muscle mass. Your hair's luscious, without split ends." Pop, gulp, pop, gulp.

Mary Ellen Tuohy, Kingsley's secretary, opened the door and tossed something into Peter's in-box. She had long curly hair, the kind Kate had tried for years to achieve with perms and curling irons. Mary Ellen wore a black mid-thigh dress, no nylons, and sandals showing her painted red toenails.

"Morning," Mary Ellen said. "Saw you on TV, Peter. Nice going." She winked at Kate and shut the door.

Peter stared at the shut door. "What's with the popsicle toes?"

"I was talking about improving *yourself*," Kate said, pointing to him. "There's always room for that, and we want to recommend—well, insist—that you see someone for self-improvement."

Peter wolf-whistled. "For a minute I thought she was wearing something different because of the red toes. She wears black every day," he said. "The same gawdawful rubber dress. Do you think we're paying her enough?"

"I think she has several of the same dress."

"How can you tell?"

"Peter," Kate said, crossing her legs. "We insist that you go to a therapist."

"Skull wants me to see a shrink?"

Kate nodded. Everyone always assumed that her orders came from Kingsley.

"Skull?" Peter laughed, and at first Kate sat there puzzled, but Peter continued to laugh, and then she thought about Peter talking a shrink's ear off and she laughed, too, but for a different reason. It was even funnier that Kingsley, whom she was about to introduce to an image consultant because J.P. insisted that his poly-blend suits and geek speak were bringing down the firm, was sending Peter to a shrink. She laughed so hard that she had tears in her eyes.

Kingsley, who must have heard them laughing, popped his

head in. He was smiling. Kingsley never smiled.

They stopped laughing, and Kingsley continued to smile. It was weird, as if he'd recently capped his teeth.

"How are we doing?" he said, still smiling. "My wife tells me that I should force myself to smile, it puts you in a better mood. Something to do with the release of a chemical. It's working, I think."

He's trying, Kate thought. She noticed that his tie wasn't bad; the small yellow flowers were almost tasteful, not the loud Hawaiian variety that he usually wore. Mrs. Gartmore had great taste in clothing, but had long ago stopped buying him clothes.

Kingsley closed the door, leaving her and Peter alone.

Kate turned back to Peter, dabbing at her eyes with her fingers. "How do you see your role here?"

"Minks."

"Excuse me?"

"I go out and capture the minks and bring 'em back for you folks to skin in the office—well, just shear, really, because I want to catch them again next year."

The phone rang. "Sergeant Mullan from the police on line three for you, Kate," James Christmas said over the speaker with zero voice inflection. His voice never changed, whether announcing a call, a fire drill, or gunfire in the ground floor lobby.

Kate rose to leave. "I'd better take this," she said to Peter. "Tell him I'll be right there," she said into the speaker.

"I keep the minks—" Peter said.

"That's good. That's very good," Kate said. "I'm going to work on finding an appropriate therapist for you, so if you could let me know your thoughts on that."

"As long as the firm's paying, I'm game."

Kate was surprised it had been that easy. Maybe Peter's dysfunction was so extreme that he wanted the attention.

"This is Sergeant Mullan from the 3rd Precinct," the voice said when Kate took the call.

"Yes, Sergeant." Two of her lines were lit up, blinking. James Christmas put all calls through no matter who she had in her office, no matter how many times she explained it to him. He was getting his Ph.D. in differential equations at Berkeley, but couldn't interject the proper emotion into his voice and still couldn't put people into voice mail. Diffy Qs, Kingsley called differential equations. "Diffy, but daffy," he complained whenever the phone went dead in his hand after James announced a caller.

Practice relaxation, Kate said to herself, taking a deep breath, and covering her phone with a sweater. One call at a time. She twirled around in her chair, wrapping herself in the phone cord.

Sergeant Mullan cleared his throat. "We don't have a forwarding address for Kim Novak. She moved out of her 33 Bartlett Street address nine months ago."

"You mean her name really is Kim Novak?. She looks more like an Alexandria or Candeleria." Kate's sweater was too translucent and the phone lines lit it up red. She lifted the edge of the sweater and peeked at the by-now three blinking lines.

"She fits your description—28 years old, 5-10, 140 pounds. Probably changed her name. You can change your name to anything you want, you know. I've got miles of rap sheets on little Vietnamese immigrants named Clint Eastwood. Everybody wants to fit in."

"I could change my name to Kim Novak?" Kate asked, thinking that she, too, could be in *Vertigo,* playing two Kims, one who was Kim, and another who wanted to be Kim.

"Just cancel your credit cards," he said. "Your bank will probably make you open another account. Watch for cancelled checks. Since we don't have a witness, it's going to be tough to do much else."

"What about me?" Kate said. "I'm a witness—I was assaulted."

"You were hit from behind. We'll never get assault. Even if we catch her with the goods, she can say finders-keepers. We might get fraud if she uses your stuff—but I'm chasing too many Clint Eastwoods for fraud. Stand in line."

*K*ate was still staring at her by-now-four blinking lights when James Christmas rushed toward her door with the fax. She could always tell it was him, the way he charged her office with the fax fluttering in his hand, stop-and-go, a flock of pigeons suddenly taking off from a park bench. He literally ran from office to office with the mail as if speed made up for all mistakes—and in some ways it did—no fax went undelivered, but often they were delivered to the wrong employee.

James burst through the office door and tossed Kate's fax into her in-box. It was his habit to toss, eyes cast down, then run, to prevent any unnecessary conversation. Last week he'd barged in when Kate was double-pumping and she didn't think he'd gotten over it.

"Thanks, James," Kate said. He was already at the door. The waist band of his plaid boxers showed above his corduroys; his scraggly ponytail, secured by a dirty rubber band, reached the small of his back. "James—"

He stopped in his tracks, facing the door. "Sorry, I forgot to tell you," he said, "Georgie Porshay's ex-girlfriend called you from the welfare office, and your mother called."

"My mother?" Her mother was a divorce lawyer in Spokane. Her phone calls to Kate had slacked off lately, which usually meant she had a new man.

"Your mother said she's decided to come for Christmas."

"My mother's talking about Christmas at the end of September?"

"Yes," James said. He always said yes, never yeah or mmm or uh huh. The formality made Kate uncomfortable.

It was actually her father's turn to have dibs on Christmas; they rotated every three years. But Kate's father, Matthew Franklin Clark, would not leave Manhattan for a San Francisco "paper-snow-flake Christmas."

"James, would you sit down and talk to me for a moment?"

James turned around slowly, tugging at one of his silver loop earrings, but didn't meet Kate's eyes. Kate met Dennis Rodman's eyes—the Dennis with pink hair—on his Dennis Rodman Fan Club T-shirt. James slipped into the guest chair and perched at the edge, ready to take flight.

"This receptionist business," Kate said. She stood and closed her office door, then sat down again. "Just isn't natural for you, is it? Do you like it?"

"I enjoy it, yes."

"Sometimes," Kate said, not sure how to put it, "the athletes like to hear more excitement in our voices. We have to be actors."

Yes, blame it on the athletes, she thought.

"They complained?"

"Not exactly." Kate twirled her pencil with her fingers like a baton. She hated to disappoint people. "Well, in their own way, yes, I guess they did. They're so used to listening to broadcasters. It's a tough role for a receptionist to live up to. I suggest stepping outside of yourself. Be a DJ. Take a few deep breaths while the phone rings—but not too many so they hang up—and smile big—they can hear that." Kate smiled and picked up the phone: "Good morning, it's a great day at Sports Financial!" she gushed at the dial tone. She set the phone back in the cradle. "I want to hear you out there. The trick is to breathe, then project, breathe and project." Kate's rib cage expanded and sunk, expanded and sunk. She was hyperventilating again.

"Who complained?"

"That's not important," Kate said, gasping for air. "I don't even remember. It's a gut feel I have about you—you can do better. Now you come around here and sit in my chair and try it." Kate stood. She was having him trade seats so he'd remember their discussion. She had talked to him about enthusiasm before, but nothing had changed.

James stood and heaved himself into Kate's chair.

"O.K., phone's ringing!" Kate said. "Sit up straight, smile and breathe. That's it. Shoulders back. O.K., you're on the air!" Kate threw her finger at him.

"Good morning, it's a great day at Sports Financial," he said.

"Better. Next time, stress the great. It's a GREAT day!"

James slapped his hands on the desk. "It really upsets me that someone complained. I go out of my way to be nice to these jerks."

"I can see why it upsets you, but you have bigger things in store for you than reception work."

"Right, it's just a stepping stone for me."

"A stepping stone, exactly." She knew it was important to use other people's words, that was a shrink trick she'd read about. "A stepping stone to, say, astrophysics?" She folded her hands in front of her on the table. Be maternal, she thought, though they were the same age.

"No." He shook this head. "I'd like to get into sales here. I could help J.P."

"Sales?" She'd thought they'd at least be rid of him when he graduated. "Sales has very little to do with numbers. You're a whiz at numbers. What about finishing your Ph.D.? Not just anyone can get one of those. Anyone can sell." She knew that wasn't true. Selling, to Kate, was Toastmasters in Mandarin. She quickly tossed some papers over the book on her desk: *Conquer Your Fears! The I Hate Selling Self-Study Course.*

James sat up straighter. "I've got the phone experience under my belt now," he said, though he wore no belt. "I know the file room front to back. I've memorized the heights and weights and stats of every player. And I think I deserve this opportunity."

It was a prepared speech, the longest paragraph she'd ever heard out of him. He'd probably overheard Kingsley offering the 200% of last year's total bonuses at the meeting. No one ever suspected the donut boy. Now she would have to tell J.P., and J.P. would have to give him a shot, because James's father, an Atlanta agent, had just sent them another client. Kate would have to find another receptionist, which was what J.P. wanted. Careful what you wish for, she thought.

*A*fter James left her office, Kate pulled Dr. Renee Fuller's card from her purse. A woman might be good for Peter, she thought. Maybe it makes sense to interview her. Not everyone would be appropriate.

As she stared at the card, the feeling gone from her toes and the fog socking in their tower, she thought about Dr. Epman's psychosomatic explanations for her numbness.

The fluorescent lights buzzed overhead. Kate folded Dr. Fuller's business card in half, then into fourths. No, she thought, picking up the phone. It was just convenient to have the referral— it saved her time. Dr. Fuller would take one look at Kate and think she'd never seen anyone saner.

Dr. Fuller's answering machine came on, but she picked up as Kate was preparing to leave a message. Yes, she could meet Kate for an informational interview during the lunch hour.

Kate called her mother's office in downtown Spokane. The

answering machine picked up.

Kate speed-dialed her mother's house and got a man's voice. "Ginnie and I aren't home right now." Kate hung up and manually dialed, but got him again, so she left a message. Something was up. Her mother had always gone by Virginia.

Kate found the gold lettering that said Renee Fuller, M.D. on the door of Room 820 in the Stanyan Building. It was a no-frills, musty, windowless waiting room the size of a custodian's closet with two leather chairs that had seatbacks at forty-five degree angles. Not that more than one person at a time could get in there.

Kate needed to pee. She needed to pee more frequently now—and unexpectedly—a symptom, according to *The American Medical Reference*, linked to a myriad of diseases. She tried to leave, but found the door locked behind her. Panicked, she studied the other door which had a light switch next to it. A tiny light bulb was underneath it—no doubt to alert the doctor that the patient was in. It was like the light switch her mother had installed outside the kitchen pantry during Kate's overeating stage in junior high. When the light was on, Kate's mother knew she was in the pantry eating.

Kate flipped the switch on and waited. When nothing happened, she turned to the magazine rack: *Town & Country, Parenting, Readers' Digest, and Body Builders. Body Builders!* She wondered if the magazines were representative of Dr. Fuller's patients. The labels had all been ripped off. So the crazies won't stalk her at home, Kate thought uneasily.

The light snapped off. Was Kate supposed to do something? She checked her watch. It was one minute to noon. She watched the second hand quiver, then spring.

Noon, straight-up, Kate heard heels clicking behind the door. Dr. Fuller was younger than she was trying to look. Her prematurely graying hair was pulled back in a severe bun. Behind her huge glasses was a calm, striking face.

Dr. Renee Fuller was the mother of all gray areas. Even her opening question, "What would you like to talk about?" made

Kate want to start talking about numbers: the Niners' Monday night score and the exact price of Motorola—if only she had her hand-held Quotrek!

"Nice place," Kate said. The style was minimalist. An airplane stainless steel sink matched a polished steel mirror. So the mirror can't be broken and used as a weapon, Kate thought grimly. Dr. Fuller was patient as a clock. She folded her hands in her lap—they were slender and veined. Her shoes were the clunky, nurse-variety, and she wore opaque support hose. "Perhaps you'd be more comfortable on the couch," she said, pointing to a severe version of a sofa that looked more like a bench for sit-ups.

"I'm not here to talk about me," Kate said, pointing to herself dramatically.

"No one ever is."

She's good, really good, Kate thought, smiling. The office was getting warm. Perhaps she would hyperventilate. Maybe the stuffy little office would act as a lunch sack restoring her carbon-dioxide equilibrium.

Dr. Fuller pressed her feet together; she was not one inclined to cross her legs. With the hair bun and glasses and the way she constantly nodded, she seemed to be going for the wise-granny-in-a-rocking-chair look. But she was too stiff, and not that old.

Kate leaned forward in her chair. "Like I mentioned on the phone, I wanted to talk to you about an employee at our firm—see if you can help him. He's one of our sales guys. He tossed a sports agent against a wall at 3Com yesterday. You might have seen him on the news last night."

Dr. Fuller shook her head. "Does he upset you?"

"Not me, really," Kate said. "He's got a temper, but he's more accepting of me than the others. He doesn't translate the sports slang."

"You find yourself interested in him, sexually?"

Kate stared at her pale deadpan face and cracked up. "You jump right in, don't you?"

"Laughter at serious subjects indicates a shallow personality, Kate." Dr. Fuller's lips formed her words as if for the hearing-impaired. She had the slow, perfect annunciation of a pre-school teacher. "I charge a hundred and thirty dollars for a fifty minute session. At three dollars a minute, I doubt you can afford to talk about my office furniture. So, does this man excite you sexually?"

"Of course not." Kate was on her feet. She threw her purse strap over her shoulder. "I came here to talk about Peter Munger. I thought I made that clear on the phone. Have you been talking to Dr. Epman?"

"What does Dr. Epman have to do with this?" Dr. Fuller asked softly. Her heavy shoes were sunk in the soothing-green carpet of quicksand.

Kate grabbed the doorknob, still reeling about the shallow-personality comment. Maybe it was a hook to get her to stay. If she stayed to find out why she had a shallow personality, well then, she didn't have a shallow personality after all, did she? Someone with a shallow personality wouldn't be so introspective. "I've been seeing him for numbness."

"How often have you been seeing him?"

"I don't see him like you see a shrink. He just treated me for numbness. And tingling sensations."

"And he suggested you come here."

"Not exactly. He couldn't help me—he couldn't find any disease. He just handed me your card with some samples of Valium."

"Dr. Epman has you on tranquilizers and you came here on the pretense of helping your colleague?"

"No," Kate said. It was getting harder to talk. "Peter needs help—" She stopped before saying "too." Maybe she did need help. A shallow personality! She thought about her decision to work instead of staying at home with her children. And her laughing was entirely inappropriate—she laughed often, even at the thought of Pinto shooting J.P. in the ass. Excessively body conscious—hadn't Dr. Epman said something about that?

"And are you numb now?"

"I don't have to tell you anything else," Kate said, squeezing the doorknob with her numb fingers. "It's a free country."

"Of course it is," Dr. Fuller said. "You're free to go at any time."

Kate didn't move.

"Well then, are we going to have our entire session with you standing in the doorway?"

Kate stopped at home on her way to Pinto's. Checking in at the house during business hours or on her way to a client event was always a mistake, and this time was no exception.

Stirling Moss was on the kitchen floor, panting, tongue hanging out. The kitchen mess was layered from breakfast, then lunch, the glass tabletop streaked with mayonnaise and strewn with morning cereal bowls, sippy cups of orange juice, and half-eaten bologna sandwiches. The milk carton dripped onto the butcher block, and the highchair tray was on the floor smeared with avocado and other unidentifiable food. Consuelo was great with the kids, but.

Kate kneeled and put her hands on the dog, shaking him. "Not dead," she assured Gus, who had started to cry. "Definitely not dead." She heaved the 90-pound animal onto his side. He lifted his head and stared at Kate for a moment, panting, then put his head down again.

"Consuelo?" Kate called.

Consuelo marched down the front stairs with Camille on her generous hip, her sweater hiked up under her arms, exposing her belly-button pierced with a gold ring. She wore wide-legged hip-hugger jeans and platform sandals; her eyebrows were plucked to thin dark lines and her toenails were a length beyond hygienic standards and painted Chanel black.

Camille shrieked when she saw Kate and flapped her arms, "Ma ma ma ma ma ma mama." Kate lifted her off Consuelo's hip. "What's wrong with Stirling?"

"*No se*," Consuelo said, shaking her head. "He don't eat. He just wants sleep. I left you a message at work."

"We've got to get him to the vet," Kate said. "Let's get him in the car." Kate checked her watch. 5:30. She would have just enough time to drop Stirling off at the Mission Pet Hospital and get to Pinto's. "You can follow me and wait for him."

Consuelo stuck out her bottom lip, which was substantial, and gave Kate her pouty look. She had just picked up Stirling from Raul's, and she hated going to the Mission Pet Hospital; she feared animals, even domesticated ones. In El Salvador, most dogs were rabid, and people did not invite them to live in their homes.

Smarter than us, Kate thought; sometimes Stirling was like having a goat in the house. She thought it especially absurd when Sandy bathed him in the upstairs bathtub. What were we thinking?

"My car still don't work good," Consuelo said, wrapping her long hair around her index finger.

"How'd you pick up Stirling?"

"Martina drove us."

"Fine," Kate said, angry at Consuelo for trying to get out of this; and it upset Kate to even imagine what went on when she was out of the house. One afternoon, when she'd arrived home unannounced, Martina and three Hispanic guys were eating mixing bowls of Captain Crunch in front of the television. Martina seemed to ferret out all the good food in the house; Kate hid the Quaker chocolate chip breakfast bars in her underwear drawer. She'd tried making rules—no friends over unless pre-approved— but Consuelo pouted and Kate couldn't stand having people angry at her.

Kate felt numb. She handed Camille to Consuelo. Camille wailed and writhed in Consuelo's arms. The children loved Consuelo—Kate could hear them laughing and playing when she arrived unannounced—but when they saw Kate they would often feign displeasure. Kate and Consuelo usually got along, sometimes too well. Consuelo told her everything—her crazy ex-boyfriend Arturo was stalking her when she took the children to Douglas Park; she was still a virgin—saving herself for marriage—but hadn't had a period in three months; when Martina crossed the border, she was almost raped by a coyote-man, who threatened to turn her in to the authorities.

"Let's go, big boy." Kate kneeled down and got her arms around Stirling's middle. Stirling kicked and clawed, tearing her pantyhose at the knee. Though he'd just returned from his second comb-out at Raul's for $195, he smelled foul—maybe he'd already found a skunk in the back yard.

Kate tried pulling him to his feet. Gus tugged on his collar. "Easy does it, Stirling," Kate said, but he plopped back down with a giant sigh. "Consuelo, you're going to have to help me carry him. He's dead weight."

Gus burst into tears.

"No, he's not dead, honey," Kate said, patting Gus on the

shoulder. Camille, hearing Gus cry, began crying as well.

"Please." Kate looked at Consuelo. "I promise he won't bite. You can put Camille in the playpen."

Consuelo said nothing, but set Camille in the playpen and rubbed her hands together. "You can take the back end," Kate said. This is why she makes the big bucks, she thought.

Together they lifted Stirling and stepped down into the garage, Kate walking backwards, Gus shuffling behind Consuelo, and Camille crying in the playpen, banging the refrigerator door open and shut. Kate was worried. Stirling had never been this listless.

They heaved Stirling into the back of Kate's station wagon. Stirling held his head up and looked around, then laid it back down. Kate covered him with a blanket.

"I'm coming with you!" Gus said, crying again. He lunged for Kate; Consuelo restrained him.

"Honey, I'll be home soon," Kate said, blowing kisses. She didn't think she'd be very effective showing up at Pinto's with Gus and a sick dog. Now she'd just have to show up with the dog, nothing Pinto hadn't seen before.

Kate backed the car out of the garage, Gus kicking and screaming. "You won't come and you won't come and you won't come," Gus said between sobs.

Kate tooted the horn—bye! bye!—guilt-ridden. She asked herself why she always ended up in these predicaments and why wasn't it Sandy taking Stirling to the ER? But did she really resent Sandy? Or was it Gus? Dr. Fuller had told her that she couldn't express anger at her children. "Spoiled brat," Kate said, under her breath, but it didn't feel right. It left a waxy taste in her mouth, like lipstick left on a glass.

You're going to have to wait here until we've assessed his condition," the desk attendant told Kate in a slow nasal voice. He had receding hair and wore an oversized Tweety-bird shirt. "At first blush, Doc thinks he's poisoned."

"Poisoned?" Kate remembered a pre-child Halloween when she'd rushed home from work thinking she'd left a bag of Reese's

Peanut Butter Cups in the garage. Too much chocolate can kill a dog, she'd read in *American Gordon Setter* when she used to read dog books. But wasn't it just last week that Sandy had set out D-Con in the garage to kill the mice? Kate had considered the possibility of Stirling eating it—though he'd have to climb on top of the water heater. Poisoning might be a good thing, she had thought, but hadn't said, and certainly hadn't meant.

Had Raul poisoned poor Stirling? No, the man was too practical. Gus would be devastated. She didn't know how to explain death to him: Stirling's gone to heaven? But they hadn't discussed heaven yet—they hadn't really discussed God, except when they sometimes said grace when they occasionally had family meals (gatherings of pop tarts around the toaster). "Yea, Big Bird!" Gus clapped after they'd say Amen. Whatever works for him, was her attitude; she just wanted him to feel safe.

Kate sat in a chair and tried to pull her skirt over the rip in her nylons, but the skirt was 30% spandex and kept popping back up. Her eyes itched, the air was thick with dog powder and sawdust. She checked her watch as she'd done every two minutes in the last half hour—6:01. She was officially late. It felt strange to be sitting there, late for an important meeting—the naughtiness of it made her feel lightheaded. She tried her cell phone. Pinto's was still busy. She tried Sandy at work, but got his voice mail. She thought about calling work, maybe Jennifer Popkins could come down, even Kingsley if she filled him in—but she resisted it. This was her deal. She tried Consuelo at home; she could demand she get down here, but the answering machine came on. "Please pick up, Consuelo, it's really important!" Nothing.

Kate sidled up to the counter where the attendant was counting out Heart Guard tablets. "Any chance I could just step out for a few minutes?"

The attendant began counting out loud as if Kate had disturbed his concentration—"15, 16..." The long hand on the clock behind him sprung another minute.

"You see, I'm late for this meeting with Pedro Araguz," Kate rambled, digging her fingernails into the wooden countertop. Somewhere in the back a dog howled in pain; luckily it didn't sound like Stirling. "Last time I met with his friend Pinto, we had to take a detour to Raul's Pet Palace on the way to get Pinto drug-tested. I'm trying to play by the same rules as the boys, but all these errands make me look like a soccer-mom. I'm going to look like an idiot if I'm late. And I'm late, so I already look like an idiot."

The attendant looked up at her and scowled; he rubbed his red hand along the peach fuzz on his chin. "You took your dog to the Palace?"

*A*t 6:30, Pinto's number was still busy and Kate still couldn't reach Sandy or Consuelo. Desperate, she called Sports Financial.

"Good morning, it's a great day at Sports Financial!"

"Excellent," Kate told James, "except it's evening now." This was worse than before. "I'd turn down the volume just a hair and work on the lift in your voice," she said, trying to lift the word "lift."

"I need help, James," Kate said. He usually left at six. Maybe she could convince him to ride his bike to meet her. He rode his bike to work from Twin Peaks every day. He especially enjoyed riding down Market Street the last Friday of the month for Critical Mass, when the bike riders of the city joined together to block traffic and protest their oppression by motorized vehicles.

"I'm supposed to meet Pinto and I'm stuck at the Mission Pet Hospital."

"Oh, it's O.K.—Pinto already called."

"When?"

"About a half-hour ago. He said you didn't show for your meeting. I transferred him to J.P."

"I thought J.P. had washed his hands of Pinto? Where's J.P. now?"

"He ran out of here after he hung up with Pinto."

"He went to meet them." Kate's heart pounded.

"It's good he was here, I guess."

The vet, a round man who was dressed like a chef, came through the doorway with Stirling Moss on a leash. Stirling was on his feet, but groggy.

"He's fine," the vet said. "We found jalapeno seeds in his

mouth. It seems he ate dozens of the little monsters. I couldn't even eat one of them. Where would he get into jalapenos?"

Kate now wished it was the D-Con. Consuelo had a cast-iron mouth and used jalapeno seeds like salt. They never asked her to cook any more, because she made kettles of boiling dog's breath chili and melt-down burritos.

"Dog's breath chili." Kate winced.

"I wouldn't feed a dog chili," the vet said. He clucked his tongue—bad girl—as if it had been Kate's idea. As if it had been Kate's idea to get the beast in the first place. Well, maybe it had been.

"He's going to be fine," the vet said, patting Stirling on the head, "if you stick to a bland diet of ground lamb—lightly browned—" he rubbed his fingertips together—"medium rare"—he didn't realize that Kate even burned toast, "for two weeks. But he also seems to have a fungus."

Kate had barely processed the part about the ground lamb. A 90-pound dog could eat a lot of lamb.

"It's a genital fungus. Sort of a jock itch."

*I*t *was* Kate's idea to have an annual marital summit, always the second weekend in November. Consuelo stayed overnight, while Kate and Sandy spent the night at the Pelican Inn, a re-creation of an English inn just across the Golden Gate. It was the only time Kate ever ate fish and chips, which she loved, breaking her rule of nothing deep-fried.

Armed with notebooks and pens, they reviewed the state of their union—the objective side: child care, career aspirations, major purchases, vacation plans. Sandy, who hated to plan, did not relish these discussions, but went along because he loved drinking black and tans in the pub and sleeping until ten. He was more social than Kate and struck up conversations about sports and the President with the Englishmen-wannabes.

They always requested the room over the bar. The din of raucous Englishmen feasting on shepherd's pies relaxed them. The noise meant they didn't have to talk any more. It masked the sounds while they had sex, and soothed their disappointments.

Kate had learned long ago that Sandy didn't like to discuss making love after the fact. He said it was like watching the videotape of a wedding—the best man's jokes were never as funny, the bride had a poppy seed between her front teeth.

To Kate, hotel sex was too much pressure; the expectation of the turned-down bed, the chocolate hearts left on the pillows that kept her wired, never spent. Frequency was what counted for her, like ski runs on a $60 lift ticket.

Last fall they had varied their marital summit by going to Puerta Vallarta, Sandy's favorite vacation—long sunburnt days of strong Cuba libres and weak hard-ons. Kate thought it was the excesses of the swim-up bars, an entire pineapple butchered for a Mai Tai, full-body ocean-side massages, and the near-death experience of the lava-tube water slide. You'd see the circle of light at the end as you careened through the slick dark tunnel—like a rescue—like a certain fate.

The hotel sex in Puerta Vallarta had been quick and incessant. Sandy's sharp whiskers scraped her sunburned skin. He breathed rum in her ear as she rinsed out her bathing suit over the sink, his hands on her waist still rough with ocean sand. "No more in-and-out privileges," Kate joked. When she had him on the floor—"just hang on"—he lamented a bruised groin. Kate rolled off him. "I thought a sore pelvis was a sign of a good vacation," she said, hanging up her dripping bathing suit on the towel rack.

When the marital summit came around this year, they were pinched for time and decided that a school-night quickie would have to do. Sandy suggested a movie, which wasn't exactly what Kate had in mind.

"We can talk during the previews," Sandy said, pulling off his suit pants. They were in their bedroom. Friday at seven. Kate had been home with the kids all day, an alleged mental health day. Now she was on the floor drinking warm Chablis from a jelly jar, putting a Barney puzzle together with Gus, who wore a plastic firefighter's hat and a gold badge pinned to his T-shirt that said "Captain Bob." Camille was trying to eat Barney's nose. A year ago, when Kate had prohibited television and doled out juice at a half a cup a day, she'd hated Barney—the blinding fuchsia and green of him—and referred to him as the anti-Christ: he was a saint compared to Captain Bob.

Kate completed the puzzle with Baby Bop's umbrella.

"Stop it, Mommy," Gus said. "I can do it by myself." He picked up the puzzle board. Camille squealed, throwing down the puzzle pieces she'd been clutching in her chubby hands.

"I like the previews," Kate said, standing up. "But I guess that's what you had in mind." She had almost given up on the marital summit. She hadn't told him yet about J.P. stealing Pedro—he was so excited about the bonus, and she wanted him to be proud.

"We can get Chinese after," he said, looking in a dresser drawer. "Where are my jeans?"

The laundry that Consuelo had washed and folded was still in the clothes basket outside their door. Just like Kate, Consuelo hated to put laundry away—Camille followed behind and pulled it out anyway—and so they mainly used the clothes right out of the basket.

"Why not this pair?" Kate asked, grabbing a pair out of his drawer. Camille pulled herself up on the dresser and stared inside the empty drawer.

Sandy patted his stomach and gulped a Heineken from his nightstand. They'd been going through a lot of beer lately; Kate knew because she did the shopping. Sandy's half gallon of Captain Morgan that he kept in the cupboard was almost empty. "Stirling's been into the rum again," he'd said earlier that week.

"Those are a little tight," he said. "Guess I'm up a size."

Kate considered his physique. He was tall, 6-3, and his broad frame could carry a lot of weight. But on closer inspection, his stomach was getting rounder. She hadn't wanted to say anything. What about this fireman thing? Didn't firefighters have certain standards? Sandy didn't believe in exercising for the sake of exercising; he'd get inspired to chop wood, but never to ab-roll, and though Kate admired him for this, she'd been finding too many boxes of pizza bones in front of the computer. Why was it that he could drop comments like "guess I'm up a size" while chugging a beer with as much emotion as "the Niners lost today" (now there he'd show some remorse!), and go to a movie and eat butter popcorn, then think nothing of eating six egg rolls?

If Kate was up a size, she'd be devastated. She'd be at the gym, then eating rice cakes for dinner—forget the movie!—because staying in shape was expected of her. Sure, Sandy had been kind when she'd gained seven pounds during the last weekend of her pregnancy, despite swimming 45 minutes every day. Sure, he said "you look the same to me," when she was up five pounds and her pants were clearly tight. But then he'd pick up a Victoria's Secret catalog and observe that some emaciated model was wearing a bigger bra. Was he flat-out lying to her?

"I wish I had time to work out," Sandy said.

"Have you ever considered a trainer?" Kate asked, taking his lead. He was in a good mood, having a beer. Make him think it was his idea.

Sandy laughed. "You mean like Madonna's trainer?"

"Regular people have trainers," Kate said, warming to the subject. Sandy liked to think of himself as a regular guy, and he certainly was that. "It might be fun for a while. I could watch the kids, say, Thursday nights. You could go out for a beer after." Until you move into the firehouse, Kate thought, then everything will be up for grabs.

She could see he was considering it. Kate watching the kids, having a beer. All very appealing. A little work out before, what the hell.

"Too expensive."

"They're having an introductory special for three sessions," Kate said. Casual, very casual. This idea was spontaneous. Don't push too hard.

"I'll think about it."

"I think we have to sign up by Monday," Kate said. Close the deal. *I Hate Selling!* was now the little devil on her shoulder.

Sandy took another swig of beer. "All right, I can give it a try."

"We've got to see *The English Patient*," Kate said, moving on before he changed his mind. She had the movie section from the *Chronicle* open on her lap. *The English Patient* had been awarded best picture a few years back and they'd missed it, opting for shorter, funnier movies that you didn't have to think about. Kate, who liked killing more than one bird with a stone—a date and a conversation piece—felt they had blown a civic duty.

"I doubt it's still playing," Sandy said, pulling a pair of jeans out of the clothes basket. "We can get the video."

"I hear you have to see it on the big screen," Kate said, checking the obscure theaters and drive-ins. "Here it is—at the Coronado in the Mission. A double feature—it's playing with *Schindler's List.*"

The downstairs door opened and slammed shut. "Can I come up?" Consuelo called, her spiked footsteps on the wooden stairs. Her perfume preceded her. It was Chanel, she'd told Kate, when Kate had admired how intoxicating Camille smelled after they were out for an evening. That always sent Sandy through the roof. They were paying her too much. She'd just built a house for her family in El Salvador and she could still afford Chanel.

"Not yet!" Sandy called, still in his underwear. He lurched for his bathrobe, then unable to locate it, shut the door and turned the bolt.

The children, weary of their parents, clamored for the door. Camille pounded on the door and Gus railed on the doorknob.

Kate couldn't take the whining and unbolted the door. Sandy dove for his closet.

"Yea!" Gus cheered, charging Consuelo.

Kate sighed.

"What?" Sandy asked from inside his closet.

"That."

"That, what?"

"I've been home with the kids all day," she said, as she watched Consuelo scoop up Camille.

Sandy poked his head out of the closet. "So take a break."

He never quite gets it the first time, she thought.

Camille giggled as Consuelo tossed her in the air.

"It makes me crabby," Kate said.

Sandy wore a red polo shirt, the color of Kate's wool sweater. He liked to match her. In general, it made her uncomfortable, reminding her of infant twins dressed by a hyperactive mother. On their night stand was a photograph of Kate and Sandy at a Puerta Vallarta fiesta posing with a bare-chested native with a shark's tooth around his neck. Sandy wore a Hawaiian shirt with tangerine-colored hibiscus flowers the exact color of Kate's sun dress. The picture advertised a closeness that Kate thought was exaggerated—Kate wanted the disclaimer: What you see going on may not really be going on.

On the way to the theater they passed the Mission firehouse. Sandy slowed down. It was dark outside, the engines put to bed. Two firemen ate dinner in a brightly lit window.

Kate watched Sandy as he looked past her. His eyes were dark and wet—muddied—his chin tilted up, a faraway look he got whenever they sang the national anthem. It made Kate feel insecure, as if he were openly flirting with another woman. She needed to be prettier, work harder, make more money.

Kate drummed her fingers on the dashboard. "Is it the sleeping porch thing again or the heavy machinery?"

Sandy gunned the engine, and they launched into the dark narrow streets with looming buildings marked by spray-can pranksters. She wished he'd say something; she wished he'd get angry.

"I feel that you're trying to leave us," Kate said, her neck tightening. She wouldn't cry. Even as a child, her mother said, she rarely cried.

"You don't understand," Sandy said. His lips were tight, his knuckles white on the steering wheel.

"I want to understand," Kate said. She touched his tense hand with her fingertips. "Help me."

"I hate wearing ties and checking voice mail and reading faxes on that slippery paper—especially the paper." He relaxed his grip on the steering wheel. "It's not like I'm a criminal lawyer saving people from the gas chamber. I need to work with my hands. I don't think I'll be satisfied until I'm around dirt."

"Or ash?" Kate said. Her mother had told her to marry a doctor or lawyer, but that was before she'd become a lawyer herself. Her mother had told her a lot of things.

"Maybe you just need a project," Kate went on. A car backfired somewhere. There were no street lights in this part of town. "We could add the deck you've been wanting. There'd be lots of dirt. Let's add another bathroom while we're at it."

"It's not the same. You'll see, I'll be around during the day. I can watch the kids more, you can focus on your career."

"My career." Kate looked out at the black street, the shadowy figures entering the Coronado with blankets and sleeping bags. "What if I don't want a career?"

Sandy faced her and put his hands on her knees. "Come on, you're terrific at it. You hate being home—it gives you a stomach ache."

"I love my kids," Kate said.

*T*he commercials had started, projecting enough light for them to find seats in the middle of the theater. Popcorn and other garbage crunched under their feet as they shifted in the lumpy seats. A jacket or towel—Kate wasn't sure—was crumpled in the seat next to her, and she tried not to look at it, though she considered tossing it over her legs, she was so cold. The regulars knew there was no heat, so they came prepared to camp. Several rows ahead a couple was making out, passionately; the fireflies of cigarettes sparkled around them. The smell of pot was like burning autumn leaves. Kate took a moment to inhale. The total effect was almost pleasant.

"O.K., let's get down to business," Kate said, pulling a typed list out of her purse. She held it up to catch some light. A bottle rolled under their seats toward the front row. "I think we can wrap this up before the previews." This was often the way they had discussions—eating dinner in front of the television and talking during the commercials. The other night during a family meal she was amazed how high the table seemed—she was so used to eating with a plate on her lap.

She dreaded telling him about the shrink. She would be flawed to him—not the glossy photo in his wallet—the one of Kate and their infant daughter, Camille's pink lips almost smiling and a perfect rosebud on her dress, Kate's face glowing (though Kate knew it was the fever from the mastitis). But he was going to find out about the shrink eventually, since he paid the bills, itemizing everything on the Quicken software, a chore that gave him a satisfaction she would never understand, perhaps the way she sometimes felt about vacuuming.

She told herself that she didn't have to go back, that the shrink probably hooked everyone with the same pitch—you're shallow. In the shrink's mind, Kate thought, Mr. Rogers needed therapy, and accountants and grandmothers and washing-machine repair men—especially washing-machine repair men.

Two rows ahead, a woman wearing a Doublemint Gum beach towel as a blanket poured popcorn out of a large refillable bucket directly into her mouth. This gave Kate some comfort, but she still felt uneasy. "You wouldn't not go to a doctor because you're afraid of finding something wrong?" the shrink had asked. And Kate had thought that maybe she wouldn't, but she knew that was the wrong answer, and, when the shrink had suggested that there were problems in her marriage, she had denied it vehemently. Why go back to that, when what she needed was someone building her up?

"Item number one," Kate read from the typed list. "Gus and church."

Sandy sank lower in his chair. "What else is on your list?"

"*Our* list, it was awful when he thought Stirling was dead. He doesn't know what dead means. Stirling's getting up there—he's 77 in dog years—what are we going to tell Gus when he dies?"

"We say he's gone to heaven."

"Is that what you believe?" Sandy never discussed God with her. It was private, he told her, even when she reminded him they'd had children together. Sometimes she felt like she was a completely separate section of his life—his life had many sections, divided up like an orange.

"Of course," Sandy said, looking at her. His eyes glowed in the darkness. Somewhere behind them a firecracker popped. "Why do you always doubt that?"

"So, will you go to church with us? I don't feel like leading the crusade on this one."

"I've done the altar-boy thing. You're the one who could use a good dose of faith."

"You think I should go?"

"It couldn't hurt. The way I see it, we can get the kids baptized and they'll go to church in several years."

"In several years!" The people lighting fireworks behind them shushed her.

"Yeah, it won't be long," Sandy whispered.

"Ask any woman how many several is, and she'll say six to ten," Kate said. She'd noted that men liked to use that word. It was indefinite, noncommittal. When she and Sandy had been dating two years, and Kate had questioned the direction of their relationship, Sandy said they'd get married "in several years." As it worked out, it was only two years later, but that was only because her old boyfriend had shown up on her doorstep, back from teaching English in developing nations, presenting her with a book of poetry he'd written that revealed intimate details of their relationship.

"It's a word meant for procrastination," Kate said. "We need church. I don't want my kids to think of their baptism like a circumcision" Sandy had been adamant about the circumcision — Kate still wanted to be convinced of its necessity. "I want them to understand exactly what it means."

"You went to Sunday school. Just explain it to them."

"I wasn't paying attention. When I think of it, I remember lemons: lemon jelly donuts for breakfast and Virginia's lemon perfume and my fingers stinging from cutting lemons with our dull knives for her Saturday night cocktail parties."

"Exactly my point," Sandy said, shaking a finger at her. "Last time we took Gus to church all he talked about was the grape juice at communion. He's too young."

A preview for *Lost World* came on, and Sandy snapped to attention, a timely commercial break from their discussion. Or was their discussion the commercial break?

"Jumping ahead to item number six," Kate said over the din of stampeding dinosaurs and a ripple of firecrackers that could have been gunfire. "I'm seeing a shrink."

Sandy didn't hear her. "At dinner," he said, putting his hand over hers, "we can do the rest of your list then."

But the time for that had passed. Kate would stop after item number five: her mother coming for Christmas.

At the end of the list — item number seven which wasn't actually on the list — she wanted to tell Sandy she was failing at work. But she hadn't even been able to type this concern; she didn't want to disappoint him. In the noisy theater, she suddenly felt all alone.

*I*t wasn't the first Christmas her mother had threatened not to come. During Kate's freshman year at the University of Washington her mother had told her that she was having Christmas in Mexico with a man named Pete. Kate was welcome to drive home to Spokane (a five-hour drive over the Snoqualmie Pass). Her mother would stock the refrigerator and trim a tree, but she really needed to develop her own life. When Kate had cried over the phone—suffering finals, acne, and the recurring nightmare of not being able to find the chemistry building—her mother had encouraged her to take her roommate— "Bindy or Biffy"—up on her invitation. "That's what college girls do," she'd said. Her mother had called a week later, saying that she'd changed her mind about Mexico and begged Kate to come home. When Kate arrived, her room had been turned into an office (only her Tom Petty posters remained), but her mother never mentioned the man named Pete again.

Her mother's not coming still quickened Kate's heart. She forced herself to remember the Christmas when she was 13, her mother freshly divorced, pacing and gulping champagne from chipped crystal, her high heels clicking on the hardwood floor, as if someone would be joining them, but nobody was. Those times were the something that kept them tied together. "But she makes you crazy," Sandy would insist, bewildered when Kate would lament her mother's absence. It was something that Sandy, with his Scrabble-playing, Jell-O-salad-eating family, would never understand.

"You're getting married, aren't you?" Kate asked, when her mother called on December 15th to continue negotiations. Her mother had been married twice before, but this was the quickest. Just when she was at her lowest, there'd always seem to be another man there to rescue her.

"You can hear it in my voice, can't you, dear?"

"I think I can."

"New Year's Day in Las Vegas," her mother said. "A stroke after midnight—too late for you to be up, dear. I know you're going to like him."

Kate glanced at her watch. Ten o'clock. Pedro would be walking through the door any second. Had she even checked to see if there were any refreshments? When were there ever refreshments? "I'm sure I will," Kate said. Was that permission to bring him?

"I'll make our reservations," Virginia said.

It was.

"Well, my client's here," Virginia said. "This guy shot the neighbor's guinea pig with a pellet gun. His wife's leaving him."

"He cheated on her?"

"The overlap problem."

It was always the "overlap problem," with annulment possibilities, when her clients did the cheating, and fornication punishable by lopping off the offender's assets, when her clients were getting cheated on.

"So what does Barry do?"

"Oh, something on the Internet," her mother said quickly, never one to take an interest in technology or anything mechanical. She didn't have the concentration to put the toilet paper on the roller or the patience to set Jell-O.

"Does he have a degree?"

"Nothing formal." Her mother giggled and Kate couldn't help smiling herself, so extreme was their role reversal. "Quickly now," her mother said. "How's the family?"

"Everybody's fine. Sandy's going to start working out."

Virginia ran and hiked and biked and admired fitness in other people. (She didn't swim, because she couldn't do it in full make-up and feared the chlorine turning her hair green; she hated to get her hair wet—she used flour as a dry shampoo.) "Good for him!" she said. "How'd you manage that one?"

"I signed him up with a personal trainer."

"Sneaky girl. Make sure he goes easy on him at first. We don't want him to have a heart attack."

"It's a woman."

Her mother sucked at the phone. "Stupid girl! I hope you made sure that she's not too attractive—though, come to think of it, that never seems to matter—but it never helps."

As Kate heard James greeting someone and then a stampede of feet, she considered the trainer, Doris Iris. She had thought of her as the kid sister—the happy Irish lassie, arms thick as a farmer's, wide-mouthed, swivel-hipped. But hadn't she noticed the *Irish*

Herald in the bathroom? What was Sandy doing with the local Irish newspaper? And then there was a bar of Irish Spring soap in the shower—the stiff-smelling, green-lined bar was unmistakable.

"I can't believe you set your husband up with a *woman*," her mother said. Since becoming a divorce lawyer, she was the affair expert. She assumed everyone was having an affair, just as she had assumed everyone was having sex when she worked at Planned Parenthood. "Permission to touch him, feel his biceps?" her mother went on.

Sandy, biceps?

"How old is she?"

Kate could hear James's shuffle-run approaching her office. "She's—" *oh shit, she's young.* "Maybe 22." Kate's voice cracked. "No, at least 24."

Her mother whistled. "Just watch out for ingrown hairs that could be hickies and inside-out underwear."

Kate slammed the phone down, her heart pounding. Her mother often had this effect on her. When she'd shown her the ultrasound pictures when she was pregnant with Camille, her mother had commented on the baby's wide-set eyes, sending Kate into a panic and ultimately down to the hospital to have the baby x-rayed again. "But I like wide-set eyes," her mother said later. Why should she listen to someone who hadn't exactly mastered her own relationships? Her mother, twice divorced, hater of cats, fired as the Campfire Girl leader for teaching the Bluebirds to make bourbon balls the holiday season Kate turned seven; shunned from the Spokane Symphony Society for spiking the brownies with marijuana she'd grown under glow lamps in their basement (the society members had known who to blame when they returned ravenous and horny to their tract mansions). But the fact was, her mother was a divorce lawyer—gossip law, she liked to call it—and had seen the personal-trainer affliction in men before. Men about Sandy's age, on the fast track to 40, without an appropriate outlet for an early midlife crisis. What had Kate been thinking, setting him up with a chesty farmhand with an Irish accent!

James appeared in her doorway. He was under stress: beads of perspiration dotted his upper lip; his Chicago Bulls T-shirt was untucked. "He wants a lemon Calistoga," he said, "And a bran muffin, if it isn't too much trouble."

Kate rummaged in her purse and pulled out a ten. "Go out the back way and find something at the deli across the street," she said. "I'll handle this." Kate smoothed her skirt and stepped out of her office and into the lobby. He wasn't there. Had J.P. grabbed him already? A *People* magazine lay open upside-down on the guest chair. Maybe she had time to go to the restroom.

Kate dashed into the single-stall women's restroom across the hall. The routine took under 30 seconds—she never understood why it took some women so long; were they wearing elaborate lingerie that snapped at the crotch? As she rushed out into the hallway, the toilet still flushing behind her, she collided with someone, someone tall, someone wearing lots of aftershave, but not Aqua Velva. Kate couldn't look. She glanced at her pointy high-heeled shoe that she'd accidentally kicked down the hall.

"I'm so sorry," he said, his big hands on her shoulders. "Are you O.K.?"

"Fine," Kate said, though she'd twisted her ankle. She tried to stand upright, but she wore only one shoe. "It's my fault," she said, tottering on one foot, finally peeking at his face. She recognized the dark eyes that had stared at her from the *Sports Illustrated* on her nightstand—the straight nose and velvet skin of a humid climate.

They're always so much bigger in person, Kate thought, glancing down at Pedro's thighs muscling through his jeans. "Kate McCabe," she said, holding out her hand. "I'm so sorry I missed our meeting. I'd like to blame it on my dog, but—"

He smiled, teeth the white of coconut, spaced wide, dimples that dented his cheeks. "Don't worry, I got your message," he said in that hint of an accent again, Spanish, but something else. Kate could see links of a chain—not gold, more like key chain—falling under his loose black cotton shirt. A crucifix, she imagined. She just knew.

Pedro retrieved her pointy black shoe—size nine and a half, she hoped he didn't notice—and kneeled before her. "Your foot," he said, looking at her with a small smile.

Kate slipped her foot into the shoe, her hand falling to his hard shoulder for balance.

The office door flung open. "There you are!" J.P. stood in the doorway with Kingsley, Deacon, and James stacked three-deep behind him, James holding a liter bottle of lemon Calistoga by the neck and a bran muffin wrapped in plastic.

"I see you've brought our guest to his knees," J.P. said to Kate, always full of compliments that failed to give her a warm fuzzy.

"Good to see you again, Pedro," J.P. said, as Pedro climbed to his feet. J.P. introduced Kingsley and Deacon, and they all shook hands.

Kate stepped over to James and put her hands on his shoulders. "And this is James Christmas," she said. "James is going to be working with J.P. just as soon as I find a replacement for his current position as communications officer."

J.P. glared at her. Practice making snap decisions, Kate thought, proud of herself.

"Good to meet you," Pedro said, holding out his hand.

James, overawed, said nothing. He held out the muffin as an offering.

"Hey, thanks a lot," Pedro said. "Raisins, too—great."

They all shuffled into the office lobby.

"We'll show you around," J.P. said. "Looks like you've already spent plenty of time with Kate here. If you need money moved around, she's the one to call. If you have an investment question, then call me and, if I can't answer it, I'll patch you right through to Kingsley."

Kingsley scraped along beside them, smiling his painted smile again, blushing to his ears. Was it Kate's imagination or was his striped tie only three colors? He seemed to be walking at eye-level with Kate—even in her three-inch pointy heels—and his shoulders looked a bit broader. Kate glanced at his feet for evidence of lifts, but only saw reasonable men's shoes, both black and tassel-less, sparkling with a recent shine.

"He'll talk to you about your future." J.P. rubbed his large, dimpled chin. "And by future, I do mean after football. It's hard to think about that now, I know—you're the bullet-man. Nobody runs with you." It was clear to Kate that J.P. intended to get credit for this deal, if a deal was going to be signed.

J.P. lifted a finger as they turned the corner into the inner office corridor. "But at Sports Financial, we don't drop you after the leagues do. We worry here about post-ball careers."

"We don't want you to end up as a *Wheel of Fortune* daytime host," Deacon jumped in.

"Is that lower than a *Jeopardy* host?" Kate couldn't resist. She could think of worse things. An ex-client, Victor Reilly, had made five million during a three-year career as a Kansas City wide receiver, then bought an auto dealership with what was left after five paternity suits, four monster trucks, and eight luxury vehicles; he was now eating out of cans and living in a can at a trailer park in Mesa.

"Looks like you guys could use a new couch," Pedro said as they walked into Kingsley's office.

"We prefer to reinvest our profits in technology," Deacon said, waving an arm at a black-and-white computer monitor in the corner, which Kingsley had finally retired. "You probably go to all these fancy-schmancy offices with matching furniture, but here we feel that a sofa is about as poor an investment as an automobile."

Pedro touched the silvery scar under his eye. That was a slip of the tongue J.P. would never have made, Kate thought. Of course Pedro was planning to buy a car. They all bought cars after they signed their first big contract. Basketball players were even worse. It wasn't just the cars for them, but the clothes and the jewelry. The credit card bills were loaded with Versace and Tiffany's charges. Sometimes Kate and Deacon would play a game trying to figure out if the clothes and jewelry were for women, but most often the purchases were for the guy. The labels were important. One Sonics forward left the suit labels on his sleeves; at first his teammates made fun of him, but then the practice caught on and removing the cloth labels became as taboo as clipping Beanie Baby tags. But for the most part, the cars established the pecking order. When Irv Johnson bought a 500SL, Trigger Smith requested that his Beamer's speakers be the size of its tires. Kate had wanted to gag, but it was never hers to decide.

As they entered the file room, only impressive for the sheer volume of files (Kingsley wanted every doodle he'd ever scratched to be at his fingertips), Peter the Red caught up with them. He was breathless. His tie was loose at his neck and his skin glowed with perspiration. Kate wondered if he'd just returned from his session with Dr. Fuller.

"Right on, Pedro!" Peter said, patting Pedro on the back.

"How's that turf toe?" The touching problem again, Kate thought. Pedro wasn't fazed, but when Peter showed him the file cabinets where his financial records would be kept, Kate bailed on the tour and locked herself in her office. She simply couldn't endure it. She'd caught the tail end of Peter's presentation to a second-string quarterback, Ken Dillon, and his wife, Maria, and had been alarmed by his prurience. Peter had explained how Ken would be loyal to Sports Financial when PaineWebber approached him—just the way he was loyal to Maria when women fans stripped to their flesh-colored panties at the visiting-team hotels—and diagrammed all this by drawing stick figures on oversized yellow paper with a green Magic Marker.

When Pedro's tour had ended, Kingsley had a bad feeling that it hadn't gone well. He didn't even want a client like Pedro Araguz and all the celebrity that went with a big star. He feared the spotlight. Big stars meant more scrutiny, and he hated minutiae. The red tape that went with being a registered investment advisor was almost more than he could bear. Why the SEC had chosen to audit him last year (he'd spent Christmas Eve digging up check copies), a boutique firm with a handful of employees, while so many numbskulls giving investment advice didn't bother to register, he would never understand. He'd found solace in a book, *The Death of Common Sense: How Law is Suffocating America,* whose author shared his views. He'd mass-ordered the book and given it to everyone he knew and anyone who offended him, to the labor attorney who told him he couldn't fire the Filipino receptionist who slept on the conference-room table during her breaks, and to the mailman who wouldn't deliver his mail without a nine-digit zip code, and to the IRS when they sent back his check because his envelope was postmarked a day late.

Kingsley just wanted to manage money. But big stars wanted more than that—shoe deals and charity nights and mosquito control. You could no longer get away with simply doubling their money. He missed the days when he sat in his little shack in Clear Lake with a battered typewriter and the *Wall Street Journal*, rarely having to meet anyone. Back then, he did what he did best. But a sole proprietor could barely survive anymore. And Mrs. Gartmore had become accustomed to San Francisco.

*B*ack in her office, Kate's phone lit up. James was nowhere. Through her window she watched Jennifer Popkins, the bookkeeper and back-up receptionist, type with the posture of a concert pianist in her ergo-chair while ignoring the incessant ringing. Jennifer was 29 and had three children who'd never been on antibiotics. She was interested in Kate's past—"isn't Rod Stewart from your generation?"—and was so efficient that she had lots of time to give Kate advice and let her in on how she'd gotten her children to sleep through the night at three months old. The inspirational quote for the day on Jennifer's sports calendar was "A winner never whines."

Why don't I fire her? Kate wondered. Her purse was stolen ten weeks ago, and, though she'd pleaded with Jennifer to get her a new key—Jennifer controlled the office keys and the coffee—every day she still had to bang on the front door. She'd even discovered Jennifer rummaging through the HR files in her office, writing down the heights and weights and childbirthing details of the women employees. Last week she'd suggested that Kate try the new clear braces to correct the "little gap" between her teeth. "That little gap's the reason Sandy married me!" Kate had spat.

Kate banged a fist on her desk, then picked up line one. "Good morning. It's a great day at Sports Financial," she said sweetly.

"Randy Nester for Kingsley Gartmore," a gruff voice said.

Randy Nester, megalo-agent, hadn't spoken to Kingsley for five years, not since before Kate had joined the firm. Kate had heard all the war stories—Randy had lured away three of Sports Financial's franchise clients.

Kate figured Randy still wanted to talk about the incident at the ball park. It was a good sign that Randy, and not his attorney, was calling. "He's in a meeting," Kate said. *With my client.* "This is Kate McCabe, the CFO, is there anything I can do for you?" She was, in fact, the CFO. She enjoyed introducing herself as CFO to people who didn't know she cleaned the company toilets.

"You sound too young to be a CFO," Randy Nester said. He was more mellow than she expected. "Betcha get that a lot."

"Well, I—"

"Maybe you can help me, Kate," he said. "I've got too much

work now. I want to get out of the tinker-toy business. I'm a sports lawyer, I'll leave you boys to push the paper. I don't need to be messing with the stocks. All's I need is a jigger-full-a-law for what I do."

Tell me something I don't know, Kate thought. Was Randy really tossing them a bone? "You want us to push paper for your clients?" Kate asked, remembering to use his words.

"Not so fast there," Randy said. "I'm like a spiritual advisor. I'm only here to inspire. They make the ultimate selection, right or wrong. So what da ya think, Kate? I gotta a Mercedes-load coming into town for the holidays. How about a presentation on Christmas Eve? Say ten o'clock. Could use a woman's touch."

"Sure," Kate said quickly, her second snap decision of the morning. She wondered why Nester so enraged Kingsley. Clients came and went, the revolving door was part of business. "Sorry about the little mishap at 3Com," she said.

"Ah, don't mention it," Nester said. "That dog don't hunt."

"Look at Nester's m.o.," Deacon said, holding up Nester's November newsletter. Someone had drawn horns and a goatee on Nester's glossy face. "Investing at the highest level," Deacon read, pointing to the drawing of a crucifix. An angel with a Tinkerbell wand hovered next to it. "God," Deacon said, who was famous for stating the obvious. "Nester says he's got God. Invest with him and you're in with God."

"We're screwed then," Kingsley said, throwing up his hands. "We can't compete with God."

"Did you give Pedro the book?" Deacon asked, tossing the newsletter on the coffee table. They all referred to *The Death of Common Sense* as "the book."

Kingsley was on his feet. "You can't give the book to an athlete," he said. "Athletes don't need common sense. They have a get-out-of-jail-free card. They think holding down a job in college is turning on the lights in the stadium."

"Sports is a job," Kate said. She was sitting next to Peter. "I think you're being a little hard."

"Since when do you defend them?" J.P. asked.

"Looks like you got all gussied-up for today," Deacon said,

and Kate caught a glint off his tortoise-shell frames. He was blind without the Calvin Klein glasses and roach-browed. His presence had the same effect as the incessant drip of her leaky bathroom faucet. She had asked Kingsley to speak to him about his suggestive comments to her and the other women employees—his weekend war stories were as contrived as porn movies—but she knew that Kingsley wouldn't know a leer from an eye tic.

"Hey, we need to focus here," Peter said.

Kate noticed that Peter was letting his hair grow again. The top was thinning, but the sides were puffy around the ears like Bozo the Clown. Maybe the shrink had made things worse; it wasn't the idea to get him more stressed out.

"How's Furious?" she asked him on a whim. She didn't think she could ask about his girlfriend (Angela, or something) when she might be two girlfriends behind. The dogs seemed to stick around longer, and, when the dogs changed, they were headed for trouble. She hoped that Furious was still eating Milkbones and that Peter hadn't taken on a dachshund (or, God help him, a Dalmatian).

Before he could answer, Kingsley rapped on the chalkboard with his knuckles. Their names were scrawled on top; on the far right was the number of clients—12, and the estimated new-client revenue, $1.8 million. J.P. and Peter the Red each had five football players. Deacon had two minor leaguers and Kingsley had no one, but a big contract like Pedro's could change everything.

Kate's name was notably missing. "What about me?" Kate pointed at the chalkboard. "Deacon's a tax accountant and he's up there."

Kingsley clicked his Bic. "Deacon has segued into client relations over a period of time."

"And you don't think I've segued into client relations?" Kate asked. "What do you call my urination work? Romantic relations?"

"You're well compensated for your work. You'll be properly bonused."

Kate didn't like the verb of that. "Yeah, like last year's gift certificate from Victoria's Secret." She stood. "Maybe lunch at Lloyd's on secretary's day?" She hadn't forgotten last year's annual review. He'd taken her to Lloyd's, where men wore bibs and ate Flintstone-sized steaks. Kingsley introduced her as his secretary to the Mafioso maître d', who oozed garlic from his large pores and knew how Kingsley took his meat. Kingsley hadn't noticed the slip of the tongue and neither had the maître d', who complimented her on her beige sweater.

"I'm the one who got the meeting with Pedro," Kate said.

"With all due respect, Kate," J.P. said, rubbing his hands together. "You didn't show for that meeting. You've got too much going on at the office—personnel issues that we couldn't even comprehend. Like the way you broke up that fight between Jennifer and Mary Ellen over the Avon cosmetics. You handled that like a pro. Irv really appreciated that we bought all that from his girlfriend."

Everyone murmured their agreement.

Kate's breasts ached. She desperately needed to pump; she'd lost feeling in her big toes. She pointed at Kingsley. "You trash me on this and you'll lose Pedro."

All of them stared at her, J.P. at her shoes. Kate could read their faces. Did she have some power over Pedro that they didn't know about? Would he come back to try on the other shoe?

Deacon spoke first, "Hey, Kate might give us a leg up on the competition."

"You're a dick, Deek," J.P. said.

Kingsley slid in his rolling chair to the chalkboard and grabbed a piece of purple chalk. He reached with his long skinny arm and scrawled Kate's name after Deacon's. "O.K., whoever gets Pedro to *sign* the contract gets the credit," he said, swiveling to look at Kate for approval.

"Now add James's name after mine."

Kingsley furrowed his forehead, his eyebrows were beetle antennae.

"He tells me he just committed a guy," Kate said. "Well, actually a woman. Theresa Paradisio, the mogul skier, is in his differential equations class at Berkeley. She's got a Special K commercial. Next week she guest-stars on *Melrose Place* as Michael's new love interest."

Sports Financial had never had a woman client. It wasn't cost-effective. Women tried hard, but still earned a pittance shooting hoops. Women had to moonlight as supermodels when they played pro volleyball. But *Melrose Place*... Didn't Heather Locklear get something like a million an episode?

J.P. rubbed his chin, for once at a loss for words. Deacon and Peter the Red sat forward on Joe Montana's sofa. Selling to a woman was different than bedding her. Kate wasn't sure they understood that.

Kate pulled a blank contract off Kingsley's desk. "It's open season on minks."

As the boys left, Kate lingered.

"Market's sliding," Kingsley said, clicking his hand-held QuoTrek. "This bear's come out of nowhere, hit us like an asteroid. Could cause an implosion in the world financial system."

Kate sat down in front of him; he studied his phone list.

"I need to talk to you," Kate said.

"I wouldn't invest now," Kingsley said, running his finger down the list. "The bear tries to pull everyone in he can before crashing the market."

"I'm not planning to invest," Kate said. She thought that Kingsley knew that she didn't have extra money hanging around. Surely she had explained this to him several times. Though she and Sandy made decent salaries, it already took every cent they had to live in San Francisco. She was repressing the financial implosion of Sandy quitting—an asteroid the size of the Transamerica Pyramid hitting their back yard.

"Are you familiar with relativity?" Kingsley asked, squinting at her.

"Somewhat." Kate leaned back in her chair.

"Light travels at a speed of 30 round trips to New York in one second. Now, if I were to get up from my chair and walk down the hall to the fax machine and pick up the fax that's waiting for me there, when I returned I'd be younger than you—relatively, of course. The trick is to keep moving."

"I'll go get the fax," Kate said, standing.

"Do you think you could unplug my laptop first?" He peered under his desk. "I never know which wire is which and I need to take it home tonight."

It was common knowledge that Kingsley was afraid of electrical outlets ever since his secretary, Mary Ellen Tuohy, unplugged her 10-key by prying the plug out of the electrical socket with Kingsley's letter opener, shutting down the power for twelve hours (including elevators) and singeing her ringed fingers. Everyone feared it was happening again whenever Kate used her electric breast pump and all the computers went fuzzy.

Kate was used to the request. Even after she wrapped his laptop cord with red tape, Kingsley pretended not to understand. He was known for acting innocent. He claimed never to have eaten at McDonald's (McDuffy's, he called it) and never to have heard of Mick Jagger; when Kate tore a picture from *People*, Kingsley shrugged, he'd seen him around, maybe he worked in the parking garage.

Kate gathered up her skirt and crawled under his desk. She yanked out the cord from the outlet. To help Kingsley match the appropriate cord to the correct outlet, she had painted both red with the nail polish that sat on Mary's desk. "I need to talk to you," Kate said again as she reeled in the cord.

His eye twitched, a nervous tic sometimes mistaken as a wink by women who didn't know him.

"Randy Nester called for you," she said. She sat in the guest chair. "Says he wants to give his clients more diversification—spread the wealth." Kate cleared her throat. "He wants me to come over to present to some clients."

"He what?" Kingsley hadn't gotten past the name Randy Nester. He tried to make himself breathe slower. He tried counting to ten. His glasses steamed.

"I think he wants to patch things up. It couldn't hurt to have me go over there and check it out."

Kingsley didn't like it at all. He didn't even like that Kate was talking about Nester, let alone getting in bed with him.

"I know you're the kind of man who doesn't hold a grudge," Kate said.

"We should send J.P.," Kingsley said. "You don't have the experience. And Nester's—" Maybe Nester had changed, though he still wasn't sure. His mind wandered to a quote by J.F.K., "Forgive your enemies, but never forget their names."

"He asked me to come."

"You take the responsibility then," Kingsley said. He certainly didn't feel like talking to Nester himself. "As long as you have your

your work done here."

The intercom buzzed. "Ms. Towne is here for you," James shouted over the speaker.

Kingsley covered his ears. Recently it sounded as if James was using a megaphone. "Bring her in," Kingsley hollered back, then to Kate, "When are we getting a new receptionist now that James has moved on?"

"I'll start interviewing," Kate said. She was doing that funny thing with her fingertips again, pressing them into a diamond shape and throwing her shoulders back.

"Search his desk," Kingsley said, cramming his shirt back into his pants. "Find out where all the bodies are buried."

The door opened and a handsome man-sized woman filled the doorway, eclipsing all but James's waving hand, a hand which seemed to point to her, as if pointing her out was necessary. Oversized guests were not new to Sports Financial, but this was a woman. Kingsley had expected someone more petite, clever in the way of seamstresses, but a bit more Betty Boop. But this woman was large, from the sweep of blue-black hair to her thickly powdered face to her frosted lips to her hands that swelled with rings. She wore a shiny carmine jacket and a fastidious strand of pearls. Her lips matched the jacket. Kingsley rejoiced in his noticing of the details.

"Ms. Alberta Towne!" James announced in his new DJ style. With a flip of her crushed-velvet scarf, Ms. Towne stepped forward with small mincing steps (for someone so large), perhaps observing some propriety unknown to Kingsley, or possibly restricted in her movement by her tight knee-length skirt.

Kingsley and Kate popped to their feet. "Nice to meet you, Ms. Towne," Kingsley said, pumping her callused hand.

"My pleasure," she said, with a voice that was deep and hoarse and older than her forty-something years—or the voice of a man. But certainly not a man. The face was too smooth, not a hair on the back of her hands. "Marvelous tie," Ms. Towne said. "That peacock stripe is your eye-extension color."

Kingsley beamed. But then he considered its deeper meaning. "Marvelous tie" could mean he'd overdone it; the colors were too bold—she saw the tie coming before she saw him. Then he recalled reading that when President Clinton said "nice tie," he really meant "screw you." But "marvelous tie," he reasoned, coming from someone in her line of work, had to be taken as a compliment.

"We've been looking forward to your visit," Kate said, shaking her hand. "I know you'll take good care of Kingsley. If you'll excuse me, I've got a presentation to prepare." Kate stepped to the door.

"Not so fast," Ms. Towne said. "I feel it's my job to tweak the image of the entire firm, not just its leader's."

Kingsley noticed that Ms. Towne wasn't quick to compliment Kate. He was enjoying himself, basking in the reflected glory of his necktie. He had his own sense of style. His 21-year-old son had recently told him that he had "zero fashion sense," but wasn't that a fashion statement in itself? And here they thought *he* needed professional help. On a roll, he asked Ms. Towne what she thought of Kate's outfit.

Ms. Towne pinched the red fabric on Kate's arm. "I think it should go away."

Kate sank into a chair, shaking out her hand as if trying to restore the circulation. She crossed her arms and legs, trying to hide. "Well I—I have something to do after work," she said, "so I needed to dress up a little."

It was clear that Alberta Towne was not the type of woman who crossed her legs or used filler words like "well" or "hmmm." She jotted something down in her notebook. "Day-into-evening," she said. "We'll need to buy for you in that category. But you do realize there's a difference between dress-up and costume."

Kate smiled, defeated.

"We have some real work to do here," Ms. Towne went on, clasping her hands together, entwining her square red fingernails, blunt instruments filed to perfection. "First, so I can get to know you, I want you to show me everything in your wallets."

Kingsley patted his back pocket and felt the bulk of his wallet; it bulged like a three-meat burrito. He wasn't even sure what he had in there. He hoarded things like free-drink coupons for a disco in Mazatlan, expired a dozen years ago, and fortune-cookie messages. What did any of this have to do with a new wardrobe? Maybe the image-consultant thing was a fraud and this was a stick-up. He'd watched varieties of con men (and women!) on *America's*

Most Wanted, but none had posed as personal shoppers.

Ms. Towne tapped her foot, looking from Kingsley to Kate. She had lots of time. They were paying her a hundred an hour to size them up.

Kingsley did a double take. Her feet could have been Georgie Porshay's stuffed into pointy shoes. Was Alberta really Albert?

"I guess you'll need to go get your purse, Kate," Ms. Towne said.

Kate stood and ran for the door like a hostage set free.

Run, Kate! Call security!

Kingsley pulled out his wallet.

"Now, dump it," Ms. Towne said.

Kingsley set his wallet on his desk. It swelled, not shutting, like the books he read in the bathtub.

Ms. Towne flipped it open and pulled out a punch card for Brian's Chinese restaurant.

"You eat here?" she asked, holding the grease-splattered card up to the light as if counting the number of holes.

"It's been a few years."

Ms. Towne nodded and folded the card into thirds. She tucked it neatly into a credit card slot in the wallet. "We'll need to re-organize this," she said, shoving the wallet back to him across the desk. "And I'll need to make an appointment to see your closet. Kate's, too. And anyone else who comes in contact with your clients."

At that moment James burst through the door, fax paper fluttering in his hand like an unwieldy bird.

*P*eter the Red knew that minks were hard to catch. They were slippery creatures, lusciously pelted but pea-brained. Sometimes they'd get close, then bite hard when they left. But they followed the pack. The key was to trap one, the others would follow.

More than anything else, Peter saw his job as making Kingsley happy. He saw Sports Financial as the last gasp on the whistle-stop-tour of his career. Kingsley had given him a chance when the others had fired him, had loaned him a few bucks even after he said it was the last time. He knew he might not be able to get another job—his résumé looked like a Chinese menu. And employers were getting fanatical about private investigators. Even at the office, he'd go to the bathroom and someone would mess with his desk. He just noticed that someone had moved the bookmark in his *American Medical Reference*. Last week his credit report was copied to him, unsolicited, and a call came in about a bill he'd already mailed. And someone was reading his mail—he could see the tiny tears along the lips of the envelopes; he now told people not only to seal his mail, but glue it down, too.

Sometimes Kingsley talked crazy about packing it in and going back to the swamp. Clear Lake. The name was a contradiction, just like Kingsley himself. Peter hated it when he talked about quitting. It was Nester that really got to him—Nester, the perennial blond, caused lots of problems for everybody. Without Kingsley there wouldn't be anything for Peter to do. Selling to athletes was the perfect job for him—the only job for him. He could understand them, while J.P. had to hit on them— nice biceps, bullet-man—and Deacon talked down to them, over-enunciating, assuming they couldn't tie their shoes.

On December 20th, Peter met Shelby Chin-O'Connor at the Bus Stop bar near her Pacific Heights apartment. It had been her suggestion. "Just around the corner from my place" had been her exact words. Peter knew what that meant. It was a rotten world. Men were often the victim, nobody realized. Folks thought you had choices.

He rubbed his beard. It was getting thicker, moving into winter (or was it really because of winter?). His head was still ringing and then there'd been the incident with Furious. Maybe he was obsessive-compulsive, with an elevated level of serotonin. He'd read that Howard Stern once felt he needed to enter every room with the right side of his body, and this reassured him. As a child Peter had counted his steps to school and back (he still counted his steps from the bed to the bathroom), and during third grade penmanship he felt he had to tap the pencil's eraser two times on the desk before making the loop of his P. He could let all this bother him, but he needed to prioritize. He had to secure this deal for Kingsley.

"I've got some great news for you," Shelby said, sitting in the

Bus Stop's open window. As Peter walked in, she sipped the head of a frothy hard cider and waved some papers in his face.

A Roadway truck, probably packed full of holiday packages, rolled by blasting exhaust through the open window.

Peter took the papers. "This is incredible," he said. "Skull's gonna flip. You sure the committee bought off on it?"

Shelby nodded, a clump of lip-length hair falling in her mouth. "They leave it to me to advise them on this stuff."

Peter whistled. "I really owe you one. Can I buy you dinner?" It was the least he could do. For the good of the firm, in the name of business development.

Shelby fingered her pearl earring, a pretty woman in distress. "I was planning a quiet evening," she said. "I've got these lovely tomatoes about to go bad. Do you want to come over for a salad? It's an easy walk from here."

The good thing about salads, Peter thought— other than their obvious health benefits—was that they took a long time to prepare. There was chopping and slicing and the ceremony of drizzling olive oil and twisting the pepper mill three times around. He thought by the time they actually got around to eating the salad they would have run out of conversation. Her heater was stuck on 90°, drying out the bare, shrub-sized Christmas tree on the coffee table, so Peter went around trying to open windows that were painted shut, crispy pine needles crackling under his feet. It struck him then that she must be alone. She didn't seem the type of woman who would be alone, there was such a put-together-quality about her. Something told him he should leave, that no affair was ever simple.

But then she offered him a glass of Chardonnay, which he tried not to drink, and a dish of salty cashews, which neither of them touched. Everything happened fast after that. Shelby boiled an artichoke, fanning herself with an elephant leaf of romaine. She complained of the terrible heat, kicked off her patent leather pumps, rolled up her pant legs, flexed those incredible calves, then finally excused herself to go to her bedroom to change, apparently forgetting she only had a studio. She returned to chop the carrots wearing nothing but a sleeveless cotton blouse.

Peter turned away, but he couldn't just ignore this. Or stand there trying to make eye contact without looking at her blond pubic hair (which was really blond—about the shade of her eyebrows) and say he was sorry about the misunderstanding. He couldn't humiliate a woman that way.

The air was hot and palpable, with only the vapor of artichoke between them. It was almost safe, until she kissed him. Her skin was soft and sticky as fresh cake, but her elbows were sharp. His fingers found her ribs, then the little bow on her bra. He moved his hand to her wrist and held it lightly, as if pinching sugar between two fingers, letting beads of sweat trickle into his eyes. He cupped her hip bones with his hands as she pulled him to bed.

*T*hat same evening, getting Gus to stay in bed was like trying to submerge a beach ball. He'd already peed, brushed his teeth, and rinsed his *Put-Put Goes to the Zoo* CD in the bathroom sink (he'd seen his father do it once after Camille had slimed it). After that Gus often scolded Kate about not touching "the shiny side" of the CD. Tonight he was particularly amped because his father had visited his pre-school that day for career day, a day when the parents talked to the three-year-olds about their professions.

Kate was disappointed she had to miss it (at least one parent from every family was there) and pleased by Gus's enthusiasm— "My Dad was the coolest!"—and Sandy taking the time, until she heard Gus saying his Dad had taught the children to Stop, Drop, and Roll.

"What was that?"

"You pretended to be a fireman in front of 30 of our friends?" Kate later said to Sandy.

"I know I haven't passed the test yet—"

His explanation was that Gus had started telling the kids at school that his daddy was a fireman, and one thing led to another.

Not a lie, Kate thought, utter fantasy. Then it occurred to her that maybe she was the one with the fantasy. It *was* happening.

Sandy McCabe, her husband; Sandy McCabe, a fireman.

Gus, now under the bed, was zooming his fire truck. He'd hosed down the bathroom with the bathtub "fire hydrant," then stopped, dropped, and rolled under his bed.

Kate understood that children loved rituals—for Gus, the getting-ready-for-bed-routine had to go in the same sequence every night (pee, brush, rinse the CD). His organic whole milk needed to be warmed in the microwave, placed on the dresser (never handed to him directly). Later, he'd set the sippy cup outside his bedroom door for Kate, the room-service maid, to collect.

The experts assured Kate that these were normal control devices, but Kate feared they were the beginning of compulsions, seeds already planted—like alcoholism—ready to germinate if something didn't go quite right, if their parenting failed in some small way. They were past the grace period with Gus. The first two years children rarely remembered anything. At three, any memory would be fair game for a therapist's couch. With Camille they still had some slack. That was the reason Sandy was the one trying to get Camille into her own bed. Kate pictured Gus at 30, recalling to some Dr. Renee Fuller-type that his mother raced through *Green Eggs and Ham,* sometimes hyperventilating after that final scene where Sam gets the picky eater to want green eggs everywhere, sometimes summarizing (which Gus always called her on), checking her watch between paragraphs. And that his babysitter, Consuelo Riviera, cleaned the bathroom wearing only her bra and underwear. She and Sandy had discussed it, and decided to invoke a "don't ask, don't tell" policy. (How could they broach such a subject with her?) After all, Gus could have made up the story about her underwear—he was prone to such myths—but Kate doubted he could have thought up the black bra and flowered underpanties. His dragons never had that kind of detail.

Kate felt she was losing control of her house. Whenever she vowed to quit and stay home with the kids, Sandy would shake his head, saying it was easier for her to stay at the office. But she wanted him to think of her as the expert on their children— sometimes she had to ask Consuelo what time Camille went down for her naps.

"Mommy," Gus said, flinging open his bedroom door.

It was his fourth time getting up. Nine-thirty and she hadn't eaten dinner. She tried remembering what she'd eaten that day—a Mocha Power Bar for breakfast. "Back in bed," she said, sternly this time, picking him up and hoisting him over her shoulder. Her breasts ached. She had cabbage leaves in her bra to ease the engorgement. She was trying to drop a feeding, one less a day would be guilt-free and would buy her some time. Camille wouldn't miss it.

Kate tossed Gus onto the bed. Forget dinner, she wanted her bed.

He landed, giggling, "I need more silly water."

"You've had enough," she said, tucking him in. She thought he'd run out of excuses. The pediatrician had recommended mineral oil when Gus refused to potty-train, held it, and stopped himself up. Kate thought that he was probably the only child in the world who asked for mineral oil ("silly water"), which she squirted in his mouth every night with a dropper. That wasn't the only thing she squirted into his mouth. The kids had constant colds, so the pediatrician suggested herbal concoctions to boost the immune system. Gus called the dark liquid in an old-fashioned medicine bottle (something that looked as if it should have a skull and cross bones) Bear Juice. Other children had described it as tasting like dirt and everything terrible in the world, but her children opened their mouths for it like hungry baby birds. She had no idea what this meant, though she suspected it had something to do with her parenting. But if Bear Juice prevented one cold, one midnight stumble into vomit-splattered bedrooms, then her treks to the medieval Chinese pharmacy in the heart of Chinatown, where there was no parking and dirty chickens hung in windows, were worth it.

Maybe her pediatrician's medicine erred on the alternative side. When the chamomile tea he had Gus drinking from a bottle at three months wasn't curing the colic, he'd suggested that Kate try smoking pot, but he was disinclined to recommend a source. She wasn't sure if the marijuana was supposed to get into her breast milk to relax Gus, or was it just supposed to relax her?

Camille wailed from her bedroom.

Sandy was lying on the cot they'd placed next to Camille's crib. According to Jennifer Popkin's self-help book on children's sleep problems, they needed to move the cot a few inches toward the door every night, then finally out into the hallway. Kate had doubts about these books. She was conflicted about the "family bed," which, counter-intuitively, was supposed to make children feel safe, hence less likely to grow up fearing being alone and jumping into bed with anyone. It was supposed to curtail promiscuity the way family meals were supposed to reduce violence and drug use. And Kate thought "Ferberizing" sounded like something done by the dry cleaner.

"Kim Novak has spent three thousand dollars in my name!" Kate said, holding up a UW Phi Beta Kappa card statement—a card she'd never applied for. "$800 at Victoria's Secret, $475 at Jiffy Lube—Jiffy Lube, for crying out loud! She must have treated all her friends to lubes. Six trips to emergency rooms—SF General, St. Luke's, UCSF—and here's three separate ambulance service charges. Is she using ambulances like taxi cabs? How has she stolen my identity?"

"Easy, Kate," Sandy said. He was studying for his fire-fighting review course with a flash-light. "She got your social security number off your Health Net card—that's all you need for a credit card. The woman's probably a drugger. She goes to the ER to get drugs—just tells them about her unbearable back pain, neck pain, whatever, and they give her Percodan."

"I could do that."

"Of course you could, but you wouldn't."

How's he so sure? she wondered. Did he know her that well? "I don't like it," she said. "Here Kim Novak is running around in ambulances, while I have to take BART!"

"Hey, come on," he said, smiling. "You took a police car home yesterday."

Sandy was sitting for the exam in the morning. He'd already taken the physical, though the boot camp portion was yet to come. Last night a woman, humorless as an IRS agent, had knocked on the door and left with a vial of Sandy's blood. Gus had asked if she was a vampire.

"She can't sleep with that light show you've got going," Kate said, pointing to the flashlight bobbing on the ceiling. Anything having to do with his fireman quest made her feel sarcastic. Camille stood, crying, rattling the wooden bars of her crib.

Sandy sat up on his elbows. "She wants a boob," he said.

Kate scooped up the baby and held her to her chest. It felt good to her, that there was still something that only she could provide. Camille shuddered, then sighed; she burrowed into Kate as if trying to fill the same space, wetting Kate's face with her tears. Kate breathed her soft vanilla hair, stroked her tender skin, feeling it give way underneath her thumb; she rocked and hummed, and they slow-danced by the glow of the flashlight. Kate wondered if there was ever a time that one felt so completely safe as when protected by one's mother.

She'd been a worrier even as a child. She'd worried about her mother not coming home, about her mother staying happy, and the way the weekend men who brought her Barbie dolls drove their beater cars. She could still picture one swivel-seated Monte Carlo with a deep key scratch on the hood and her mother's stiletto sandal in the middle of the driveway the next morning for the whole neighborhood to see.

But her mother had always been there to talk, and she stayed home if Kate asked her, and taught her that drinks taste better out of pretty glasses. She was never too busy to stop what she was doing—put down the phone or the eyelash curler, turn off the Jane Fonda work-out video—and give Kate her full attention. She would answer Kate's questions. And there were never sugar-coated answers: she used the word "vagina" in conversation, explained what a tampon was before Kate needed to know....

If anything, she talked too much. Kate would never know if she was trying to be a friend or desperately needed one.

Kate remembered asking her mother how many times a week God expected you to pray—even then she'd been looking for a number—and about the dinosaurs being killed by a meteor. (That end of the world still bothered her.)

Sandy snapped off the flashlight. "This cot's so cramped," he said, rustling the blankets.

"Better get used to it," Kate said, lowering the sleeping Camille into her crib. She tucked a white-eyelet pillow under her head. "I doubt they'll have a queen bed for you at the firehouse." Kate pictured the mustachioed men welcoming him to the sleeping porch. "Come to think of it, maybe there will be a few queens."

*A*t two a.m., Kate still couldn't sleep. Sandy breathed evenly, like a child. He was always first to fall asleep, and this irritated her. She often lay awake, staring at the sparkles on the ceiling, remnants of the constellations, stickers that glowed in the dark placed there by the prior owners, two gay men having more fun than they had. When they moved in, Sandy and Kate scrubbed and scrubbed, but several stars and a crescent moon remained.

Kate hated to wake him. "Honey," she said, shaking his shoulder gently.

"What, huh?" he asked, rubbing his eyes. "Go to sleep, Kate."

"I just wanted to ask you something?"

"Let's not talk about your mother. Just stock up on toilet paper." Sandy complained that her mother used several rolls of toilet paper *a day*. And that she was a slob, leaving toothpaste in the sink and underpants in the bathroom, which Camille wore around her neck—in preparation for boas, he feared. He claimed that her mother had sullied his Rose Bowl sweatshirt with "pancake make-up or menstrual blood," he wasn't sure.

"No, the personal-trainer thing," Kate said.

"I told you—it's fun," Sandy said. "I'm making progress. I've lost twelve pounds. I think I'll stay with it."

"But you don't need it. You look great."

Sandy reached out and tried to pat her, but patted her pillow instead. "That's nice of you to say, but I could stand to improve. I still have that boot camp to get through."

"Well, I don't think Doris has much experience," Kate said. "She's kinda young—probably has lots of buffed boyfriends hanging around." Kate stared at the ceiling. She spotted a small galaxy over the dresser that they'd missed. "Probably just one serious buffed boyfriend—I think she mentioned him. For what we're paying, there're some pretty knowledgeable guys there who could help you."

Sandy pulled the blanket up to his neck. "Maybe an amateur's good for me. She really cracks the whip. I haven't worked out this hard since high school."

High school? Kate sat up. What was he getting at? Weren't high school boys sexually at their peak? Couldn't they keep an erection for something like a whole night—you'd knock it down, and it would pop right back up like Gus's Oscar Meyer punching bag. She remembered the rides in their fathers' cars, their slobbery kisses, like eating a peach.

Kate reached for Sandy under the blanket and stroked his leg. They needed to have sex, and they needed to have it now. He needed to understand that she could crack the whip, too, when she wanted to. She felt that if they didn't do it enough, it would slow to a trickle, like her breasts drying up without Camille's suckle. "I don't know," Kate said. "I feel like I forced you."

Camille whined in the next room.

"Shhhh," Sandy said, rounding his back away from her. "I guess Doris tired me out. Let's go to sleep. I swear I like it. I don't mind it at all."

*P*hillip the Dog Trainer insisted that if they made continual eye contact with Stirling Moss he wouldn't be so naughty, sniffing crotches and snatching mozzarella sticks that Sandy planted on the arm of the sofa. This he demonstrated with the demo-dog—a foot-soldier rottweiler named Elias.

Kate felt that continual eye contact with a 90-pound animal in a household with two small children was ambitious. She didn't get enough eye contact during her bullet-point conversations with Sandy—certainly not continual eye contact—so she resented these efforts with Stirling, though she was having an increasingly difficult time coexisting with him. The dog had separation anxiety. The Clomicalm wasn't helping; she often had both children and the dog in the bathroom with her while she peed, and the dog would follow her around the house with the click-click-click of his unclipped toenails—*can I get you something? a drink of water?* He'd block her entrance into the kitchen, panting, *Your baby's crying! Your baby's crying!*

Kate had heard that the neighbors' German shepherd was 19 years old, which in and of itself was alarming—Stirling Moss could live to be 133 in dog years! But the worst part was since she'd had children she herself seemed to be aging in dog years. The last year had brought an exponential number of wrinkles and sags that

Sandy refused to acknowledge.

Most mornings when Consuelo opened their front door, Stirling Moss did a nose dive for her crotch. But, occasionally, and without notice, Sandy would decide that Stirling needed discipline. Those times Consuelo opened the front door to Sandy restraining Stirling with a choke collar, shouting commands—down, boy; hurry-up (in a tiny voice); goooood, Stirling—stuffing pepperoni treats into his mouth. "This is what we're trying with Stirling today," he'd tell Consuelo, never breaking eye contact with the dog.

Kate was no psychiatrist, but she guessed that Sandy took Stirling's failures personally. Stirling was meek, neurotic as a show dog, afraid of the voice on the answering machine, and generally afraid—there were birds not hunted, things left undone. Maybe these drill-sergeant mornings were about Sandy's guilt (he'd insisted that Stirling preserve his balls). Or perhaps it was that Phillip the Dog Trainer had Stirling walking on his hind legs within five minutes of arriving at their house (for a fee of $125 an hour), and Sandy still had no control over him. The dog hadn't retained much from the training sessions, but Sandy was certain that he was only biding his time. He needed more time. After all, every evening Stirling would run out in the backyard and flush Mike the cat from the bushes. He didn't point (though Sandy swore that he had once pointed when Kate had been working late—"Did you see that, hun?" though Kate never did. Too bad they didn't have replay capability), but the flushing of the cat indicated that an instinct was there, buried in the everyday burdens of a city dog.

Like Stirling Moss, every night Sandy retreated to the backyard, Stirling to flush the cat and Sandy to chop wood in his Home Depot metal shed. Wanting to give Sandy his personal space, Kate never entered the shed. She envisioned it as dank and smelling of rain, clipped grass, and swollen paperbacks. She avoided that part of the yard, afraid that if she got too close she might hear the rustle of Irish newspapers or the slosh of a rum bottle, dark secrets too burdensome to the delicate balance of her life.

But Sandy would emerge from the shed relaxed, with an armful of wood. He'd make a fire in the living-room fireplace almost every night unless, for air-quality control, the city had prohibited it. He felt that he needed to comply with the city—he wanted no black marks against him when his civil-servant application was reviewed. Kate was certain they would find nothing (she racked her brain to come up with something—anything!), but he was a regular Boy Scout, Sea Scout, really.

Saturday morning, Sandy appeared to be in a shed mood. He was confident that he would pass the fireman test. It was December 22, two days before her mother's arrival, and the house was foul. They had one bathroom and Kate didn't enjoy sharing it with strangers. In particular, her mother's boyfriends, who'd leave whiskers in the sink and the toilet seat warm.

"It's filthy," Kate said, storming around holding a bottle of Windex like a gun. It was the only cleaning product Consuelo Riviera ever used. Kate had even seen her cleaning the highchair tray with it. They went through it like they went through organic whole milk (that and paper towels, which Consuelo used to dry dishes). Kate had hired "The Brawny Boys of the Castro" to clean on Christmas Eve (they cleaned wearing G-strings, but Kate had heard they were thorough), when she realized that Windex was the only cleaning product they had on hand. When she'd interviewed the boss-man (he was fully clothed and looked as if he could carry a piano on his back), she had at first been suspicious of his smooth hands. "Gloves," he'd told her, a bit snidely. Obviously. Kate knew no mother who took the time to don rubber gloves. That's why his look like that and mine look like this, she thought. Her knuckles had started to crack from the cold.

She'd been mortified as they walked through the house taking inventory of the cleaning supplies. They did not even own a mop. "Must be in the garage," she'd assured him.

The boss-man explained that they cleaned in G-strings so they wouldn't get bleach on their clothes. Maybe that was Consuelo's theory, too, Kate thought with some relief.

Kate picked up Sandy's dirty socks, and threw them into the fireplace. Gus took the cue and began throwing toys and newspapers into the fireplace as well. "The insect problem is unacceptable," Kate yelled up the stairs to Sandy, who was getting ready for his exam. "First the fleas freeze, now we have ants. The floor moves!

"Our Christmas tree is infested," Kate went on, as Sandy rolled down the stairs, fast and lumbering as a freight train, with

Camille tucked under his arm.

"Take them away, please," Kate said.

She couldn't look again. The frosted Christmas cookies that she and Gus had hung on the Christmas tree (a rare Martha Stewart moment) — the colorful Santas, and stars, and candy canes — were covered with ants.

"What would your mother think?" she asked him. Her voice shook on the edge of sobbing. She felt the shadow of Sandy's mother, who anesthetized her household ants with lemon juice, pulverized rose petals for potpourri, and could fold the fitted bed sheets into phyllo dough triangles.

Sandy handed Camille to Kate and quickly plucked the cookies from the tree and lobbed them into the kitchen garbage can.

"Did you mail the Christmas cards?" Kate asked. She'd written and addressed 75 cards (30 to people from his office).

"Sure," he said, shaking the ants from his hands, then wiping them on his jeans. But she knew he hadn't. Maybe it was intuition, or maybe it was because she was looking for reasons to be mad at him. Let it go, she told herself, we don't have to send holiday cards every year. But getting the children to pose for the picture, faces animated and without smudges, Stirling Moss between them and grinning, had required almost more patience than she had had. Then she thought of the painstaking morning of writing out the greetings — Happy Holidays!! Sandy, Kate, Gus and Camille (and Stirling Moss too!!!). Such enthusiasm it had taken, licking and stamping, licking and stamping, the cramp in her hand, Camille trying to climb her, her coffee gone cold. She would feel better if she was certain that the cards were in the mail. With Camille still on her hip, she went down the stairs into the garage.

It had been a poor show of faith, Kate knew, but the red envelopes, licked and sealed, were still in the back seat of his BMW.

"Sandy!" Kate marched up the stairs.

Sandy was at the refrigerator pouring vanilla Yo Soy on his Captain Crunch. He'd been opposed to Kate's efforts to incorporate soy into their diet until he'd accidentally used it as a creamer one morning and discovered the fatted vanilla flavor tasted much better than nonfat milk.

"You lied to me," Kate whispered, cramming Camille's chubby legs into the Johnny Jump-up that was hanging in the kitchen doorway.

"I was going to do it this morning. They'll get there. I didn't want to make a big deal."

"The big deal is that you lied. What else would you lie to me about?" Kate stormed around the kitchen wiping food off the counter with a sponge. She stuck the box of Captain Crunch, still wide open, back in the pantry.

Kate knew she was getting nasty. To her knowledge, Sandy had never lied to her. She had fallen for his goody-two-shoes character. He trusted everyone. He gave handfuls of coins to every bum on the street; he even gave twenty bucks to a man who came to the door claiming car trouble, and didn't laugh in his face when he came back again. The fact that he always answered the door— Kate hid inside—and listened to the Jehovah's Witnesses and redwood-forest activists was testimony to his earnestness. He had even reported the $400 he won playing video poker in Reno. But the thought that he could lie, that there was this quality she didn't know about him, made her mind reel. What was out there that was out of her control? Should small lies be given less weight? She remembered how she'd once caught a bookkeeper who'd been kiting receipts: Kate had first stumbled on a small lie—her son didn't go to the school she said he did—then one thing led to another.

Gus appeared in the kitchen. "Mommy, I'm thirsty. I want some juice."

Kate yanked open the refrigerator and grabbed a box of Welch's grape juice. She jabbed in the straw and handed it to him.

"It was a white lie, Kate," Sandy said. "I didn't want to upset you."

"Not white," Kate said. "White is when you tell me that I don't look fat when I ask you."

"You've never looked fat."

"You know what I mean."

Sandy plopped his cereal bowl on the table, splashing Yo Soy over the sides. "I wanted to avoid the tongue lashing, that's all."

"You wanted to fire the president if he lied, but it's O.K. when you do it? Frankly, I care more about what my husband does."

Sandy laughed. "I hardly think this is comparable. My forgetting to mail the Christmas cards is not a matter of national security."

"But it's still a lie. It's the same thing. Lying to prevent embarrassment, lying to avoid a tongue—"

"The president was under oath. I can't believe you're this concerned."

Kate grabbed the ropes of the Johnny Jump-up to stop Camille's incessant ponging. Camille shrieked. "So, as long as you're not under oath, it's O.K.?" Kate said. "Do we need to get a judge to come over and swear you in every morning? *I'd like to remind you, Mr. McCabe, that you're still under oath.* Is this what it's come to?"

"Daddy, you're hurting Mommy's feelings," Gus said.

"I'm sorry," Sandy said, slapping his knee with his hand. "Kate, I'm sorry."

And Kate felt that he was sorry. But it was a battle she hadn't wanted to win. He had lied to her; he was capable of lying. Would she always forgive him the way she forgave Gus for whacking Camille, then repenting in the corner for 30 seconds? Gus knew better, too. Was sorry too easy?

*K*ate took Gus and Camille to her office after Sandy left for his exam. Kate was behind at work and thought she might be able to get some tasks off her desk, while the children milled around enjoying the holiday decorations. It was always the fantasy: achieving Brazelton "touchpoint moments" while accomplishing something.

Kate was deep in year-end minutiae. It was the time of year when she was most needed. She wired money, opened IRAs and children's trusts that had 12/31 deduction deadlines, and led the crusade to find secular, non-aggressive holiday cards, which she signed and mailed to the athletes. She'd mastered the boys' signatures: Kingsley's looked like a cursive X; Deacon's was "Deek" with vibrating e's; Peter the Red was illegible; and J.P.'s had the upright loopy quality of grade-school penmanship. She sometimes wrote, *With love, J.P.,* just for kicks.

During December the athletes always needed a lot of cash. Peer pressure was heightened to a frenzy. What to buy the significant other was foremost in their minds. Last-minute splurges meant selling off securities. It was a period of poor planning and penalties and short-term capital gains. Athletes she hadn't heard from in months dropped by in droves for cash handouts. Many were inspired to donate bell towers to their churches or build gymnasiums for their high schools. Kate took calls from athletes wanting directions to the nearest Charles Schwab branch—in say, Chevy Chase. She sweated and consulted maps. She licked envelopes and drank too much office coffee and wrote letters to Mississippi churches and North Dakota high schools. She ate rotting apples from the office fridge and wondered what went on in these places.

A few athletes insisted on composing the generous gifting letters themselves, so Kate reviewed them, eliminating exclamation points and other excessive punctuation. For some reason she had a hard time convincing them to set up IRAs and children's trusts for various DNA-authenticated children around the country before year-end. *It'll save you sixty-thousand dollars!* Kate would tell them as she FedExed more applications. When they arrived in person for cash handouts or holiday cheer, she'd corral them in her office and stand on her desk waving the application (the signature lines all highlighted in yellow), but most attempts failed.

It was the time of year when the athletes, bombarded with glossy catalogs, cold-callers, and Victoria's Secret million-dollar bra possibilities, could not find enough places to spend their money, so they sent holiday gifts to Sports Financial. Kate's office bulged with zippered footballs stuffed with toffees, autographed posters, crates of Harry & David pears, garbage cans full of green and red popcorn. She hoped that Gus and Camille would be awed.

It had been a slow boat from the office lobby. Gus had insisted on pushing Camille in her stroller—without Mommy's help—and knocked over two elves and a papier-mâché reindeer from the Franklin Tower holiday display.

Kate's desk was piled high with papers and coffee cups.

"This is messy, Mommy," Gus said.

Camille pointed to a fish bowl full of red pistachios from Georgie Porshay. "Nice," she said.

Camille was talking—it hit Kate like an epiphany. A "touch-point moment" if she ever saw one. "Pretty, aren't they?" Kate said, lifting her up to touch the bowl.

Kate set Camille on the carpet and checked her voice mail as Gus dug Styrofoam peanuts out of boxes that Kate had started to open, but had abandoned when she ran out of time and interest. She had ten messages, the first from Pedro Araguz. "Hi, Kate," he said. "I need to talk to you about something. Give me a call."

He'd left the message Friday night, and, since it was Saturday, she didn't know if she should wait until Monday to call him back. Was calling on Saturday outside the confines of business development? But she needed this deal. So far, even James was ahead of her, and Pedro was her only prospect. Sandy was a smart guy and would likely pass his exam; he would quit his job at the law firm and they'd have a tough time paying their bills. Peter the Red and J.P. did most of their signing after hours; J.P. would go for it, she thought.

Kate looked up Pedro's number in the small black phone book she carried around (athletes never left their numbers) and dialed. The phone rang. She thought of Pedro on one knee, slipping the shoe on her foot. That wasn't sexual, was it?

Gus stopped dumping Styrofoam peanuts on the floor and looked over at her. "What is it, Mommy?"

"Nothing," Kate said, smiling at him. She'd learned in her leadership training classes that you could block things out (like mean thoughts about staff people) by simply cancelling them, touching the same spot on your temple, visualizing them slammed shut in a vault. The problem was that the thoughts weren't so easy to hide, and always came back, like bounced checks posted in a dry-cleaner's window.

His answering machine picked up.

She tried his cell phone. He carried it sticking out of his back pocket like a teenager's comb. She pictured him reaching behind himself to grab the phone, holding it with a finger and thumb like a toy.

"Yo," he said after two rings.

"Hi, it's Kate from Sports Financial," Kate said, with spring. She tried sitting upright in her chair—posture was important, according to *I Hate Selling!* Camille pulled up on her leg and swatted at Kate's breasts.

"Little Flower," Pedro said. "We need to talk about cars."

Kate scooped Camille up onto her lap. "An early Christmas present for yourself?" Kate asked, unhooking her bra with one hand and holding the writhing Camille with the other. Kate refused to wear nursing bras—she was never able to line up the nipple with the peek-a-boo hole.

Pedro laughed. "Guess Santa's coming early this year," he said. "J.P. said you guys could get some good deals."

"We do," Kate said, thinking that J.P. would hate this. He would somehow turn it around that he'd told Pedro to call her for the "paperwork," when the truth was that J.P. knew nothing about buying cars. Kate wasn't intimidated by the cheery, wet-combed car salesmen. She managed to get them to stop talking long enough to set her terms. They were nothing compared to the agents with their run-on sentences and vibrating ties who talked for hours without a breath or a blink and would keep refilling your Diet Pepsi until you had to pee so badly you couldn't think straight.

Car purchases weren't a matter of negotiating (Kate wished she could take credit). She simply didn't negotiate. The vehicle was to be loaded with every possible (and impossible) extra, for a price she set from extensive *Blue Book* research over the Internet— or she would take her client and his cash elsewhere.

As Camille suckled, it occurred to her that Pedro could be buying the car for his mother, or girlfriend. Maybe it was for Laura, the mysterious name he'd uttered when Kate had first called him. She'd be able to tell from the color and model—more so the color. She was an expert on the psychology of cars. White, silver, and bikini-yellow were gifts for females. No one ever gave a black or red car as a gift. Red was a show-off, black was jealous. Models were tougher. From Kate's experience, quarterbacks bought sleeker cars—Jags and Beamers. Baseball players bought more muscular *American* vehicles.

And the Hummer. They all wanted the Hummer. A guy wins the Super Bowl and what he really wants to say when Disney asks is: "I'm going to buy a Hummer!"

Sometimes Kate was wrong. She'd been blown away when Z Pitt, a 280-pound linebacker for the Cowboys, had purchased an itty-bitty Miata. When she'd balked—"those curves are so soft and female"—he said he liked to feel his knees against the steering wheel. Kate, sometimes an armchair psychiatrist, thought it was separation anxiety, something to do with being in the womb.

But they all bought cars sooner or later. When Sandy's firm had offered to buy him a car, Kate had been touched that he said a sports car wasn't him. She liked the idea that he was above all that. "Maybe another wagon that has room for the kids and the dog," he'd said. Then he came home with the black Beamer, which really threw Kate, because he wasn't the jealous type at all. Maybe he'd take the kids around in the fire truck—in the back swivel seat—Kate recalled thinking, the mother of all crotch-rockets.

"What kind of car are you looking at?" Kate asked.

"I was thinking a Corvette. Maybe red."

"That's so Clarence Thomas," she blurted. He could afford so much more, she thought, a rare thought when it came to professional athletes. Baby-faced minor-leaguers drove Corvettes. Middle-aged men who packed guns and Binaca drove Corvettes. Pedro hadn't struck her as wanting a muscular vehicle—so vanilla American. She'd had higher hopes—something exotic and wingless. Maybe it was just her aversion to Corvettes: every time she saw one she touched her temple and canceled.

In high school she'd cruised Spokane with boys who drove tricked-out cars that looked like Corvettes—maybe they were Corvettes, their fathers'. Recalling the chewing gum stuck on the floorboard and the bourbon in the Tab cans, and how her jeans pinched her waist and the button—fastened with pliers—pushed into her navel, made her nauseated. But something in her craved that nausea like the secret excitement of a new pregnancy, or the ache of muscles stripped out at the gym, as if something about it had been good for her.

Those feelings were now a false alarm. She knew herself too well. Her shoulder hurt from lifting Camille; her period was just late. Still, she'd get a whiff of Aqua Velva and think back to when a car's pine air-freshener doubled as fuzzy dice. And the taste of cherry Lipsmackers on her lips. A sip of bourbon, cold hands squeezing her breasts till she flinched. The thrill was real, but always fleeting, like defective fireworks, falling off in the dark, because she knew she had to get home. She would plead curfew—and still get home before her mother.

*K*ate sensed there was more to Pedro's Corvette than a flashy car. Why buy a Corvette when you can have the Concord?

"Clarence Thomas?" Pedro was laughing. "What do you drive?"

Kate hesitated, relieved that he was amused. *The client is never wrong!* Poking fun at a man's car preference was probably second-guessing his manhood. "I'm a bad example," she said. "I drive a Taurus station wagon."

"I might have known. Miss Practical."

"I've got two small children and a large dog. And I don't have unlimited funds."

"Don't Corvettes have a back seat?" he asked.

Kate glanced at Gus, who was stuffing his mouth with green popcorn. It wasn't just two kids in two carseats. Children expanded, like exploding Pampers in a swimming pool. It was the cheddar goldfish, the sippy-cups of grape juice (Kate, who often spilled, even used a sippy-cup for coffee while driving), the bottles of soured breast-milk hidden under seats—for weeks. It was impossible to explain to someone who didn't have children.

"Trust me, it's of no use," Kate said.

"I've got my heart set on the red Corvette," Pedro said. "Like the song."

You deserve it, was almost out of her mouth. It was what she said to all of them. But she stopped. She wanted to understand. "Why are cars so important?" she asked. "Do you have to keep up with the teammates, is that it?"

"I can afford to buy a nice car," Pedro said, a hint of insult in his voice.

"Of course you can," Kate said. "But why the obsession? The way I run around finding cars for you guys, you'd think I was finding ovum for your sperm. What's the message everybody's trying to send?"

Pedro was silent. Camille was asleep, lips pink with sucky-blisters, head arched back. Only the unpleasant sound of Gus stepping on Styrofoam peanuts could be heard, like feet crunching live eggs.

Pedro sighed. "The message is: You're out. You made it out."

"O.K.," Kate said, pulling down her sweater. She stood, phone cradled under her chin, and lifted Camille over to her stroller. She reached behind herself and hooked her bra. She could appreciate the boys from the projects making it big. *Hoop Dreams*, and what have you. "But not everybody comes from poverty," she said, tucking a Winnie the Pooh blanket up to Camille's chin. "And everybody wants the car."

"Wherever you come from, you made it out," Pedro said. "You need something that reminds you."

*K*ate was certain, three days before Christmas, she wouldn't be getting any deals on cars. The anxious car salesmen, who buzzed her like gnats, would have the upper hand this time. Maybe they'd throw in the giftwrap.

"And Little Flower," Pedro whispered.

"What?" She no longer had a problem answering to this name.

"Are you wearing black stockings?"

Kate felt blood rush to her face. She jammed her hands into her Levi's pockets. Camille was asleep, in her innocence. Gus, not quite as innocent, but still innocent, whacked at the empty boxes with a solid chocolate bat, courtesy of some baseball player whose name she couldn't remember.

"Uh, no," Kate said. The floor of her office was covered with green and red Styrofoam peanuts.

"You remind me of this school teacher I used to be crazy about," he said. "She had this kind-of reddish hair and small white hands. She seemed so sad, like you. Sometimes she wore these black stockings...."

No one had ever described her as sad. She wouldn't have described herself as sad, exactly; it was more of an exhaustion, a feeling of pushing herself all the time. Sandy didn't see the sadness in her; he didn't even ask a-penny-for-your-thoughts when he came upon her staring out the window. She had warned him once that some Monday morning he was going to find her in the basement painting pottery. He'd only laughed: "What, and miss your investment meeting?"

Kate chalked Pedro's insight up to athlete-weirdness. Many trash-talking athletes stumbled occasionally onto soothsayer accuracy.

Maybe that was it: she was sad. She wouldn't have put that name to it, but there it was.

"Did you get my box?" Pedro asked, onto the next subject, as if he often put his finger on a person and touched something missing.

"What box?" In the context of their discussion Kate thought *present*. Since her in-box was not discernible through the clutter, her mail was piled on her credenza.

Kate grabbed a large shoe-box-size box addressed to Kate (no last name) and ripped off the brown paper. It was a shoebox, a Nike shoebox. It was stuffed with receipts. At the bottom were some Merrill Lynch statements and Empire Sports documents—Randy Nester's company.

"Can you help me?" Pedro asked.

Kate pulled out a receipt. Big Nate's for $269! Groceries at Diamond Heights Safeway for $422.

"Help me figure out my finances," he said. "Don't you need those receipts for taxes or something?"

Taxes! She hated to tell him that those receipts for slabs of beef would be of no use. Why was it that everyone assumed she did taxes? People always made assumptions about her just because she was a CPA.

But he was asking for her help. Trust, according to *I Hate Selling!* meant you were there.

"I'll see what I can do."

"The car, too?"

Kate straightened her back; she felt every notch in her spine. "Of course."

"Call me."

"I will," Kate said. "Bye." She hung up the phone. "Come on, Gus, stop that. It's making me crabby."

Camille snorted in her sleep. Gus stopped whacking the boxes and took a bite of the chocolate bat.

As Gus ate the chocolate bat like corn on the cob, Kate recalled the shrink saying that she didn't show any anger toward her children. Well, she was feeling a tad angry now, sitting in a room covered in green and red Styrofoam peanuts, her son eating a chocolate bat before lunch.

"Gus, I get mad at you sometimes, don't I?"

"Nope."

"That's ridiculous. I know I do."

"Not really."

"What about the time-out I gave you last night?"

Gus shrugged, wiped chocolate from his mouth with the back of his sleeve.

Kate stepped over to him, kicking Styrofoam peanuts out of her way. "Enough chocolate," she said. "If you don't stop eating that bat right now," Kate wagged her index finger, "I'm going to have to get really mad."

Gus stopped midair, his mouth wide open on the way to another bite. "Are you going to get mad or is Daddy going to get mad?"

"*I* think we need to understand why he's afraid of you," Dr. Fuller told Kate later that afternoon.

"What about him lying to me?" Kate asked. She had skipped the gym and used her marital credit to see the shrink. "Is that irrelevant?" Kate stared at the ceiling from the shrink's makeshift couch and thought about doing a few ab-curls.

"What sort of tongue lashing *would* have been in store for him?" Dr. Fuller asked.

Kate swung her legs around and sat up. "I thought you were supposed to be on my side. I'm paying you enough to at least recognize my hardship."

Dr. Fuller crossed her legs. Today she wore a plain gray suit (even on Saturday) and formal scarf pinned fastidiously at her neck. Kate was certain it was a shrink-trick: Dr. Fuller was trying to be unmemorable. Years later someone would ask Kate to describe the shrink and Kate would have to say, I don't recall.

Kate wondered if there was any way a mother could pull off the same thing—basic black sweaters, meatless casseroles—anything to avoid being the future topic of discussion on a shrink's couch.

"Haven't you been trying to get him to lose weight?"

"I've been encouraging exercise and healthy eating, yes."

Dr. Fuller clasped her hands together, an annoying habit comparable to a bell going off when she reached some new level of understanding. "I think he's feeling too much pressure from you," she said. "It's probably the reason he's choosing to move into the firehouse."

"Are you saying that this is some sort of cowardly divorce?"

"Why are you calling it cowardly?"

"Why are you calling it a divorce?"

"You called it a divorce."

Kate pulled on her thumb, trying to crack the knuckle. "Is it common for husbands—approaching 40—to want to move into firehouses? In your experience?"

"I wouldn't say common, but it's not unusual."

Not unusual. Kate tried weighing this assessment—an assessment that probably cost her $15—as her knuckle finally cracked. Her fingertips felt frost-bitten with the hot, prickly sensation of thawing.

"All that I'm saying is that Sandy's under too much pressure. You set very high standards, and he needs to get away."

"It's nice he has that option." Kate sat up. "I'll tell you about pressure. Here's the snapshot: I arrive home after ten hours at the office into the eye of the storm. The dog has torn apart the diaper pail, Gus and Camille are clamoring for dinner, the tip of my $100 kitchen knife has mysteriously broken off, and Sandy's upstairs trying on fireman's thermal underwear. Meanwhile, he tells me that I shouldn't be so shy around the athletes and really go for it."

Dr. Fuller pointed a finger at her. "Are you saying that you want to quit work?"

"I'd like to know that I could."

"What's going on at work?"

"Nothing." That's how it always started—nothing—then it catapulted into divorce and despair. "I need to buy a Corvette for a potential client," she said, for something to say. "He's a nice guy."

"A nice guy? In what way?"

There were things that you didn't even tell shrinks, Kate thought. She told herself that under no circumstances would she mention the shoe. "He says please."

"Do you perceive that he's more courteous than Sandy?"

"A little," Kate said, feeling herself slide into the trap. "But I don't see why that's relevant."

"More polite, and maybe more understanding?"

"You really have me pegged as a tramp, don't you?"

"I'm trying to understand your relationships with men, and automatically you assume it's sexual."

Kate's face burned. *Are you wearing black stockings?* "I spoke to him for maybe ten minutes."

"I don't think that quitting work would be healthy for you. I think you need to be in a place where you're being admired. Who would appreciate all your exercising if you stayed home?"

Admired? How could this shrink in her rat-hole office, who'd probably never sat in a crowded movie theater or shared a pitcher of beer, make such assumptions? But deep down she knew that she didn't want to quit work: she didn't want to drive car pools and clean the mice out of the garage. Maybe the shrink had a point. She thought of Pedro and her shoe, that had seemed so petite in his big hands. What was missing from her life? Maybe her marriage *was* in trouble.

"Stay at work," Dr. Fuller said. "Maybe you'll get to ride in a Corvette."

*K*ate decided to surprise Sandy with his mother's Jell-O salad on Christmas Eve. After leaving Dr. Fuller's office, she went to Bell Market and bought a box of lime Jell-O, a can of pineapple tidbits ("not chunks"; her mother-in-law had been very specific), a jar of maraschino cherries, two pints of whipping cream, whole-milk cottage cheese, a bag of mini-marshmallows, and eight rolls of toilet paper. Kate hoped that she wouldn't screw up: making Jell-O was not a skill passed down in her family.

As she lugged the two bags of groceries up Castro Street, a bike and two strollers rolled past her. She liked that Noe Valley was full of children—Fertile Valley, it was nicknamed. The day was cool and windless. The fog had settled in the eaves of Twin Peaks, the two mountains that swelled above Noe Valley, the breasts of Mother Earth, her nipples to the sky.

San Francisco was festive during the holidays. The row

houses that had once seemed so impossibly mashed together—
"You couldn't even floss them," Kate had complained when she
and Sandy had moved there from Seattle—were decked out in
wreaths and bows. The front-porch pillars of 19th-century
Victorians were wrapped to look like candy canes. On 21st Street
two gay men decorated the front of their house with a 30-ft. tree
and giant gift boxes and stuffed animals. They took turns every
night in December (unless they were attending dinner parties)
dressing up as Santa and passing out candy canes to the startled
children. It was such a fantastic spectacle that people tried giving
them money. The *Noe Valley Voice* printed their request just to
donate to a favorite charity: "We're a couple of wealthy fags and
we don't want to take any money from anybody. This is our
present to you. Use it as an example of doing good."

The house next door to them boasted so many red lights—
the owner kept them up year round—that sometimes the power
flickered and the television zapped off when Kate and Sandy were
watching *The X-Files*. Kate had grown up with white Christmases
in Spokane and believed that Christmas lights were supposed to
glisten through snow. But the city's efforts were inspiring, and Kate
sighed deeply when she saw that the weather vane on top of the
turret of the Victorian across the street had been changed from a
rooster to an angel.

Except for the lack of seasonal snow, Kate felt that San
Francisco was an ideal place to live. That and the earthquake risk,
but she'd taken precautions to alleviate that. She'd counseled the
children and Consuelo on how to stand in doorways to avoid
falling bricks; she'd prepared (and dated) gallons of water in the
basement, adding a teaspoon of chlorine bleach for preservation.
There were jars of aspirin and peanut butter, cases of Spam (who
would eat it otherwise?), Carmex for lip blisters, Vaseline that had
many uses, and two boxes of Super Kotex to soak up blood on
wounded heads. And if the house collapsed into the basement,
burying her stash, she had the back-up plan of the Eddie Bauer
knapsack under their bed. It was stuffed with campers' dried food,
water, a Swiss Army knife and a hundred dollars cash that Sandy
kept using for pizza money. Kate was good at shutting down risks,
at back-up plans. And how often do I need to pray? she
remembered asking her mother. She felt confident about

earthquakes. It was those risks she couldn't do anything about that troubled her.

The bags were getting heavy as she passed her Taurus wagon parked on the street a half-block from her house; she pulled the bags up closer to her chest. It occurred to her that she didn't remember locking the car. By leaning against the car she balanced the groceries between her and the car and jiggled the door handle to see if it was locked. It was. A man in his late thirties with a pointy beard and wearing a wool cape nodded at her as he passed. Usually she gave little thought to people walking out of the Castro district—naked painted men on roller skates, men dressed as women, women dressed as men—all on non-Halloween days—but this man gave her a peculiar feeling.

As she flailed with the bags, attempting to heave one to her hip, she dropped one, and the jar of maraschino cherries exploded on the sidewalk.

The man turned. He grabbed the can of pineapple tidbits before it could career into the street. He helped gather up the rest, and, urging her to take care, continued on his way.

Later that evening, when she went to get a book she'd left in the car, there was a business card tucked under the windshield wiper:

Axel Staperfene
Psychoanalyst

430 *Folsom Street Suite* 430
415.747.9836

"Give me a call," he'd written on the back in black letters as perfect as if he'd typed it.

Kate normally disregarded things left on windshields, but she had a strong feeling it had been left by the man in the cape. Had he noticed the way she shook out her numb hand before trying the door handle? Maybe it was the red jacket that had attracted him—she'd been wearing a lot of red lately (against the advice of Rocky the color analyst: men saw sex when they saw red) and considered that she might be trying to send a subliminal message. A cry for help? She knew she was going to have a hard time letting this one go.

Saturday evening, after finding Axel Staperfene's card, Kate prepared for Alberta Towne's arrival. She'd agonized over what to wear and decided to dress down, hoping that Ms. Towne couldn't find fault with jeans and a turtleneck.

Sandy was overseeing the children's dinner of Consuelo's *cocktel de fruta* and a doggie box of crispy beef from Noe Valley Chinese. Camille had just uttered another word—"Suelo." Kate had been overwhelmed by guilt and pride and sour grapes.

"A shoebox, that's unbelievable!" Sandy said, patting Kate on the arm. "We won't even miss my salary the way you're going. Can you pass me the soy sauce over there, Gus?"

"His shoes were once in it," Kate said loudly, wondering if he should be jealous, if she should feel guilty.

"I know," Sandy said, dribbling soy sauce on a piece of crispy beef and onto his already stained white T-shirt that was hanging out over his jeans. He popped the piece into his mouth. He was still losing weight, and he wasn't dieting. Kate thought that the exercising must be more rigorous than she knew. "The guy trusts you," he said, shoveling more crispy beef onto Camille's highchair tray. "Your Mommy is a big executive," he told the children.

"Yea, Mommy!" Gus said. "Happy birthday to you..." he started singing.

"Doesn't it seem sudden that he would just send me his personal receipts?" Kate heard the click-click-click of Ms. Towne's heels on their wooden front porch.

"You must have made quite an impression."

"He called me up to chat." She wanted to say, *He asked me if I was wearing black stockings.* She wanted to confess that the question had made her skin prickle. And the children had turned, in their innocence, to stare at her silence. But the context was wrong. And she hated it when women teased their husbands with elevator romances—*the soft-spoken older man on the BART train said my shoulders were a perfect T.*

"That's what you've got to do," Sandy said, punching the air. "Maybe you should listen in on J.P. Try out a few of his tricks on Pedro."

"He's not a zoo animal," Kate harrumphed. "Pedro, I mean."

"Seems to work for J.P."

Excuse me! Kate thought. We are talking about Pedro Araguz—a charming superstar with a sloe-gin smile and a six-pack of stomach muscle—probably a half rack—making ten million a year. Does your trust run that deep? Are you so perfect a man, so painfully optimistic, that you always expect the best from people? From me, for example? Or, was it that he hoped Kate would fall first. Her failures would assuage his guilt—she'd heard about things like this. Or possibly he was so buoyant from finishing the fireman exam early that his confidence had soared. Kate secretly hoped his early departure from the exam was a sign he'd missed some big concept (those who'd swaggered out of the CPA exam early hadn't known what they didn't know).

"Aren't you going to answer the door?" Sandy was asking her. "Your fashion consultant is here. I don't want to get in the way of her critical eye."

Kate started for the door.

"Keep her away from my T-shirts, will ya?" Sandy yelled after her. "I have a certain look."

Ms. Towne appeared in the doorway, pressed and powdered and well-heeled in a gray-green duster with faux-fur collar. Her last words to Kingsley that Kate had overheard: "If you're down to your last $2,000, for gawdsakes get yourself a decent overcoat."

Ms. Towne eyed Kate's waist. "If you have belt loops, you've got to use them," she whispered in her throaty voice, touching Kate on the shoulder. She smelled of expensive perfume and Tic-Tacs.

Kate hooked her finger on an empty loop and tugged. "Beautiful coat," she said, stepping away from the door.

"It's the mystery color," Ms. Towne said, as she heaved an iron clothes rack into the entryway with one hand. "Satisfies every need. That way you only need one. We'll teach you."

In the master bedroom, Ms. Towne complained about Kate's wire hangers. "Always discard them," she said, flinging them onto the bed. "The dry cleaners use them because they're disposable. Like these," and she threw Kate's flip-flops into the garbage.

In a flash, Ms. Towne organized Kate's clothes into four categories: summer, winter, rotate out, and gone—gone was the category piled highest on the bed on top of the wire hangers. In San Francisco, where summer could feel like winter, Kate only wore one category: all-year-round. But she didn't mention this to Ms. Towne, who had started sub-categories of "weather-permitting," "event-appropriate," and "resort wear." All this time, Kate had been wearing "resort wear" to work on casual hump-day.

"I need to see you in all your jackets," Ms. Towne said over her shoulder as she organized the sub-categories. She'd taken off her jacket, but was still wearing a silver scarf around her neck. She'd also worn a scarf at the office, and Kate wondered what she was hiding under there. A chicken neck? Jowls? An Adam's apple?

Ms. Towne made "collections of colors" that could all be mixed and matched. She was most proud of the "sunset collection" where the purple-blue pants were to be worn with a rose-colored sweater. Kate could hear Sandy's bad jokes: Hey, surfer dude! He could never do the paisley & plaid thing—he thought those guys were crazy or vain, or crazy because they were vain, and sometimes Kate found his fashion lameness sexy. He was strictly a khakis and polo-shirt guy—in a suit he was comfortable when a stripe in the tie matched his jacket, the tie patterns repeating in dizzying symmetry. He'd try to match her with his primary colors—and never know he was clashing.

Kate modeled her jackets, and Ms. Towne thumbed up or down or marked them with chalk, then pinned. Kate tried on her remaining pants, trying to cover her bra and zebra-striped underwear with her arms. Ms. Towne tore out hems with neat flicks of a razor, cut pants into pedal-pushers with a pair of sterling scissors. Kate learned that a purse was "a bag" and that "tonal" was in, matching was out. "Think casual elegance," Ms. Towne said, snapping her fingers, "not Girl Scout."

Ms. Towne unzipped a Neiman-Marcus plastic garment sack, thick as a body bag. "I bought you some things to fill some holes in your wardrobe," she said, handing Kate a light yellow dress with a V down the back. "It's a slip dress," she said, reading Kate's confusion. "Redheads always think they can't wear butter. It'll be marvelous with your bony chest. *You* could even wear it backwards. We'll throw a cardigan over it for the office, and there's your day-into-evening."

"There's not much to it," Kate said, touching it with her fingers. *Transparent* was too obvious to say.

Kate wriggled into the dress. Ms. Towne whirled her around

with a push of her heavy, callused hand. "Lose the bra," she said.

Kate reached behind her back and unhooked the bra, then tossed it onto the heap on the bed. She stared at her reflection in the mirror, unsure. "Don't you think that my nipples look... prominent?"

Ms. Towne considered this, a hand under her chin. "You either wear it with nips like you don't give a damn or you don't wear it at all. It's critical how you wear something. You never see Kate Moss all hunched over, now, do you?"

Kate didn't want to tell her about the possibility of leaking—or the shrinking of her already "bony chest" when she quit breast-feeding.

"I'm liking you in nips," Ms. Towne said in her deep husky voice; her gold eyes were fixed on Kate's chest. "Even the mannequins are wearing them now."

"*T*hat voice," Sandy said, when Kate stepped into the kitchen. He held Camille, still wearing her Barney bib, on his lap. Gus was rolling Play-Doh snakes on the kitchen table. "I kept thinking you had a man in there." He stared at the yellow slip dress she still wore. "Is that a dress or underwear?"

"You're jealous?" Kate asked, clicking the heels of her extreme shoes together, feeling like Dorothy trying to find her way home.

"Of the fashion consultant?" Sandy was flabbergasted. But the exaggeration in his voice made Kate think that maybe the potential was there.

"Never mind," Kate twirled around. "What do you think?"

Sandy studied her up and down. "Human beings don't have feet like that."

Kate ignored him and opened the refrigerator. Camille toddled over and tugged on the dress; Kate scooped her up and squeezed her hand which was sticky with *cocktel de fruta*. Kate could return the dress with the price tags still on.

"She didn't like much," Kate said, shifting Camille to her hip, "but she said my Christmas dress this year was a twelve on a scale of 1-to-10."

Sandy rubbed his eyes. He looked as if he would fall asleep if he became horizontal for any reason.

"You can't picture it, can you?" she asked. In her mind's eye she had seen him thinking of her in that dress, the lusty way she'd looked with a flute of champagne in her hand—she'd hoped it was a mental snapshot he carried around. But it was sometimes better not to know. "I only wore it to the four Christmas parties we've gone to," Kate said, slamming the refrigerator door.

Sandy took a swig of Yo Soy out of the plastic container. "Don't let it hurt your feelings," he said. "I can't even remember if I had lunch today."

Singing in the church choir on Sundays, unless the Niners played on the East Coast, was a Kingsley-defining activity, along with investing and swimming. He was a natural loner; the choir was his one effort at making sense of a group. But even in church he was afraid that someone might tap him on the shoulder and want to know why he was there. If pressed, he might confide that the chorus, repentant and human, yet somehow divine, lifted him up to a version of stardom, but a more palatable stardom, assembly-line style. Sooner or later, someone would ask, and he planned to explain that it was easier to have convictions when they were recited with others—with the tactical pronoun—"we believe"—than face them alone.

Sunday morning Sandy took the *Examiner* and locked himself in the bathroom while Kate got Gus ready for church. Sandy had bounced out of bed that morning humming "Whistle While You Work," and he continued to hum as he brushed his teeth, stopping only to spit in the sink. Kate knew that he was certain he'd passed the firefighter exam.

As Kate struggled to shoehorn Gus's feet into his party shoes, Camille, apparently displeased with the attention Kate was giving Gus, threw a hissy fit on the floor, rolling and yanking at the pair of Kate's pantyhose she wore around her neck. Sandy had been in the bathroom for 20 minutes and from time to time Kate would hear him turning the pages of the newspaper.

"Where's Daddy?" Gus asked, which he asked every morning while Sandy had his private bathroom time.

"He's having a little coffee break." Kate was still in her bathrobe. Her hair was wet. The kids needed breakfast, then she and Gus had to be out the door in 15 minutes. She felt that Gus needed the Sunday school experience, and she was going to do that for him even if Sandy wouldn't participate.

Kate didn't want to begrudge Sandy his bathroom time— surely there had to be some anatomical reason why it took him so long. If it wasn't anatomical, it was a terribly inefficient way of multi-tasking. Kate was out of the bathroom in less than five minutes; it never occurred to her that she might need to go and sit on the toilet for half an hour, reading or filing her nails while the world banged on the door—most of the time the children and the dog accompanied her.

Camille stopped crying. Her white wisps of hair had gotten wet with sweat or milk and had dried in stiff pin-curls. Kate pulled her onto her lap and finished tying Gus's shoes. Kate could understand how, without language, babies were easily frustrated. Kate was frustrated and she had a credit card and an Internet connection.

"Mommy, I don't have any underpanties on," Gus said.

Kate pulled at his waistband and checked. "Go get some out of your drawer."

"It's empty."

Kate hauled Camille over to the drawer and stared inside. "Well, go Commando then," she said. *Commando at church?* Kate weighed propriety over digging through the basement laundry basket. *What the hell.*

"Yea!" Gus strutted around the room. Swinging, Kate thought. She wondered if that free-and-loose thrill ever left, or did men get used to the tucked-in security of briefs, like Z Pitt's knees tucked up inside the Miata womb.

"What's that smell, Mommy?" Gus asked, scrunching his up-turned nose.

Kate brushed the lint from his corduroy pants with her hand. "Probably just your father."

"Mommy, look! Smoke!" Gus jumped up and down, pants falling off his skinny hips.

Kate jerked her head toward the bathroom. Smoke was leaking out from under the door. "Sandy!" Kate yelled. She ran to the bathroom with Camille on her hip. She tried the doorknob. Locked.

The toilet flushed.

"Stand back, Kate!" Sandy yelled from within. "Get the children downstairs." The smoke alarm chirped, then roared. Camille started crying again, digging Kate's arm with tiny jagged fingernails.

Kate grabbed Gus's hand and pulled him toward the stairs. "Come out of there!" she yelled at Sandy.

The bathroom door burst open. The wall-to-wall carpet, once heather-blue, was ablaze around the toilet. The fire was racing toward the hallway. Still wearing his terry-cloth robe, Sandy leapt over the flames and onto the toilet seat; he whacked at the fire with Kate's embroidered white guest towels.

As the flames died out, the smoke alarm became increasingly annoying.

"How do I get this thing to shut off?" Kate dropped Gus's hand and fanned the smoke alarm until it stopped.

Gus dropped and rolled toward the stairs. "Good job, Gus," Kate said. "Now go downstairs and wait for me in the living room."

"What is going on?" Kate demanded of Sandy, who was opening the bathroom window.

Sandy was soot-faced and sheepish, but oddly excited.

"The fan's broken," he said. "So I lit a match."

Kate saw the gaggle of used matches around the toilet basin. "This obsession with fire," she said, shifting Camille, who was still whimpering, to her other hip. "Don't you think it's gone too far?"

"Did you see how I put it out?" he asked, grinning. His straight teeth that had almost no overbite sparked as he smiled; his wavy hair looked aflame under the heat lamp.

"Yes," Kate said slowly, eyeing the charred guest towels. "It was very clever, but we have one bathroom and company coming tomorrow. It's Christmas—"

She stopped to listen to the glass breaking downstairs. She

heard the door fly open—the whooshing noise of Castro Street rushed upstairs.

"Gus!" Kate ran down the stairs, Camille bouncing on her hip, as half a dozen firefighters stormed in with their equipment.

"He put it out!" Kate called to them sweetly. "We're O.K." She made an O.K. signal with her free hand.

They stopped and looked up at her, squinting. She ran a fast hand through her wet hair.

One large firefighter mumbled something, stamping his heavy boots excessively on the entryway welcome mat.

At that moment Sandy appeared at the top of the stairs just in time to take credit for his feat. His terry-cloth robe, loosely tied and parting dangerously, was blackened along the hem.

Gus reached out and yanked one of the firemen on his plastic sleeve. "My dad's a fireman."

*P*yromania had to be the explanation, Kate thought, with some relief, as she gunned her Taurus wagon down 24th Street toward Saint Joseph's Episcopal Church. Pyromania was probably treatable, unlike homosexuality or a general disenchantment with her. There'd been another telling incident just last Saturday. He'd been weeding the back yard, when evidently it occurred to him that kerosene along the perimeter would do the edging job quicker. In the process of dripping kerosene along the edge of the yard, he'd accidentally dribbled on his khakis, and when he and the children had picked her up from her hair appointment that afternoon, his pant leg was still smoldering.

It was a cool sunny day in the banana belt, and the 24th Street coffee shops spilled joggers, ponchoed guitarists, transvestite bagmen, and polka-dotted strollers onto the sidewalks. A Santa sipping from a Martha & Brothers coffee cup sat in a wagon pulled by a fleet of four big dogs. More dogs blocked shop doorways, like gargoyles. Kate had observed that city dogs were mostly large— fussy standard poodles and stately Great Danes—as if city dwellers were trying to bring the wilderness inside. A dog was tied to every parking meter between Noe and Church, and a meter maid with a wreath fixed to her hood slapped a ticket on any car straddling a corner or encroaching on what seemed to be randomly painted red curbs. The jeep in the handicap zone, Kate chuckled, better get its checkbook out—she'd never live that dangerously. She craved a black coffee.

As it was, she and Gus would miss the family service but, torched bathroom or not, Kate was determined to get him to Sunday school. The last two times they'd gone to church, it had been for memorial services, which weren't representative of the church experience. She wanted Gus to hear parables from the Bible, which were good stories that enforced strong morals, and sing happy songs, and to learn to love everyone equally, because God was there for them. She did not want him to grow up without religion and the security it provided. Maybe Sandy was right and she could use a good dose of faith, though it irritated her that he felt he was above that. She hated when he said that he wasn't a worrier, as if being not a worrier, was some grown-up altar-boy status that she would never achieve. The non-worriers let things happen—like artery plaque and late charges—feeling no need to intervene in the passing parade. Perhaps, if she had paid more attention in Sunday school, she wouldn't be sentenced to keeping sentry watch her entire life, as if her very presence might control the stars. Maybe it wasn't too late.

"Where are we going?" Gus called from the back seat.

"To church, honey."

"Who died?"

"No one died. You don't go to church only when someone dies."

"I want to go home and see the firemen."

Kate downshifted to first gear. They were driving at a 45-degree angle. A diamond-shaped sign warned **HILL** in red letters, and someone had scribbled NO SHIT over it.

"The firemen went home. You'll love Sunday school. Everybody's really nice."

"No!" Gus shrieked. "I want my daddy."

"You will go to the fucking Sunday school whether you like it or not."

*W*hen Kate retrieved Gus from the custodial closet, the teacher told her that he'd refused to participate in the discussion so she'd given him the task of identifying all the broken toys in the classroom. "No songs?" Kate asked her. "No lessons? Not one parable?" Wasn't this whole thing supposed to be for him?

In the car on the way home, Kate called her father, Matthew Franklin Clark, in Manhattan. At one point during his marriage to Kate's mother, he had wanted to be a minister; at other points, an encyclopedia salesman, a Montana forest ranger, and a gynecologist; he ended up in real estate. Kate had always taken comfort in his faith. He said grace before big holiday meals and knew all the words to the hymns in church. He'd believed it was important for her to attend church and she thought that, as her father, he'd know what was best for her. *I'm Kate Clark's father* was the caption next to her picture that he'd worn on his jogging shirt throughout the divorce wars. It seemed logical to Kate that at a pivotal point in her child's life—how and when should Gus attend church?—he could help her.

"Hi, Dad," Kate said, gunning the weak-hearted Taurus up another hill.

She could hear water lapping and the engines of his indoor hot tub humming. On weekend mornings in winter he started his day in the hot tub with a Bloody Caesar (a black olive, a marinated mushroom, and an almond on the toothpick) and the *New York Times*. It was always unsettling talking to someone while they bathed, even her father, especially her father. But if she called in the evening, he was into the licorice liqueurs, sampling them from mosaic crystal glasses, comparing the properties of ouzo, anisette, and his favorite, Sambuca, crunching the three coffee beans that floated on top.

"I just took Gus to Sunday school," Kate said, hopefully. In the back seat, Gus had rolled down his window, and wind ripped through the car.

"Oh?" The hiss of jets filled the phone like static.

"Don't you think it's time he went?" Kate asked, idling at the stoplight at 24th Street and Dolores.

"Mmmm, the Bible has some very interesting stories. I read it again last year. Did I tell you that? Made a hobby of it."

Her father had the uncanny ability of turning the conversation back to him. He'd been the star of Kate's wedding, the first time he'd seen his ex-wife in years. The relatives had gasped when they saw him—permed and dandified in white tux with tails—walk Kate down the aisle. He'd lost 29 pounds in two months, or so he claimed as he greeted the guests from the receiving line.

"You make it sound like a Stephen King collection," Kate said.

Her father laughed, swallowing water. *Thinner,* by Stephen King, was his favorite book. It occurred to her now that he'd pulled a *Thinner* at her wedding. "I think Gus should learn the stories," her father said. "But I don't see any reason you should go."

"Why not? You always thought I should before. What's wrong? Don't you believe in God anymore?" She asked it quietly, holding in her breath, like one asks a husband if he's having an affair.

"I wonder sometimes," her father splashed around, "if it's all just some big experiment and God doesn't think about us very much."

"No. That can't be true."

"The world is only 5% Christian. Not that I believe in that reincarnation crap. What would it matter anyway, since you wouldn't remember the other lives though is interesting to think about who died the year you were born. Ever consider that, Kate?"

"How can you say—"

"I don't think God'll hold it against me for not being sure."

"*D*ad's gone agnostic," Kate reported to her mother over the cell phone. She and Gus were parked outside Martha & Brothers' coffee shop. She had promised him hot chocolate with extra whipped cream if he'd sit tight for two minutes and not unhook his seat belt and leave the vehicle. Her mother was packing, Kate knew. She was breathless, shoving things into her suitcase without folding.

"I'm not surprised," her mother said. "Is he still dating the horn blower?"

"I thought you said he was going to be a minister," Kate said. "What was my childhood all about anyway? Don't you remember all the Sunday mornings at church? The commandments I memorized for a Payday bar? The lemon jelly donuts?" Kate was losing her voice.

"Christianity doesn't have all the answers," her mother said. "You always want to tie everything up, Kate. You can't wear a belt and suspenders."

Kate could handle her mother taking Sandy's side — the fireman thing would let him sow his oats and all that business, or it's the hero thing. But Kate wasn't comfortable with her mother defending her father. This show of unity drained her, made her feel alone. She had a sickening feeling that their nasty divorce, 18 years earlier, was still propping up her relationship with her mother.

As she and Gus sat outside Martha & Brothers in the ticking, gutless Taurus wagon, Kate with her wind-whipped hair, Alberta-ized in a tangled wrap-around skirt, Gus in his party shoes, she felt stranded.

*C*hristmas Eve morning, James was at the reception desk. He'd cut his hair and shaved the top into a J.P. buzz, and he wore a tan-and-rose-toned sports coat complete with a neatly folded pocket hankie and a burgundy V-neck sweater. Kate stopped to stare. The ensemble had the impact of paisley worn with plaid, but somehow worked. Where did he get the confidence to clash? Ms. Towne had to be behind it. They would all start to look alike in their collections of sunset colors. Kate couldn't help but think they were all being worked into her paint-by-the-numbers master plan.

"Nice combo," Kate said, which was all she could think of to say. She clutched Axel Staperfene's business card in her hand.

James blushed to his ears. It occurred to Kate that she'd never seen his ears. They came to points on the tops with small tufts of white hair. "Your eight o'clock interview is waiting in your office," he boomed. His on-the-air voice had extended into conversation.

"I took the liberty of arranging an interview for my

replacement," James said, on the verge of a sneeze. He yanked the pocket hankie from his breast pocket and sneezed into it, then blew his nose. "Oh!" he threw up his arms, waving the hankie in surrender. "I forgot. Captain Mullan sent you a picture of that woman who's been using your I.D. Guess a dentist she went to for teeth bleaching got suspicious and took the picture. Sorry, I accidentally opened it."

"Now we're getting somewhere!" Kate said, grabbing the envelope. "Wait till you see her. She's got some nerve stealing my identity. I'd like to see this hanging in a few post offices."

J.P., who was headed for the restroom with a *Muscle Week* magazine tucked under his arm, looked over her shoulder. James flailed with the pocket hankie, attempting to jam it back into his breast pocket, as if stuffing a Kleenex back into its box.

Kate pulled the glossy out of the envelope. It was an x ray, a shot of the bones and teeth of a mouth and a jaw.

"Well, you're better looking," J.P. said, snapping his red suspender against his chest.

"What do they expect to do with this?" Kate said, still staring at the x ray.

"It's clear you don't look like her," J.P. said, pointing at the x-ray, then touching it with his finger. His fingernails were actually dirty, and Kate turned to see dark circles under his eyes. "Check out those sharp incisors," he said.

"No," Kate said, grinding her teeth. "You have it backwards. She's the one who doesn't look like me. I'm the victim here."

"Whatever you say, Kate," J.P. said, flipping through *Muscle Week* as he continued on his way to the restroom.

"I'm paying her bills at Victoria's Secret and North Beach Leather," Kate yelled after him. "I paid for injecting her lips!"

The door shut behind him. "The collagen—400 bucks a vial!" Kate yelled at the shut door. She picked up her briefcase and took a breath. "Hold my calls, please," she told James, who was no longer at the reception station. She was talking to herself again, just a crazy officewife, muttering under her breath about her bunch of dysfunctional husbands who'd left her home to manage the kids. Husbands who got to focus on one thing, while she kept the place together and cleaned the toilets.

Kate wanted to call Axel Staperfene. The impulse was not

unlike the urge to push in childbirth. Resist it, resist it, she heard the doctors telling her, and they knew what was best. The urge to call would have to wait until she could get the young woman out of her office. Kate introduced herself and practiced being pleasant. There were no Scrooges on Christmas Eve, she told herself.

"I was just interviewed by an elf," Heidi Oliver said, handing Kate her résumé. She was about twenty, with short cropped blond hair that fit her pretty head like a cap. And she had impossibly large breasts under a fitted lavender suit. The tiny heart-shaped buttons were about to burst.

"That was just Kingsley," Kate assured her, as she skimmed the résumé. "He's just dressed up for Christmas."

Heidi had two years' experience as a receptionist. Her former boss was a plastic surgeon, she told Kate; she'd had an affair with him. "He was trying to make me into Barbie."

"I see," Kate said. She cleared her throat. "I mean, I don't see—I understand."

"He turned out to be a jerk."

Never trust a candidate who puts down her former employer, Kate recalled from some manual, but at least Heidi was honest. And she enunciated carefully, putting emphasis on certain words. The athletes would enjoy that. "I'll need to check references," Kate said, "and verify this salary."

"They'll probably just want to say I worked there," Heidi said. "You know how stiff they are these days. But you can call Michael, Dr. Austin, I mean. I have a letter from him."

I'll bet you do.

Heidi pushed a piece of paper across the desk to Kate. Her fingernails were stubby and painted bubblegum pink.

Kate read the letter. On his engraved stationary Dr. Austin gushed about Heidi's pleasant personality and organizational skills.

"This looks good," Kate said, setting the letter on her desk. "I guess you can start Wednesday, subject to my reference check." Kate slid open her drawer and pulled out some forms for Heidi to complete and a video tape of Deacon winning $55,000 on *Jeopardy* six years ago, which she gave all the new employees before he could give it to them. He'd won the Famous Accountants category hands down. "May as well get started on this," Kate said, handing her the video. "Do you have any questions for me?"

Heidi was chewing gum, which Kate noticed for the first time. "Is there, like, a dress code here?"

Kate hesitated. "Not really." She thought of Mary Ellen Tuohy always in black, in perpetual mourning, except for the popsicle toes. It was almost too specific to prohibit. "We all use our best judgment and dress for business."

"Like what you're wearing."

"Right," Kate said, pained that her outfit seemed so conservative. The above-the-knee black flip-skirt and the aubergine blouse was one of her least conservative looks. She'd tossed her closet the night before looking for something hip to wear to her meeting with Randy Nester.

Heidi's lip gloss caught the fluorescent office light. Kate wondered if Sandy would find her attractive. There were probably many of these Barbies at his law firm. What would he say if one felt sorry for him that he was stressed, and offered to get him off, under his desk. Would that be all it took? For someone to ask?

Kate decided to punish her. "Let's do a real interview question, shall we?" Kate said, pressing her fingertips together. "If you could improve anything about yourself, what would it be?" This one was the best, Kate thought, because an arrogant, potentially team-destructive candidate would claim no flaws, while a weaker candidate might give away a career-limiting deficiency, like illiteracy. The trick was to use the weakness to your advantage and say something like, "I'm a perfectionist and have a hard time letting go of tasks," which bosses loved.

Heidi rocked in her chair, thinking, her mouth in a tight pink line. "It wouldn't be my breasts or glutes," she said, with certainty. "They're already enhanced."

*K*ate dialed Axel Staperfene. As the phone rang, she changed her strategy. Anger. That was it. She didn't appreciate the strange note left on her windshield. It had upset her husband! She wasn't the type of woman who would call phone numbers from flyers left on her car as if they were for dating services.

An answering machine picked up. A hollow computer-generated voice (which was exactly as she remembered the bearded man's voice) requested her to leave a message. "Of any length," it said.

Kate liked that he'd offered "any length." It suggested a propensity to listen, a likelihood to understand and commiserate. Still, she was determined to sound angry.

The machine chirped and Kate let him have it. "This is Kate McCabe," she said. "You left your card on my windshield at the top of Castro Street, and I want to know what this is all about. I expect a return phone call. My work number is 735-3000." She hung up.

*A*s Kate drove across the Golden Gate Bridge to Randy Nester's office, she decided she needed to think like a man. She needed to think like J.P., who would never have thumbed through a color chart and pulled 13 outfits from his closet, finally settling on the aubergine. She'd already blown it. J.P. would not be breathless, sleepless, caffeine-deprived, with lipstick on his teeth. He would not practice his speech; he'd intend to shoot from the hip, if intending at all. He would listen to the CD and sing along with Guns and Roses and not consider all the ways that Randy Nester might humiliate him.

The day was blustery and the bridge creaked, and Kate considered—which is what she always thought about when she drove across the Golden Gate—what the poor souls had been thinking as they jumped to their deaths into the choppy black water. It was a brave thing, but cowardly at the same time. Last week, when she'd crossed the bridge, a hooded man was standing on the ledge, and traffic had sat for two hours. "I hope he jumps," some woman, terribly late for work, said over the radio.

Kate hit the speed-dial button for Lonnie's Autos in Serramonte.

"Lonnie, please," Kate said, rolling down her window, thinking that she might throw up. "It's Kate McCabe."

She was making good time—too good. She needed a detour. She needed McDonald's.

"No Big Mac, my ass," she said to Lonnie's hold music, as she took the next exit. Sandy would move into the firehouse and she would stop nursing. It might be her last Big Mac then, and her last baby. She would be a woman past child-bearing and junk food. She would savor the final moments, the hamburger relish and pink baby feet.

"Merry Christmas, Katie," Lonnie came on the line. "I expected a call from ya, seeing it's Christmas Eve and all."

Kate pulled into the drive-through lane and idled behind a Celica. The choices were numbered, packaged for her convenience.

"You know me," Kate said to Lonnie. "I need a red Corvette with all the trimmings. Delivered today."

"Corvette?"

"You heard right."

"Haven't asked for that one in a while. Tell you what, though," he chuckled, "I've got one under the tree right here for you."

"Can I help you?" The voice box on the display menu had sensed her presence.

"Big Mac, please."

"You're going to have to speak directly into the box, Ma'am."

"Big Mac," Kate said, louder. "And a Diet Coke."

"You want seat warmers?" Lonnie asked. "This one's got 'em. I can take 'em out."

The athletes loved seat warmers, which worked better on a date than running out of gas. She had to give them credit for multi-tasking: you could seduce a date and warm up at the same time. Kate and Kingsley had taken Georgie Porshay to dinner and he'd insisted on driving Kate home in his new 500SL. As they approached the freeway exit, her bottom began to heat up, becoming so unbearable that she squirmed in her seat. It was in no way intended to look erotic, but probably did. She was so embarrassed when Georgie smiled at her—the tiny mustache like a shadow on his lip—that she'd leapt from the car as he slowed down at the first stop light off the exit. She'd cabbed it home, and when she'd examined her buns in the mirror, they were still pink. It was a dirty, dirty way to get into a woman's pants, but probably effective in certain situations.

"Better make it dual control," Kate said. "And no onions!" she shouted at the box. J.P. would eat onions before a meeting, but she would draw the line.

"Would you like fries with that?"

"Do you want the ABS, DVX, spoiler, neon trim, and the warranty extension, that's extra? We can cherry-dip it, too. And what about the stereo—small or large?"

"A large," Kate said.

"How about a Happy Meal? Comes with a Rug Rats squeaky toy."

"Fine," Kate said. "Give me the works."

*A*t one minute to twelve, Kate sat in Nester's parking lot with half a Big Mac. Now she really felt queasy. It was never as good as she'd imagined it to be.

Nester's mouthwash-blue glass building loomed like a mirage against the olive-tree backdrop. There seemed to be no doors or windows, or maybe it was all windows.

Kate was determined to be late. She checked her voice mail: "Yes, this is Axel Staperfene, returning your call. I have an opening later this week—Wednesday at 2 p.m." He sounded strong, but feminine—a good foot rub, Kate thought. He was probably gay. Gay was good. "I'm rather booked for the next few weeks," he went on, "and I'm sorry, but I don't do phone consultations. Let's plan on that, unless I hear from you. Bye-bye."

Bye-bye? Was she crazy? Was she absolutely out of her mind, or was she writing the appointment down in her datebook?

Kate deleted his message from her voice mail and canceled the thought.

"*M*iz McCabe!" Randy Nester was on his feet, his golden arms outstretched. Another love fest, Kate thought grumpily. His tan, glowing face was peeling from his infamous helicopter skiing, and his compact body looked fit in a powder-blue polo shirt. He wore crisply pressed cords, and no socks and no shoes. Kate tried not to look. He was barefoot. The two tall rangy men who stood when she entered were also barefoot. One of them she recognized as Reggie Adams, a big bat at Arizona about to turn pro. He was devilishly handsome and already a notorious rogue, dating female rappers and frequenting the pages of *Sports Illustrated* with his six-pack of stomach muscle and starved cheekbones. Black as coal, her mother called him. He wore lime green pants, a sherbet-colored paisley shirt, and a tangle of gold chains around his neck—golf clothes—at Sports Financial they would mouth those words to each other when the clients arrived at the office wearing such combos.

The other one was Pedro.

Kate's lips parted to speak, to say something in recognition, but Pedro just nodded pleasantly, all business. His outfit was more subtle: khakis and a black button-down shirt. These men are enormous, Kate thought.

Kate held out her hand to Nester, who still had his arms outstretched.

"Kate McCabe, I want you to meet Reggie Adams and Pedro Araguz."

Reggie and Pedro took turns shaking her hand. "Hello, hello," Kate said, not looking at their feet, feeling like a woman reporter who had taken a wrong turn in the locker room.

"Take the load off, Miz McCabe," Nester said, pulling out a chair. "We're trying on some shoes that Nike sent over. Pretty decent of 'em on Christmas Eve. Don't think we have your size, though." He chuckled.

You'd be surprised, Kate thought, tucking her feet neatly under the chair.

"Here, Pedro, you need socks with those," Nester said. When he turned to grab a pair of socks off his desk, Pedro mouthed hello to Kate. It felt like a wink, the footsy of it made her blush. She imagined his eyes on her pantyhose, which fortunately were nude, and the way her foot had fit in his hand. She wanted to legitimize it—I bought your Corvette!—but this was her job and she would follow Pedro's lead. Sports was not a normal world. The principles of client lunches and follow-up phone calls did not apply. She could read all the books and follow them step by step—the way she lived her life—but success in this business came down to special attention: a shoebox of receipts and bare feet in an agent's office. It hit Kate then, how J.P. survived, shooting from the hip.

She would give away nothing to Nester.

"Look at these feet!" Nester said. He stood, staring down at his own feet. "Jesus had feet like these. See the gradual slope of the toes. The big toes are the longest. Perfect symmetry. Compare them to Pedro's here." He sidled up to Pedro, and they stood foot-to-foot, Pedro a head taller. "Now, he's double recessive. His second toe is longer than the big one, and it's also double-jointed. I'm not even going to get near Reggie's. Get yourself a pedicure," he hollered at Reggie with his hands cupped over his mouth like a megaphone. "You're a superstar, for gawdsakes. Nike wants your feet! If they could only see them." He slapped Reggie on the back.

And there was his charm, Kate thought. He made the athletes feel like the stars they were, while telling them what to do. At some level everyone wanted to be told what to do.

Nester stepped behind a sprawling desk decorated with photographs of a beautiful young woman who Kate hoped was his daughter. "This is a historical moment you all are witnessing," Nester said. "Reggie has decided to sign with the San Francisco Giants. I'm about to present him with his first hat." Nester reached under the desk and pulled out the official Giants hat and handed it to Reggie.

Reggie took the hat and touched it gingerly, no outlaw in a sherbet-colored paisley shirt, just the kid he'd been when he'd started tossing the ball around as a toddler. One in a million little boys eventually turned pro, and far fewer bypassed the farm system. The first hat would mean a lot. Kate knew that it was not lost on Reggie that Randy Nester had given it to him.

Reggie set the hat on his head and bent down the bill, the ritual of new hats. Nester had created a bond that went beyond the agent-client relationship.

Nester stepped around the desk and landed in a chair. They sat in a small cozy circle. "Kate's gonna tell us about what her firm, Sports Financial, has to offer," he said, swinging his right leg over his left, so she faced the smooth pink bottom of this right foot. He beamed at Kate. Pedro, in athletic socks and no shoes, and Reggie, barefoot in his pristine new hat, turned to her and stared. Their knees jutted out, higher than their waists. Reptilian, Kate thought.

"Sports Financial has an international presence," Kate began. J.P. always said to speak in laymen's terms and to paint a picture—

a paint-by-the-numbers picture—but Kate refused to insult them. "We have a relationship with a hundred-year-old bank in Japan that has its thumb on the pulse of international trade. Kingsley Gartmore is the founder of our company. He's spent his life becoming an expert in finance. He spends the day following the markets and reading the financial papers. He will personally design your portfolio and monitor your in—"

"Let's take a break," Nester said, standing up suddenly. "Reggie, you're looking a little parched, there. How about a Coke?"

"I'm not really thirs—" Reggie began, but Nester was already slapping his phone. "Martha, can you bring some Cokes in here?" He slapped it harder. "Martha? Martha?

"Huh," Nester said. "She must have stepped out to the little girls' room. I'll go check." He dashed from the room, still barefoot, the jaws of the dinosaur doors snapping closed behind him.

Pedro leaned forward in his chair, elbows on knees. "Kate, save your breath," he whispered. "Nester's not giving you any business. This is a beauty contest. He's just parading a bunch of advisors in front of us, then he makes up some pros and cons about each one, then he tells us what to do. He's already decided who he's using. He did the same thing last year."

Kate was furious. It was Christmas Eve. She thought of the speech she'd memorized, the closet she'd tossed before settling on the aubergine, and the interview with Barbie she'd rushed. There was a half-eaten Big Mac sitting on the passenger seat of her car, and her mother was arriving at SFO in 90 minutes.

"Then why are you here?" Kate asked.

"I saw your name on the schedule," Pedro grinned. "I'm shopping."

Kate considered storming out, but here she was with two of the top athletes in the country. Nester had taken his comedy routine out of the room, and they were bored senseless. Their minds were presumably on the holidays: stocking-stuffers and slabs of beef and Christmas Day football. Anything she could do to entertain them was giving candy to babies.

Kate reached in her briefcase and pulled out some business cards and brochures. As she passed them out, she talked again about Kingsley Gartmore the wizard, but not the Wizard of Oz.

He was accessible. As she spoke of him she fell into a euphoria-generated Peter-the-Red kind of love. At Sports Financial they were all available to serve. They were friendly and flexible and would earn them top dollar. Have it your way and Jingle All the Way.

As she was wrapping it up with a Q&A period—Reggie inquired if Sports Financial validated parking—Nester returned with four long-necked bottles of Classic Coke on a tray, open and breathing bubbles, with no glasses. Never drink from a long neck, Kate's mother, the divorce lawyer, had warned her. The bottle thing again, Kate thought, a booby trap more subtle than dual-control seat warmers.

"Time's up," Kate said, standing. Nester shrank from her, speechless, the Classic Coke bottles quivering on the tray. "Make your own choice," she said to Pedro and Reggie.

As she pulled on her coat, she noticed behind Nester's desk two more baseball hats splayed on the floor: Minnesota Blue Jays and New York Mets. He probably collects them at airports, Kate thought. She felt dirty, as if she'd just watched Nester give a blow job.

*I*n the parking lot, Pedro appeared as Kate slid behind the wheel. "The Corvette's in the mail," she told him stiffly. She needed to get on the road. "I've had about enough of agents and athletes and their dog-and-pony shows."

"Sorry about that." Pedro touched the edge of the half-open window. The metallic chain that looked like a key-ring chain hung under his polo shirt—the crucifix she imagined was obscured. "I really did want to hear what you had to say. I think Reggie's impressed."

Kate, prey to compliments, hesitated, her hand still on the key. "What about you? Were you impressed?"

"I was wowed."

Kate turned to him. He was looking straight at her, his face unshaven, his bomber jacket hanging open. He rubbed his chin nervously, and Kate noticed the wrinkles in his khakis. She doubted that the woman named Laura—the name he had uttered on the phone—lived with him, or lived with him very often. Not that women necessarily ironed, Kate thought. She couldn't iron, the creases always ended up in the wrong places, but still.

"Is that your Happy Meal?" Pedro asked.

"As a matter of fact, it is."

Ask for the sale! an annoying voice chided her.

"So what's it going to be, Pedro?" She was still annoyed, which made the question easier; she saw him not as the superstar he was, but the man. "Are you coming with us?"

Pedro took a step back from the car and shoved his hands in the pockets of his jacket. "I'm leaning that way." He smiled.

"Good. Let me know what I can do to help your decision process along. Merry Christmas."

Pedro grabbed the window. "Yeah, what are you doing for Christmas?"

Kate put the car into gear. "For starters, I'm picking up my mother and her boyfriend at SFO. I might try dragging her to midnight mass."

"There's a great midnight mass at Our Lady of Fatima," Pedro said. "All my family's in Argentina this year, so I'll probably go alone."

Kate glanced at his hand that was still resting on the window edge and saw the torn cuticles. Christmas Eve alone? The man on the cover of *Sports Illustrated?* Would he watch satellite TV and microwave a chicken potpie? Kate remembered the Christmas the year her mother left her father and signed up to *adopt* an Air Force man who was stationed in Spokane for Christmas dinner. She had cleaned and cooked for days, leaving Ajax in the toilets and rolling ladyfingers on the dining room table. Kate remembered her mother's disappointment: the skinny kid at the front door, the crunchy rice pilaf, the "thank you, Ma'ams."

Should Kate and her family adopt Pedro for Christmas?

"The service starts at 11:45," Pedro said, stepping away from the car. "Come by if you like."

"We'll try."

*K*ate swung by Fisherman's Wharf to pick up the salmon she'd ordered. The men shouted at her—"The freshest!

The very best price!"—dangling bulging-eyed snappers, and crabs in deep pink armor.

She took solace at the Wharf on Christmas Eve—its brackish smells, its dirty gulls diving from weathered pilings, sailboat rigging clanging in the wind like distant carolers.

Christmas Eve dinner would be simple. Kate had a recipe for salmon filet from her friend Nadine, who collected recipes with three ingredients or less and had turned her on to the cookbook *Desperation Dinners:* whack several times with a rolling pin, butter, then shove in the oven with baked potatoes. Kate liked the finality of it. That anxiety out of the way, she tried thinking pleasant thoughts about her mother's new fiancé, Barry. It bothered her that he sounded like Mr. Rogers on the answering machine and had moved in within three weeks of meeting her mother. Now he worked out of her mother's house doing "something on the Internet." So he was always home, screening her mother's calls (he picked up on the first ring) and packing low-fat meals for her lunch.

Her mother had met him through a *Weekly* ad: Fit devoted fiftyish heterosexual man seeks extraordinary woman 35-55 with similar physical abilities. Her mother had also placed an ad and had met several men on park benches, but she'd asked that Kate not tell Barry. Kate liked having these "little darlings" on her mother, not to use—she wasn't that mean—but to carry around if her mother decided to air Kate's dirty laundry. Her mother's soiled laundry, next to Kate's, was fit for a Clorox before-and-after ad, but there was always a shady story (like the time she'd gone to a movie with her college English professor, before finals even!) that Sandy didn't know about.

"My ear hurts," Gus said.

Kate glanced in the rear-view mirror. He'd bent his head to one side; it rested in his hand. Camille, in the other car seat, whacked at her own ear, in devilish mimic (Kate hoped).

Kate had 45 minutes to pick up Sandy at work, then get to the airport. Her mother liked a crowd at the airport. Dinner was still in the back of the car.

"Does it hurt just a little bit, or a lot?" Kate asked. It was next to impossible to figure out what was going on with children. She likened it to being a vet. She calculated the fastest time to drive to the pediatrician and then to the pharmacy for antibiotics. If she didn't get the ear treated today, they might have to take him to the emergency room on Christmas. Like last year.

"A lot. It hurts a lot."

Kate made an illegal U-turn at the corner of Mission and 24th Street and drove to the clinic. Her pediatrician did not offer drop-in privileges. She pulled into his parking lot and called from the cell phone.

Virginia refused to take the SuperShuttle after dating a man she'd met en route to Kate's house on her last visit. The man had brought her home before midnight, then sent Kate a Van Gogh self-portrait postcard. "No good deed goes unpunished," it read. "I promised you I'd get your mother home on time, and she didn't like that." So Kate, Sandy, and the kids (Gus on his first dose of antibiotics) inched down Highway 101 at 1:45 in the afternoon.

Kate cracked her knuckles as they came to a bumper-to-bumper stop. She'd planned to meet her mother at the gate—everyone fresh, the children with clean faces, hair wetted and combed. Kate hated to be late; it tortured her to think of people checking their watches, wondering if she'd stopped for a latte or pedicure. Her mother would be disappointed, and have to make excuses for her to Barry.

Kate hadn't nursed Camille before they left, and she spoke over the child's mounting cries. "Every time Virginia gets a new man, it's like she's joined a cult," she said to Sandy. She leaned into the back seat and shook a Barney rattle in front of Camille's face. Gus slurped a boxed grape juice with his pointy chin tucked to his chest. "Now it's marathoning and fast food," Kate went on. "I can't believe they go to Arby's—Arby's! Who goes to Arby's?"

"Somebody must go," Sandy said. "Maybe we should have an intervention." He was still pouting. Last night, after hearing about the engagement, he had taken Stirling Moss out for a walk in the fog and came home reeking of beer. "The Dubliner?" Kate had asked, when she saw the book of matches on the nightstand. Sandy collected matchbooks that he stuffed into a Martha Washington sewing cabinet from his mother; it used to be his condom drawer. "What happened to The Rat & The Raven?" The new interest in the Irish was puzzling, and alarming. Kate thought of Doris Iris in Lycra. More alarming than puzzling.

The Barney rattle sounded like pennies in a Coke can. Sandy flipped on the radio. "I don't think it's brainwashing," he went on, scanning the stations. "Your mother's just a bum-magnet."

"Not bums—artists."

"She can't afford an artist."

Gus grabbed the rattle out of Kate's hand. "Mommy—I want more juice," he said. "Stop it, Camille!—I'm talking to my Mommy." Sandy found a static station on the radio, and Camille calmed down to a whimper.

"Dr. Jim says only half a cup a day," Kate told him, knowing that he got at least four times that. Her negotiations with Gus weren't going well—she'd resorted to the pediatrician for authority.

"She's picked up these little phrases," Kate said. "Don't go there, she'll say. I tell her about all my friends divorcing and she says, *don't go there.*"

"Well, she should know."

"Come on," Kate said. He'd broken the unwritten rule about ganging up on someone else's parent. "Remember what they say about the third time."

"A charm," Sandy said. "But why Christmas?" He punched the dashboard for emphasis. Cleaning solution squirted onto the windshield. "Shit," he said, flipping on the wipers.

"Shit!" Gus piped from the backseat.

"Gus, we don't say shit," Kate said, rubbing at a chocolate stain on her skirt. Camille's crying had made her milk let down—her breasts had recoiled into lumpy, desperate shapes, the nipples haywire—and she tried to dry her blouse by sticking her chest up to the heater. Heat brought on more milk, she remembered, recalling the geysers that erupted from her nipples in the shower. Still, she was determined to dry it. It's absurd to wear silk when you have children, she thought, sinking back in her seat, but she'd hoped that Barry would first see her as a graceful young woman with long legs and thin ankles, a butterfly in her little flip-skirt, darting after the children—"now how could she have two kids?" But she looked grungy: she'd bungled her eye make-up as she'd tried touching it up in the pediatrician's parking lot; the dark half-moons she'd concealed earlier that day appeared again under her eyes.

"Daddy says shit," Gus said. "Mommy says shit. Shit! Shit! Shit!"

Sandy revved the engine and jammed Big Bird's Christmas tape into the tape deck. "Christmas is a private holiday," he said, raising his voice over Big Bird's. "I don't want to sit around in my bathrobe trying to make conversation. He probably hates football."

"Daddy, you're hurting Mommy's feelings," Gus said.

The heater was on full blast, pulsating Kate's blouse.

"I just want Mommy to admit that Grandma's rude," Sandy went on. "She's so worried that Grandma'll get mad at her."

"She's rude because she's not showing up with her husband of 40 years?" Kate said. The static off, Camille was crying again. "We need to decide what we're going to say to them about the wedding." She turned around and rubbed Gus's face with a Handy Wipe.

Sandy honked at a stalled van in front of them. "How am I supposed to explain him to Gus?" he said. "*This is Grandpa?* No way."

"Grandpa—no way, Jose!" Gus shouted.

They weren't moving. "We don't mention the wedding," Sandy said, turning off the engine in the middle of the freeway, two miles from the airport exit.

A siren was coming up behind them.

"You always have to joke about her," Kate said. "So she doesn't send us toothbrushes and hot cocoa for Christmas Eve like your mother. You just can't accept that she's still a babe."

"She's a grown-up," Sandy said, sticking his head out the window. "I don't care what she does as long as it doesn't upset you."

"I just see her with someone more established," Kate said. "Maybe a doctor. She's going to end up supporting him."

"You never like any of them," Sandy said. A police car drove by them along the shoulder. Sandy started the car again, although traffic hadn't moved. "She drops you every time she gets a man."

Something *else* must be bothering him, not her mother, Kate thought. She wished she could think of an opening. Then he blurted out that he had failed his test.

"No way—you studied so hard."

"Not the written test," Sandy said. "The physical. My blood work came back and my cholesterol's 320. They called me this morning."

"They called to tell you this on Christmas Eve? What kind of outfit is this?"

"One that doesn't take holidays."

Kate rolled down the window. She hadn't thought of that—the firefighters with low seniority working the major holidays. "How can it be so high? You don't even eat cheese. I'm the one always eating the cheese."

Kate told herself she would make only fat-free meals: egg-white omelets and cheeseless pizza. She would steam vegetables and press lemons. His cholesterol would be down in no time. But it was going to be a drag: Sandy, depressed at Christmas dinner—teetotaling—refusing to eat her Jell-O salad, scraping the filling from the deviled eggs. She found herself disappointed. What was the matter with her? It was Christmas Eve and her husband's health was in jeopardy. 320? What had he been eating?

But she'd won, hadn't she? He wouldn't be going. Only now she realized, part of her had been looking forward to him moving into the firehouse. Like a little divorce.

*B*arry, the wacky tom, walked out of Gate 89 with a thick red arm draped over his fiancée's shoulders. He wore a Seattle Marathon finisher's cap, a GOT PROTECTION? anti-virus-software T-shirt, and a camera slung around his neck. He was tall, but paunchy for a marathon runner. Kate recalled that he had a naked-lady tattoo somewhere (her mother had not been specific) that had recently acquired a bikini.

"Kate!" Virginia called, lifting her Nordstrom shopping bag in the air. Her face looked thinner—no doubt from the jogging regime—and she wore an ostrich-blond leather jacket, baggy oatmeal-colored slacks, and sensible closed-toed shoes. This wasn't like her mother: she wore cigarette pants and insisted on toe cleavage—even in winter. Her hair was still sugary blond, and her eyelids a rainbow of shadows—but he was already changing her.

"You look so stressed, darling, what's wrong?" she asked as Kate leaned to kiss her on the cheek.

Kate shook her head, smiling at Barry. "We had a detour at the pediatrician's. We were almost late."

"Almost late?" Her mother laughed. "That's like almost pregnant. It all seems overwhelming right now, doesn't it? Just chunk it down—that's what I do. Now, where are my little lambs?"

Before introductions could be made, Barry was snapping pictures of the two of them. "Sandy's with them down in baggage, so we should hurry," Kate said. "You look wonderful—so thin." Kate touched her shoulder. "That jacket's a knockout."

Virginia set down her bag and wriggled out of the leather jacket. "Try it," she said, handing it to Kate. "I was thinking of you when I bought it."

"No, no," Kate said, handing it back. "You'll freeze your skinny butt off." Her mother was not attached to material things. Door dings on cars and broken stems on wine glasses never upset her. She accepted gifts from boyfriends, but would often misplace them or give them away. With Kate she was indulgent, buying gifts she couldn't afford. A few months ago she had given Kate all her size 4s, and Kate had hemmed all the pants and shortened all the sleeves. Now that her mother was thinner, she hoped that Barry wouldn't encourage her to ask for them back. If she could just avoid returning the clothes in the first six months of their marriage, her mother would be back to a size eight. The relentless exercise that was now a special torture for her would go the way of the mountain bike hanging in her garage.

"Nice to meet you, Barry."

"Likewise." Barry lunged and hugged her, bear-style. Kate winced; her breasts were cement.

Barry pulled out a container of Binaca and spritzed his mouth. "I thought this would help you out," he said in a nasaly sing-song *(It's a beautiful day in the neighborhood....).* He handed Kate a typed document:

```
Christmas Eve Dinner
    Ahi with Peach Compote
    Caesar Peas
```

      Beet and Carrot Casserole
      Shoestring potatoes
      Homemade Pumpkin Ice cream
   Christmas Breakfast
      Dutch Babies with Crab
      Herb Sausages
      Mini gooseberry muffins
      Orange Juice
      Coffee
   Christmas Dinner
      Angels on Horseback (appetizer with oysters,
        water chestnuts, wrapped in bacon and
        secured with toothpicks)
      Pork Roast with Cranberry Sauce
      Candied New Potatoes
      Creamed Spinach
      Mexican Chocolate Mousse

What the hell? Kate thought. "Thanks," she said and folded the piece of paper into her purse. "I guess Gus can eat noodle fingers." Kate had just convinced him that he liked salmon.

"Gus won't eat Angels on Horseback?" Virginia asked, rummaging through her purse. "I hope he's not becoming one of those picky eaters." She pulled out a lipstick and rubbed it along her lips as they scooted along toward the baggage claim. Her lips were large and chapped like puffed pastries. "They're so annoying to have at dinner parties. Pretty soon he just won't be invited anywhere."

"He's three, Mother," Kate said.

As they rode the airport's conveyor belt, Barry took more pictures—so socially challenged, Kate thought, he has to have a camera between him and everyone else. Her mother pulled a floppy straw hat out of her bag and set it on her head (she feared the California sun).

"Isn't she adorable?" Barry said, snapping her picture. "She wears that hat in her convertible. Everyone knows her around town."

"You bought a convertible?"

"Just a little one, darling," Virginia said, holding her thumb and index finger together, the size of a matchbox car.

Every time her mother paid down her debts, a new

something—car, man, it didn't matter—would come along. With all the divorcing going on, Kate kept hoping she'd turn a profit.

Her mother held her arm as Barry photographed the Coit Tower construction display. "You'll die for Barry's Dutch babies," she whispered. "And his starfruit"—she patted Kate's arm—"just came into season. He's very into things in season. It'll make him so happy to be waiting on you. He's going to be your stepdaddy, you know."

Instant stepdad. Kate thought of the sea monkeys she'd tried to grow in her closet as a girl. She'd ordered them from a magazine—*just add water!*—and had checked them daily; each time it disturbed her: they might have grown large and be hiding amongst her clothes. But they never amounted to anything more than fish food floating in a goldfish bowl.

Kate was concerned about the menus—she was allergic to shellfish; in fact, so was her mother. "What about our shellfish allergy?" she whispered.

"That's always been in our heads, dear. We all like to blame our acne on something."

Kate knew that she should object. She already had a turkey thawing. The table had been set for two days. She couldn't imagine not having the cooking to keep her busy and focused. Sipping hot spiced wine in the living room while a stranger banged around in her kitchen made her hysterical. Say it, she told herself. Tell him, *no, thank you.*

But her mother would be angry. Kate had seen ones like Barry come and go and had even shared Christmas dinners with a few of them. The conversation was always strained (talk of child support and New Year's resolutions). Kate had done her time waiting up for the weekend men to bring her mother home in their beater cars. Sometimes her mother didn't come home, but called to tell Kate about the Lean Cuisines in the freezer. Kate liked post-break-up the best, when her mother bad-mouthed the boorish men and Kate joined in—what a loser, Kate loved to agree.

None of the men had ever worked out, so why should she care what Barry thought? Miss Manners would suggest, in her exasperated way, that Kate pretend that she hadn't understood that he wanted to cook and thank him kindly for the recipes. But she couldn't do it.

*T*hey stopped at Safeway on the way home. With both children in the cart, Camille in the front basket and Gus getting buried in groceries, Barry shopped from another typed list. The items were gigantic—a half-gallon of soy sauce and a family-size catsup. Kate would look in her refrigerator and see the strange brands long after he was gone. They had agreed to split the bill and, like splitting dinner in a fancy restaurant, everyone tossed in items they could have done without: a plastic Christmas tree full of chocolate kisses, a potato-chip-size bag of gummy bears, and a half-rack of Christmas beer.

At home that afternoon, everyone watched Barry, the Pillsbury Dough Boy, in the kitchen. He was in a chopping frenzy, mopping his sweaty brow with Kate's poinsettia dish towels. Kate wondered how they would endure three meals with Camille generally dissatisfied in her highchair and Gus refusing to eat—with about one meal's worth of conversation.

By four o'clock, on her fourth cup of coffee, Kate felt that she needed a task. She wanted to get her hands on a paring knife, or even a carrot peeler. After making the life-size Santa puzzle with Gus four times and doing push-ups on the living room floor, it occurred to her that Barry would have no gifts to open.

Kate collected Sandy and the kids and shepherded them to the car.

Sandy was more than happy to leave the chefs. He liked to have a hand on a steering wheel; it was something left over from high school.

"He's a guest in our home, isn't he?" Kate said as Sandy backed the car out of the driveway.

"I suppose you could call them guests," Sandy said. "Geraldo's guests have less baggage." He scanned the radio stations for that perfect mix that could buoy him into a good mood. They were different that way, Kate thought. She was a repeater, playing the same song over and over.

Kate liked having the kids strapped in the back seat; it made her feel that the parents were in charge again. Sandy landed on *Carol of the Bells*, and Kate relaxed. She would freeze the salmon (if she ever remembered to remove it from the back of the car) and maybe she would get to go to midnight mass. Sandy always volunteered to stay with the kids, and Barry didn't do church, according to her mother. Kate hadn't decided if she and her mother should go to Pedro's church or Saint Joseph's. What did it matter, anyway? It was all church—the midnight voices around the city would rise up as one, welcoming Christmas. If she went to Our Lady of Fatima to take care of a client, who cared if she killed two birds with one stone? God didn't care, she was almost certain of that. Gus was medicated and no longer holding his ear. The fog had lifted, and it was a sunny Christmas Eve afternoon, the air warm and expectant, the telephone poles decked with red bows.

*W*hen they got home, Barry was frying potatoes; they needed to be candied, he said, then chilled for the next day. Pots and pans on all six burners sizzled and sputtered. The garbage can was on top of the kitchen table brimming with soda cans and other recyclables—the newspapers were mixing with hamburger wrap! Peels and coffee grounds covered the counters.

Barry threw a fistful of salt into a pot. "We've got it all taken care of here, Kate. Don't want to cause you any anxiety." Why was she getting the feeling that her mother had told him that she was seeing a therapist?

Virginia was stirring the muffin batter wearing a ruffly apron that said "Ginnie's Kitchen" in frilly cursive. Cooking? Kate thought, remembering her mother's turkey roll on Chinette. He probably had her cleaning, too. Underneath the apron she wore Sandy's University of Washington 1992 Rose Bowl sweatshirt and a pair of black Lycra running shorts. Her legs were thin, ribboned with muscle, and tanned, a state difficult to achieve in Spokane during December. And her mother never tanned. She'd either spent her life wearing Block-Out or she had no pigment, Kate still wasn't sure. "How'd your legs get so tan?" Kate asked.

"Barry works wonders, doesn't he? It's Sudden Tan. It took him an hour on each leg."

An hour? On each? Such delicate work! Kate thought of the gentle street vendor in Union Square—"Let me paint your name on a grain of rice." She thought of foot rubs, of cunnilingus. She remembered the couple in Puerta Vallarta who'd taken pleasure in greasing each other's backs with sunscreen. At the time Kate scoffed that this was the type of man who bought paint-on chocolate, the type of woman who wore garter belts—with black stockings. Maybe she'd missed something. She had left Mexico with sunburn splotches on the blind spot of her back, an area she'd tried to reach on her own.

"They're on a first date," Kate whispered to Sandy. "What does she really know about this guy? I told her to get bank statements and health records." Kate craned her neck to see her mother banging open cupboards.

"I don't think that's going to do it," Sandy said sadly.

"This kitchen is so disorganized," her mother said, and Kate stared at the back of her mother's head, the dark roots showing through the blond. "And did you see the bathroom? Looks like they had a fire in there."

Barry huddled over a pot, looked up, his face wet from the steam. "This kitchen isn't laid out all that well," he said. "It's not Kate's fault."

"*F*ish is poopy," Gus said, picking up his piece of ahi and dropping it onto Kate's plate.

"No bathroom talk at the table," Kate said, lifting the fish back onto his plate with a fork. "You love peaches." She looked at Barry. "Sorry, Barry, the ahi is gorgeous."

The view of the greasy pots and spoons crusted with sauces made her heart pound; Barry had seared the ahi with the iron and its cord dangling off the oven made her want to hang herself. The casserole had required food processing, several pans, and a cup of butter. Why couldn't her mother ever say no?

"What type of computer business are you in, Barry?" Sandy asked, a forkful with two peas on its way to his mouth.

Poor guy, Kate thought. She knew he was starving and here she'd given him the task of finding out if Barry was actually making a living in the computer business.

"Screen savers, novelty sponges, memorabilia," Barry said, squirting ketchup on his shoe-string potatoes. "There's a huge market for it. My website gets at least two hundred visitors a day."

And how many actual customers? Kate wanted to know.

144

Camille whined, banging her hands on the tray. Kate knew that she wanted to nurse. Later, Kate thought, shoveling Caesar peas into her mouth.

Her mother stared at Kate's breasts from across the table; Kate felt them plumping up in her red satin sweater. Their eyes locked. Kate shook her head, no.

"*My* Kate," her mother said. "I've never seen you so radiant."

Kate narrowed her eyes.

"Voluptuous," her mother went on. "Wouldn't you say so, Barry?"

Barry nodded, his mouth full of food.

Her mother reached for the bottle of wine. "Kate never had breasts until she met Sandy and started eating at McDonald's."

Camille wailed, saving the day, and Kate tossed her an Arrowroot Cookie. Enough, Kate thought. She wanted them out of there; she wanted to hate Barry. See, Mom, he's all wrong for you. He'll bore you in a minute and he's bossy and broke. But what did she know about a screensaving business? After all, people bought T-shirts that said SHITHEAD.

*A*t quarter-past eleven, Kate gunned Sandy's BMW into the dark night. Virginia grabbed Kate's rear-view mirror and pushed a red lipstick over her lips.

"They're getting on so well," Virginia said, done with the mirror (though it still faced her) and lighting up a cigarette.

Kate turned onto 24th Street. She still hadn't decided which church. She pictured Pedro alone in a pew, his damp hair curling slightly on the ends, fresh from a shower. Would he watch the door for Kate? "Nothing wrong with a bits-and-bytes guy," Kate said.

"I just don't know if it's for me."

"What are you saying?" Kate stopped at 24th and Mission, the fork in the road. "You're engaged," she said. "He obviously adores you."

Virginia crossed her bare legs. The Sudden Tan legs, Kate thought. Even at her thinnest, her mother was more voluptuous, with a soft swell of breast and high athletic arches in her feet. The floral dress (a gift from Barry) rolled off her white shoulder, exposing a black bra strap. Kate smiled. A little of the old Virginia shining through the Spic 'n' Span.

"It's too much sometimes," her mother said. "He's not respecting my space."

Consider my situation, Kate thought, *my husband wants to move out.*

"Why are we stopped here?" Virginia asked.

Kate revved the engine. "I can't decide which church."

"Don't you have a church?" Virginia stubbed her cigarette out in the ashtray. "What about the little place we went last year with the attractive minister?"

"Yes, well."

Her mother touched Kate's chin and turned her face toward her. "You do look radiant tonight. Maybe it's not the breasts. It's something else."

Kate turned off the engine. It was quiet; the car ticked as it cooled. "I was just thinking about a client who asked that we drop by his church. He's a football player, all alone."

"In my experience football players are never alone."

"He is tonight."

"Let's go then."

*I*t was reckless to be here, Kate thought, it was sex without a condom.

The church was bigger than she had expected, seating over five hundred—everyone else Hispanic. Toddlers in red taffeta gowns climbed the pews and rubbed their eyes. Kate could appreciate the parents' commitment: the cost of these elaborate clothes, the hardship of carrying sleepy children, the fight to keep them quiet.

A thousand votive candles lit the black recesses of the altar, where a porcelain Jesus was nailed to a cross, dark wounds in His palms. A carafe of red wine and stiff white linen napkins sat on a table in the middle of the aisle. Incense and wax and lilies and dime-store perfume ebbed and flowed. A harp purred from the choir loft.

Pedro was not alone. He was with Pinto and they had saved seats in the second row. As Pedro and Pinto escorted them forward, Kate felt people staring. When Kate looked, heads quickly turned, faces disappearing behind fans, under silk scarves brimming with pink sponge curlers. She tried to imagine what these people might think of her and her mother—on the arms of two attractive Hispanic men. Mother and daughter on a double date?

It was like the summer after her freshman year of college. Her mother had arranged a double date with two brothers, both youngish criminal lawyers—one married and one cohabiting—facts that came out later, emptying like the bottle of tequila that the men pumped into their margaritas. They'd all gone swimming at, of all places, the lawyers' father's house (who was also married or cohabiting). Kate changed into her bathing suit in the bathroom; later, the married brother emerged from the bathroom with a leg-hole of Kate's underwear around his index finger. "Which one of you left these?" he asked, twirling the panties. Her mother laughed and Kate looked the other way. "I would have guessed they were your sister's," he'd said. *Bookends*, he'd called them.

"But I'm a redhead," Kate was saying to Pinto as she pushed toward the pew. After all, she was basically a redhead, though she hated that term. He'd said something about her and Virginia looking like twins. She's a blond, Kate thought. A winter-correction blond, but nonetheless. There were no similarities.

Kate decided it was Pedro everyone was looking at. Never date a man who turns more heads than you do, her mother had once told her, certainly some of her better advice.

Virginia slipped into the pew, wiggling by a family with three small children. Pinto followed. Bookends. Bookends, Kate tortured herself. Determined to make the men sit on the ends, she climbed over Pinto and squeezed in next to her mother. Pedro, seeing an easy entrance to the vacancy at the end of their pew, went around the front and sat on Kate's right. Kate smiled, pleased with her lab-rat manipulation. She pulled off her long coat and draped it over her lap.

The congregation stood, crossing itself in unison, and began *Adeste Fideles*—in Spanish. Glancing at her red program, Kate realized that the entire hour service was in Spanish. This wasn't necessarily bad. Not understanding the words heightened the senses. The choir moaned from the rafters, weeping about Jesus and sin—*pecados*—that much Kate got. It sounded to her like the English word peccadillo, which she already associated with sin—though lesser sins—white lies and midday fantasies and sideways glances in elevators. The smell of lilies (which had always reminded her of funerals) made her dizzy, but cleared her sinuses.

"*La paz está con nosotros*." Everyone was shaking hands; coins jingled. Pinto and Pedro were already working the row behind them. Kate shook her mother's hand, which seemed too bizarre, so she hugged her. Then she turned around to the row behind her and held out her hand to a teenage boy. "Peace," Kate said. He looked at it for an instant, then grabbed it, smiling with two gold framed teeth.

"*Paz*," he said.

"*Paz*," Kate repeated.

Pinto reached across Virginia and squeezed Kate on the shoulder. Then Pedro hugged her, his hands lingering on her back for an instant.

"*Hola*," Pedro whispered. "Are you O.K.?"

Then he started translating for her, whispering in her ear: "Lord, send me where you would have me, to a village, or to the heart of the city; I will remember that you are with me."

When Pinto passed them the basket, Pedro tucked a $1,000 bill under the pile of ones. It was folded tightly to look like another one, but Kate had spent her whole life being an accountant.

*A*t that moment Kingsley was at Grace Cathedral, a handsome late-Gothic replica on Nob Hill. He was in the choir, standing shoulder to shoulder with the other tenors in their fussy red robes. He couldn't stop thinking about what Peter had just told him: Peter had committed Kingsley to sing the National Anthem at the next play-off game. The programs had been printed! During the opening hymn, he had imagined that everyone was there to see him, which he knew was a sin of pride. As he belted out the words, he felt as he would in the stadium when he would face them alone, alone except for three network cameras in his face.

In the front row, Peter the Red—in full tuxedo—clutched the arm of his girlfriend, Angela. Her black curly hair was large and messed-up looking. Peter always had bosomy women who had a sexual force about them, the type of woman who smelled of gardenia perfume, who leaned across laps to whisper to someone in a crowded theater, exposing violent purple underpants under black jeans. This type of woman scared Kingsley. He preferred not to look at them directly; he found Mrs. Gartmore's sleek good looks much more manageable.

Angela's aging parents slumped beside her. Her father had nodded off during the Communion prayer and now rubbed his eyes.

Peter waved at Kingsley wildly, squeezing Angela's arm even harder. Kingsley pretended not to see them, though the tenor at his right shoulder nudged him ever so slightly. My God, it's the benediction, he thought.

Peter, apparently frustrated that he couldn't catch Kingsley's eye, whistled—a wolf whistle heard often in the office at the copy machine, directed at various receptionists. Kingsley frowned. Had Peter lost his mind? Kingsley continued to watch Father John Hardcastle, who cleared his throat and repeated the verse. Then he had a thought that made him smile. A fan. That's what this was all about. Peter the Red was a fan. A stalker, even!

*T*he two back wheels of Sandy's BMW were gone, and the car's rear end rested on the ground. Someone had scratched the black paint, making a parallel pin-stripe.

"I guess we'll need a cab," Virginia said.

"No, no, we'll take you home." Pedro stepped around the car and jiggled the trunk. "They didn't get in."

"Sandy's going to kill me," Kate said, her hand on the car's hood. "We can't leave it here."

"You got Triple A?" asked Pinto.

"That'll take forever," Kate said, running her finger along the scratch that went all the way from bumper to bumper. "If they even work on Christmas."

"I've got a couple of spares in my garage," said Pinto, jogging backwards. "I'm just a block from here—we'll have you out of here in no time."

"I'll go with you," Virginia said, taking Pinto's arm. Before Kate could object, they were off.

"I'm real sorry about this, Kate," Pedro said as Pinto's and Virginia's footsteps echoed off. "I feel like it's my fault. I shouldn't have asked you to come. I want to pay for this. I insist."

"No. Thank you but no." Her breasts ached. It was definitely the Cinderella hour. She wondered what would happen if she simply didn't pump, cold turkey. Would her breasts explode or simply dry up?

Kate sat down on the curb and dug her heels in the mud. It smelled of rust and chocolate and leaking oil. "I wanted to come," she said. A stream of water trickled from a nearby fire hydrant. She wondered if there'd ever come a time when the sight of a fire hydrant wouldn't take her breath away.

Pedro sat down next to her and offered her a peppermint. The 48 bus banged past them, shooting sparks from its cable.

"Do you ever go to church with your husband?"

"No, he doesn't really like to go." She didn't like talking about Sandy with Pedro or even saying Sandy's name. She was certain that all affairs evolved out of talking about spouses, so she didn't think she should mention Sandy at all.

Pedro reached out and touched her hand lightly. "But you'd like him to?"

"I'd like him to understand why *I* want to go."

"Maybe he's afraid of what you'll find. People turn to the church when they're restless in their lives."

"I'm not *turning* to the church," she said, hugging her knees. "I just want my kids to grow up with faith. It makes life a hell of a lot easier."

"What about you? Would it make life easier for you?"

Kate grabbed her knees tighter. She felt tired. Life didn't have to be this hard. "I don't know."

"You're stubborn. A challenge."

Kate sighed again and shrank away from him, as if absorbed by the sliver of moon that polished the rooftops of four neglected Victorians across the street.

A car backfired in the distance. Pedro set his warm hand over her cold one. "Do you ever think about me before you fall asleep at night?"

Kate turned to see if he was teasing. But his small smile was serious.

There was a strange thumping sound down the street. Thump. Thump. It was ominous, like an elephant charging.

Thump. Thump. Thump.

"Kate!" It was her mother's voice. Her mother and Pinto appeared a block away, her mother ablaze in her white fur coat like an apparition. She was jogging in her stiletto sandals next to Pinto, who was dribbling two tires down the street. Thump. Thump. Thump.

Give him five years," her mother said.

"What?" Kate turned the car up Castro a block from her house. The telephone-pole candy canes were starting to peel away to dirty weathered wood, like advertisements for after-Christmas sales, boxes crammed with tinsel and Glo-bulbs that tricked you into believing they were beautiful.

"If he's still pursuing the fireman thing in five years, leave him."

Kate's vocal cords went tight. Her mother often surprised her, the way she stepped on toes and tripped on the heart. "Is that your professional advice?"

"No, that's advice from your mother."

"That's the way you've always handled things," Kate said, pushing the garage-door opener. She told herself she wouldn't think about Pedro the same way again. She would get him to sign the contract, then turn him over to J.P. She would return his shoebox.

"Just make sure you're not trading one set of problems for another."

The day after Christmas Kate found Sandy eating cottage cheese with sliced pears in the kitchen. Camille gripped

Kate's hip with her chubby thighs, her pink leggings riding up past her knees.

"They read me someone else's test results," Sandy said, jabbing his fork at her. "My cholesterol's only 172."

Though Kate had secretly wished for something like this—a reversal of fortune or someone else's misfortune—it was not relief she felt. It was the original sense of doom, the original rejection. She spotted Gus's fireman badge—Captain Bob's—next to the container of cottage cheese. "So you're off to boot camp?"

"Tomorrow." He smiled so wide she could see his gums and the silver in his back molars. It was not the smile of the man she'd married. It wasn't the tight smile of a scared lawyer who feared missing an issue of *Lawyers' Daily*. It was the smile of someone free to windsurf on weekdays.

He seemed to be waiting for her to congratulate him, and when she didn't—setting Camille on a chair and gently tying the laces of her pink tennis shoes—he stood and rubbed her back. "You'll see," he said. "It'll be O.K. We'll adjust our schedules. The kids'll get a kick out of it. Who knows—you might get a kick out of it."

The truth was, Kate thought, Sandy would get a kick out of it. She concentrated on looping Camille's shoe lace into a bow. She held her breath as Camille thrashed on the blue velvet seat cushion; she refused to cry. Tears, Sandy might read as sadness—and some of it was sadness—that she'd left something open when she'd fled the house one day, something raw and shiny that had caught the attention of another man.

Mostly, though, they were angry tears; she was letting him abandon her, even if it was just for the nights. It was just the way her mother had abandoned her, going out every night, so that now she compulsively checked locked doors and sometimes under beds.

Worst of all, it was pride; he was abandoning their way of life, the life they'd created together. Apparently he still longed for a freer existence. Apparently he wasn't having any fun, either.

"It's not how it's supposed to happen," Kate said, and maybe that's what bothered her most. "If it's free time you want—take it," she said, hooking her hands under Camille's armpits and setting her on the floor. "Take my play-off tickets for starters. I can watch the guys on TV."

Kate caught a glint in Sandy's eye. The gesture—the attempt at finding his heart—was not unnoticed. "No," he said finally. "Career before fun."

Kate winced, his sacrifice on her behalf not having its intended effect. "Take a vacation then. I'll stay with the kids. It doesn't have to be a life-event."

"You don't want to be married to a lawyer."

She glanced at him to see if he suspected something—her own dissatisfactions, the vastness that lurked behind her day-to-day life—but his face was turned to Camille, his sturdy man-fingers running through her downy blond hair. Was he thinking that Kate didn't want to be married to *this* lawyer?

Gus plunged a spoon into a container of Trix aqua-colored yogurt. "Don't cry, Mommy."

The children always knew. "I'm not," Kate sniffed, bending over and pulling cans of green beans and mandarin oranges out of the grocery bags.

"Would you just stop for one minute," Sandy said. "Look at me." He reached out and touched her face. "It drives me nuts the way you're always moving. You want to force all of us into your little plan."

Everyone, including Camille, stopped and stared at Sandy. Even he seemed surprised by his outburst.

Kate set the garbage bag down on a chair. All the years she'd been trying to get a rise out of him, he'd never gotten mad at her. But now that he'd expressed his anger, it didn't give her the refreshing feeling she'd imagined. How dare he be mad!

"It won't be forever," Sandy said, softly again. "I've always gone along with your stuff."

That he had, Kate thought. Yet "her stuff" had involved licensing and certification along a vertical ascent that had brought the family more financial security. "Her stuff" had not been stuff that she'd really wanted to do. "I don't make enough money," Kate said.

"But you will. You're so good—you're going to make more. Things have a way of falling in your lap."

What Kate knew about herself—on the tip of her tongue like her shoe size—was that nothing had ever landed in her lap.

*T*he four-story brick building at 7th and Folsom was crumbling into the sidewalk. The city had marked the battered entrance with orange slashes: condemned. Why Axel Staperfene, who worked there, would have some kind of magic fix for her, she couldn't say. He'd given her a peculiar feeling when she saw him, and that was the feeling she was banking on.

Kate pressed the button next to 430. Would he even show up? She checked her watch. 2pm. She was exactly on time. The door buzzed, rattling as Kate pressed it open. The lobby was tidy, but dark and moist with incense and the type of restroom hand-cream she most hated; a terrarium in the corner was full of night-loving ferns and jasmine, the flower that craved darkness.

The window at the end of the hall was shattered, and shards of glass covered the floor.

Kate took the metal stairs to the fourth floor and opened the fire-exit door to an empty hallway. She stood outside the door for three minutes, until exactly one o'clock. Then she turned the doorknob and stepped inside.

A leather, L-shaped couch wrapped the room. Everything was leather: a wing chair with dramatically arched armrests, the cushions of four stools that were equidistantly spaced against the wall, and the curved window treatments. The room smelled of licorice and shoe polish and old leather. A stub of incense smoked on the coffee table next to an orderly fan of magazines: *The New Yorker, Light & Healthy,* and *Working Parent*—it appeared no one had ever read them. In the corner that faced Folsom, a wrought-iron bird cage held twin yellow parakeets. Where were the framed certificates—degrees from respected institutions that Axel Staperfene had attended? Where were the trinkets? Baubles from trips? The paperweight from Northwestern or Stanford? There were no trinkets of any sort, not even a discreet No Smoking sign. Kate had a sudden urge to light up.

She stood in the middle of the room, feeling overdressed in her light-yellow wool pants and peach cardigan sweater. She felt like an Easter egg. This place was tougher than that, and a little morose. It was the type of place you wore black jeans and a tight black T-shirt with a leather jacket. Don't-fuck-with-me boots would have been appropriate. She'd have liked to put her Don't-fuck-with-me boots up on his leather sofa. She'd do better next time, she thought—if there was going to be a next time.

The gas heater next to the double doors rasped; the birds in their cage crunched bird seed on dirty newspaper. Kate didn't like birds—even fluffy yellow birds seemed like flying rats that would land in her hair if given a chance.

"Hello, Kate," a calm voice said. It was a familiar voice and it was coming from everywhere: from under the closed double doors, scraping through the grates in the heater, lilting up from behind the L-shaped sofa, and spewing out of the mouths of the horrid parakeets. Hello, Kate...

Kate wheeled around. Axel Staperfene glided toward her. His cropped black hair, neatly trimmed mustache, and pointy goatee were just as she remembered. There was no cape this time—he wore baggy black leather pants, indescribable chartreuse running shoes (nothing her athletes had ever endorsed!), and a tight-fitting white dress shirt. (Was it a blouse? It most certainly was a blouse!) What was she doing there?

"I didn't hear you open the door," Kate said, shaking his hand, which was dry and calloused. She would offer to pay him for the hour and claim that she had to go—her children had the stomach flu—there would be no need for further elaboration.

"I just went down the hall for water. Have a seat." He pointed to the sofa. "We have lots to talk about."

"Why do you go around leaving cards on people's cars?"

"Are you married, Kate?" He didn't sit, but stepped closer to her with his arms crossed. Despite the severe beard, his face had a softness, the long eyelashes were feminine. His muscular shoulders strained the fabric of the tight blouse.

"He's not gone yet. Saturday maybe. Saturday he moves into the firehouse."

"You think he doesn't want to be home?"

A parakeet twitched in the corner. Kate sat stiffly on the couch and crossed her legs.

"You have sexual problems," he said, squinting down at her. It wasn't a question.

Kate turned her head away. Right out of the gate—sexual problems. Did she exude this problem like oil from bad pores? "Of course I have sexual problems. I can't get the toddler out of my bed. Why did you put your card on my windshield?"

"It's my job to understand these things. The compulsive way you checked your car door. You can't leave anything alone."

"I lack faith?"

He smiled an upside-down triangle. His eyes bulged. Kate thought: perhaps he has a thyroid condition. But by now she knew the rules; you don't ask shrinks anything. "I probably wouldn't have put it quite that way," he said, "but, yes. Faith. Put your feet up. I have something nice to go over your eyes." He leaned over the coffee table and picked up a lavender-colored silk bean bag with a Chinese tapestry design and sniffed it deeply. "Lilac," he whispered.

"I'm allergic," Kate said. She wasn't about to cover her eyes or let down her guard in this place. He could off her.

"At least lie back then. You're nervous. Look at your knees." She'd been unaware she was clenching her knees together. She'd been grinding her teeth, too.

The leather sofa squeaked as Kate leaned back and rested her head on the armrest. He's way too new-agey, Kate thought, with his lilac-scented bean bags and squeaky leather. She could smell the cloying bean bag from where she was. And Axel himself was exuding dime-store cologne—and way too much.

Axel disappeared for a moment, then soft music filled the room. A piano and breezy horn. It sounded French. "Do you like Edith Piaf?" Kate asked. The French singer was one of her favorites.

"I'm not familiar with her."

That's weird, Kate thought. Weren't shrinks supposed to know everything?

"Has your husband always been a fireman?" Apparently he was going to continue standing behind her.

"Sandy's always been a lawyer—before that a law student." Kate stared at the ceiling. The beige paint was chipping around the recessed lighting. "He's never really liked it. The hours, the billing pressure, the continuing education.... He thought it would be different. The fireman thing came on suddenly—like the stomach flu."

"He'd never taken an interest in fighting fires before?"

"In fires, yes," she said. "But that's a whole session's worth of discussion." Like most of her conversations, she felt they only had time for the bullet points.

Axel cleared his throat. "You don't have intercourse very often?"

He was too close to her age. It felt like the time in college when the impossibly young doctor at Planned Parenthood—at least she hoped he was a doctor (perhaps a security breach?)—had given her a pelvic exam. "What's often?"

"You tell me."

"Often would be more often than we have it." She could tell her cheeks were turning pink. She was uncomfortable with this line of questioning—the shrink standing above her with a bird's-eye view of her crotch.

"What about masturbation? Would you rather masturbate than have sex with Sandy? Maybe you're hoping that he stays at the firehouse, so you can be alone."

"No, I—is nothing off limits here?" Kate grabbed her knees to her chest, knocking the bean bag off the table. A sex toy—that's what it reminded her of. "You're not a sex therapist, are you?"

"I'm not sure what a sex therapist is, Kate."

Oh fuck. He *was* a sex therapist. Here she'd thought that he'd observed something true about her and then he'd launched into his thesis on masturbation. She feared he'd want a demonstration— or worse, to coach her! Or whatever sex therapists did. There was something peculiar about him all right. And his spooky music. It was the same peculiar feeling that had attracted her when she'd seen him on Castro Street. She felt a little scared; it was like a sudden draft in the warm room. "I have some questions for you," Kate said, deciding to test him. "Have you ever heard of the TV show *The X-Files?*"

"Is that a game show?"

"*Seinfeld?*" Kate held in her breath.

"I think we need to talk about you, Kate."

Do you know what year it is? Kate glanced at the closed front door. Would it be locked if she tried turning the knob?

"Who do you think about when you masturbate?"

"I don't." Kate sat up and grabbed her purse.

"But there's someone, isn't there?"

Kate wrapped the purse strap around her hand and stood, not

looking over her shoulder.

"I'm ready when you want to talk about it."

"How much do I owe you?" Kate fled to the door and found it open. She turned around to look at him. He sat squarely on a stool that he'd positioned next to the couch, looking ever so slightly concerned about her. *Who are you?* She could drink up his concern. It was hard to get concern. She wanted to ask him how he knew there was a Pedro.

"Pay me next Friday," he said, hoisting up a leg and resting his foot on his leather-clad knee. "You can come at the same time. But I won't give you a break for leaving early. What are you used to paying?"

"I'm not a regular at this. I used to pay someone $130 an hour."

"I'm only slightly more expensive. A hundred and fifty."

Kate pushed the door open. "I'm done with therapy anyway." She couldn't possibly afford him.

Axel held his head at a tilt. "I think you've come here to confess something."

Confess? It hadn't occurred to her to confess. What was he imagining that she planned to confess? Confession was something you did with a priest in a booth, not a sex therapist.

"I'll send you a check," Kate said, stepping into the hallway.

"Quitting is really an issue with you," Axel said, wiggling on the stool, which also squeaked.

"I think you can overdo therapy," Kate said, holding the door and preparing to slam it. "It's like too much plastic surgery. Pretty soon the scars are as bad as the wrinkles."

Axel lifted a hand to his brow, shielding his eyes from the sun that crept through the blinds. "We'll talk about that next time."

*A*t three o'clock Virginia cabbed it to 430 Folsom Street. She had to get out of Kate's house anyway. Barry had taken a junket to Fry's Electronics, and she'd been making Consuelo nervous, smoking in the kitchen. When she'd gone out to the front porch, Gus had brought her Axel Staperfene's pretty business card.

"Can you come now?" the man had asked. "I have a cancellation."

The place was a dump. A hooker had shown her how to get in. Could her daughter have hit rock bottom and not be telling anyone? She always seemed on the verge of crying, which was new for Kate. You'd ask her if they were out of orange juice and her eyes would rim with tears. But Kate with a shrink? It made no sense. Kate was too tough for a shrink, she'd never needed coddling; she'd even survived high school without protein. As a teenager she'd never once called Virginia "bitch." There were a few shrieking fits, but no rehab and not much pimple-hysteria. Kate had thrived on anxiety. She'd turned to it when Virginia divorced; it had saved her from drugs and maybe teenage suicide, tornadoed her through straight A's, a dolphin dancing on its tail. She'd made it into something good. Or had she?

"Are you sleeping with my daughter?" Virginia lay on the squeaky leather couch with the lilac-scented bean bag over her eyes.

Axel Staperfene's stool whined behind her. He could be Kate's type, but she wasn't sure. The problem seemed to be with the football player, but in her book shrinks didn't make things any easier.

"I thought you wanted to talk about yourself, Virginia," he said. "Are you married?"

"On New Year's Day. But you didn't answer my question."

"I can't talk about my clients."

"Listen here, you prick." Virginia sat up. "I asked you if you were fucking my daughter."

Axel was unruffled, his hair held a kink of electricity from the stale room. "I think it's safe to say I'm not."

"Fair enough." Virginia lay down again and adjusted the bean bag over her eyes. It smelled nice, the way gasoline smelled nice when she filled up her car—the way she knew she shouldn't breathe it. And his voice was pleasant, it flowed lavender into her pores. "Why is she coming here, then?"

"Why does that bother you?"

"I can't understand why'd she'd see a shrink unless it has to do with her marriage. In my experience, marriage is the most likely reason you'd see a shrink."

"And the easiest."

"What's that supposed to mean?" Underneath her legs, the leather was lumpy. "Maybe I wasn't there enough for her," she said. "The eighties were tough times."

"Well, you're here now."

The floral voice. He forgave her, she felt it. He'd heard worse things—murder, implants, bulimia—maybe even from her own daughter. She felt her toes push into the flesh of the leather armrest.

"Why'd you decide to get married this time?" Axel asked.

"Is there a thing as simple as love?"

"You tell me."

Off to her left, parakeets skittered over newspaper. "Kate always had her reasons for marrying Sandy. She wrote them down, can you believe it? I say, once they make it past the initial screening, if you have to have reasons—you shouldn't do it. When she was 15, she made a list for me before I married my second husband. *Nice jeans* was on the pro side, and *no more baked potatoes for dinner. Swivel seats, watches TV while he eats, three's a crowd* were on the con side—go figure. I always admired her for that, she checked under every rock."

For the first time Axel Staperfene said nothing.

Virginia went on: "I never told her I was terrified that she was too strong."

*K*ate punched in the number. The phone rang three times.

"Yo," Pedro said.

"Hi, it's Kate from Sports Financial."

"I know where you work."

Kate lifted the Nike shoebox onto her lap. "I've got your paperwork together. A hundred thousand in contributions to Our Lady of Fatima. Nice of you. Did you know you spent over seven thousand on your Land Cruiser last year? By the way—how's the Corvette?"

"I got it, thanks," he said. "Wanna go for a spin tonight?"

"I've got swimming lessons with the kids. Sandy's—"

"I'd like to stop time then. For a few hours. So we could be together."

Kate was silent, clutching the phone. She thought of the way he'd looked at her as they sat on the curb on Christmas Eve. It had almost been a kiss. It might as well have been a kiss. She wondered if she would have done anything to stop him.

"I thought you might want to check it out for the warranty," Pedro went on.

"I didn't buy you the extended warranty. Did you really want one?"

"O.K. What else did you find in my shoebox?"

"Lots of mysteries in there. You like banana smoothies and hotel movies."

"I spend too much time alone."

"That's hard to believe," Kate said, sliding into the trap. She'd been so sad that he had to be alone on Christmas Eve and sadder that she had to leave him. "Hey, Pinto sent me a picture of us from Christmas Eve. It's good except I have devil eyes. My eyes are always bright red in pictures."

"It must be the flame in your heart."

She switched the phone to the other ear. "Will you autograph it for me?" It was the voice she used to congratulate the athletes on their games or thank them for tickets—slightly playful, a bit obsequious.

Pedro was silent.

"Pedro?" Kate said. He was mad, she knew.

"O.K., Kate. Stick it in my shoebox, and I'll have my secretary stamp it."

"I'm sorry—"

"How's your husband anyway?"

"Fine."

"Glad to hear it. Happy New Year. I'll call you if I ever need another car."

"You're not happy with it?"

"My Dad always wanted a Corvette."

"You can afford to buy him anything. Corvettes are everywhere now. They're nothing."

"When he died in '69, they were something."

Kate gulped. "I'm sorry."

"Yeah, well, I've gotta get to practice."

"Good lu—" she started to say, but he'd already hung up.

*P*eter the Red was poised outside Kate's door, his arm suspended in the air, about to knock. She waved him in. He looked terrible, as if he had the flu. His natty sports coat and pocket hankie did nothing for his doughy, almost mustardy face, crows' feet like riverbeds feeding the broken capillaries on his cheeks.

He sat stiffly in her guest chair.

"Did you miss the flu shots this season?"

He raked his hand through his Bozo the Clown hairdo. "I'm the control."

Kate swiveled in her chair. "You look...."

"I'm experiencing severe musculo-skeletal discomfort."

"So, how's Dr. Fuller?"

"She's a tough nut, but I had her peeing her pants last session. She's from Detroit, too, you know. Did she tell you she was Miss Michigan?"

"She didn't mention it," Kate said. Had they talked about Peter at all? More disturbing was that the shrink had apparently considered Kate the more desperate patient in need of traditional therapy. Worst of all was the certainty that Peter was a better salesman. Kate could have sat in Dr. Fuller's office all week and Dr. Fuller would never have peed her pants.

"She said you kinda flipped out and stopped coming."

"What else did she tell you?" Kate pushed back in her chair, banging into her file cabinet.

Peter waved a hand, shaking his head. "I just have the feeling you've got the inside track on this bonus race." He rammed his elbow into his groin in the disturbing way Sandy had done when illustrating sex on the kitchen floor. Did all men do this? Was this like a fraternity handshake? Some insider thing like ankle tattoos and hats with antlers?

Kate pointed in the direction of the chalkboard that Kingsley had rolled out into the lobby. "I'm not even on the map. James has pulled ahead."

"James is a kid. Skull and I—" He twisted his index and middle fingers together. "What I got cooking is gonna get me partnership. That means I'll be your boss, Katie. I don't think you want to blow your wad."

For the first time, he worried her. She twisted her wedding ring around her finger, flashing to chocolate kisses and sawed-off shotguns. She had defended him. She had dismissed the brain virus as "talk." They had wanted to fire him, and she'd convinced them he was harmless.

"What's cooking, Peter?" She tugged at her ring. It still wouldn't come off.

Peter's smile was boiling over. He was dying to tell. "I met this gal on the 49ers' board," he said. "This Shelby Chin-O'Connor." He moved his hands through the air, tracing breasts and hips.

"She hyphenates?"

"Second generation."

"Aaah." Kate gave up on her wedding ring and dropped her hands in her lap.

Peter leaned forward in the chair, his red hands squeezing the arm rests. "So this gal Shelby helped me put Skull in the lime-light," he whispered. "He's the main act—singing *Stars and Stripes* at the last play-off game."

"He's singing?" Kate was horrified. It was too awful to picture: the comb-over like a ragged mop, the French blue on French blue. He'd be on national television, the camera too close—his icepick pores, tonsils quaking in his throat. "Can he sing?"

"Like a nightingale," Peter said, rubbing his hands together. "Picture it. Sports Financial all lit up on the scoreboard." He lifted his arm, then let it drop, slowly, fingers quivering like twinkling stars.

It wasn't just seat-of-the pants that got you ahead in this business, Kate thought. You had to be desperate, and a little insane.

Peter reached across her desk. To Kate's horror, he yanked on the edge of the photograph of her and Pedro that was sticking out from under the desk blotter.

"He hasn't signed a contract with you?"

"No."

Peter lifted the edge of her blotter and shoved the photo

underneath. "I didn't think so. Once a Nester boy, always a Nester boy."

He clapped his hands. "So I got it wrapped. There's no need for you to embarrass yourself anymore."

He looked at her, cocking his head. "You've got lipstick on your tooth," he said, tapping his left incisor with a jagged fingernail. "Pull yourself together, would ja?"

*W*ednesday night, Sandy's law firm gave him a going-away party after work at Campton Place, a super-chic restaurant just off Union Square. Consuelo had a date with the UPS man (a "citizen man" Consuelo called him), so Kate stayed home. Sandy took BART to work that morning, anticipating a drunken night of the fraternity sort. Why not? Kate thought as she put the children to bed. His life had become a fraternity—sleeping porch and community condiments, bathroom rules and the one-cup concept, serenading troubled women off ledges and cats down from trees, chanting a fight song just for spirit. It sounded like fun. He'd figured out how to have it.

Kate was relieved she didn't have to attend the party; she feared the closure of expensive Russian caviar and the bad jokes. She could imagine the fireman-groupies, the hyper-responsible paralegals transformed into women who jumped out of cakes. They would love the hero in Sandy, and the fun guy he was going to be. They would want to be close to him, as everyone wants to touch the new bride. They would twirl their long hair and strands of pearls, stupefied: gosh, they never knew that firemen wore flame-retardant underwear and sprayed their naked selves with protective coating that looked like PAM cooking spray.

Kate hadn't even asked him how he'd quit—what had he said, exactly? Had they begged him to stay? Had he enjoyed dumping them or had he wavered just a moment? Maybe they'd gotten on their knees—told him how he'd be missed. But he seemed immune to flattery.

At 11:30, Sandy still wasn't home and Kate couldn't sleep. Camille hadn't made her way into the bed yet, so there was only Sandy's absence. She knew that she would eventually take over his space. At first she'd be awkwardly spread-eagled on the bed, staring at the glowing planets on the ceiling as she listened for sirens passing by; then, as time went on, she'd be belly-flopped diagonally, the sirens becoming white noise.

Kate sat up in bed, thinking of the things that were best accomplished while the children slept. Well, that would be almost anything, save vacuuming—Gus liked to ride the vacuum as Kate pushed.

Kate went downstairs to get the mail, wearing underwear and one of Sandy's old sailboat-racing T-shirts from years earlier— before Kate, before children. It had been washed a hundred times and the purple boats on the front were faded, the cotton worn soft. Sandy liked it when she wore his clothes. Hey, you look like me, he'd say, poking her in the shoulder with a finger.

As she passed through the kitchen, she noticed a paper Safeway bag on the table. She'd seen it earlier while she and the kids ate dinner at the table; she'd let it sit there like funeral flowers amongst the salt and pepper shakers and the platter of macaroni 'n' cheese.

Ever since the cholesterol scare, Sandy had given up Big Macs and Mystic Mint cookies. He ate only fruit, tuna fish packed in water, and cottage cheese; when he came home from his sessions with Doris Iris he gulped liters of water from a plastic bottle, patting his shrinking stomach and flexing his swelling biceps.

The bag was full of cantaloupes—eight of them. Eight seemed excessive, even if he planned to share. Eight cantaloupes were a mid-life crisis.

Kate went down the back stairs into the garage, ducking through the spooky labyrinth of unfinished pipes. A trickle of moonlight leaked in from a mud-splattered window. Sandy's workbench, where he'd intended to finish a stained-glass window, was stacked with Costco packs of Huggies, Christmas wrap, and beach toys caked with sand. Boxes were stacked to the ceiling, some labeled with Magic Marker—*Gus Clothes 6-12 months; bad wedding gifts/white elephants; old shoes.* Kate's wedding dress, boxed and hermetically sealed with a peek-a-boo window of white lace, hung near the yard tools. Another box, labeled *Kate's Real Lingerie,* boxed during the fourth month of her second pregnancy, was also gathering dust.

The cement floor was cool on her bare feet. The mailman had crammed the mail in the chute again, afraid of their cat-fearing dog. She gathered the mail, finding a piece of junk mail under Sandy's car.

It occurred to her that she hadn't been inside it since Christmas Eve. She wondered if the passenger seat was still adjusted for her height and if the car still smelled of new leather. Sometimes when she'd buckle up in her station wagon after Consuelo had been driving, the seatbelts reeked of Chanel. What woman's scent might be on that passenger seatbelt? Maybe her mother's tart lemon from Christmas Eve—or something sweeter. She imagined Doris Iris's fragrance powdery and girlish.

Kate set the mail on Sandy's workbench and opened the BMW's passenger door. She climbed inside and shut the door behind her. There was still a trace of the new-leather smell. Kate flipped on the overhead light. The inside of the car was so adult compared to Kate's: a notepad suction-stuck to the windshield was covered with Sandy's tiny gas-mile entries in impossibly straight lines. There were no sippy cups, Happy Meal prizes, or milk stains.

Kate's head was too close to the roof: Sandy's latest passenger had been shorter. Doris Iris was tiny. Sandy had taken the time to adjust the seat for someone who rode frequently—for her comfort. Or for the ease of sexual acts. Stop it, Kate told herself, buckling up. He takes clients around.

Short clients. Kate smelled the seatbelt: nothing. She sniffed harder, disappointed.

Suddenly there was a great clamor in the garage, someone tripping over boxes and rakes.

Kate popped the car door, poking her head out and flinging light into the dark garage. "Sandy?"

A sound of metal and thrashing through newspaper. Someone was making his way toward her, fighting the recycled paper and aluminum cans.

Sandy appeared before her wearing a black-and-yellow firefighter's hat at an odd angle, as if to rescue her from the car.

"Going someplace?" he asked.

He was grinning; Kate could see the white glare of his teeth. He looked cute in the hat. Wacky, yet brave. Maybe they could talk about what she was doing in his car. She would just ask him about Doris Iris, and he would reassure her. "Just smelling your seatbelts,"she said.

Sandy laughed. She could smell the booze on his breath.

"I was hoping you weren't asleep," he said, crouching to be next to her.

"You had fun," she said, pressing the release button on the seatbelt and watching it shrink away.

"Yeah, I won't be sorry to leave that place, but I kept hoping you'd show."

"You knew I didn't have a babysitter."

Sandy clutched Kate's knees, steadying himself. "For a second I thought you *were* there. There was this woman with her back to me—she had your hair."

Kate's hand flew to her hair, smoothing it. "I'm sorry," she said. She was sorry that she hadn't gone (really, it was a kind of betrayal), and that another woman had her hair.

"You're wearing my shirt," he said. He leaned toward her and kissed her hard on the mouth. She normally didn't like it when he'd come home drunk and amorous—he'd find her groggy in the bed, sober, and more than a little pissed off. A blind fuck, her mother would call it, pinning the tail on the donkey. But tonight there was something playful about him that she liked. The harsh taste of rum in his mouth excited her.

He pressed her down, fumbling with the sailing T-shirt, yanking it over her arms until it hung around her neck. As he found a nipple and traced it with a finger, the console jabbed into her back. "Let's go upstairs," she said, lifting the hat from his head and setting it on the dashboard. His face was buried between her breasts. She touched his baby-fine, straight hair, so uniformly black it was almost blue. It smelled of fried tortillas, but it could have been calamari fritti at Campton Place.

"This is so cozy," he said, raising his head. His breath was wet—a drunk fog in her face. He reached toward the passenger door and whacked at some levers; the seat popped back. It lay flat, like a lounge chair. Would she ever have discovered this feature on her own?

Kate squeezed past him and lay down on the bed he'd made. She pulled off the T-shirt and watched his reaction. If her memory served her, they'd never done it in the garage. The garage was almost outside, one step away from public nudity.

Sandy was at her knees, his mouth set in a serious pout. Sex should be serious, he'd once told her. He yanked off his lawyerly tie, then dove for her, his pants falling down around his shoes. Sex with shoes was O.K. with Kate—it was random, elevator sex— while stockinged feet was rolling over into a bored spoon.

Kate tugged at his briefs, hooking her fingers under the waistband and pushing them down to his knees. His working out had given his muscles an unfamiliar definition that she wasn't sure she liked. Her hands roamed his smooth back; she was alert, knowing it was still him, but uncertain what she might find. She liked the way he rolled down her panties with his open palm, his fingers discovering she was wet. Then he stuck his tongue in her ear.

Kate almost sat up.

In all the years she'd known him, he'd never tongued her in the ear. She'd heard stories of unknown twins sneaking into their brothers' houses and making love to their unwitting wives, passionately and possibly better than they'd ever had it. There was always something like this—some ear-licking peculiarity—that gave it away. But Kate knew Sandy. Of course it was him. Anyway, she'd glimpsed the question-mark-shaped scar under his jawbone. There was no mysterious twin.

Sandy's lips drifted to her neck. He balanced above her in a one-armed push-up, then lowered himself onto her (no doubt some fireman regimen, Kate thought. *Show-off.*) She arched her back to receive him, knowing that she wouldn't come now, not with her whole life tugging at her.

She flinched as he entered her. Everything was too hard. She thought of how she'd taken Gus to church, so he could be stronger than she was.

He went on for a long, long time. "Wow," Kate said, when he finally came.

"I had a lot to drink," he said, collapsing on her. "It helped to throw up."

Kate's chest was pinned under his enhanced pectoral girdle. She lifted her head. "You ralphed at Campton Place?"

"In the toilet," he said. He seemed delighted by the experience. "There were daisies on the seat cover."

Kate could barely breathe; his weight was crushing her. "You think you might have been in the women's bathroom?"

"Too many daisies," he groaned. His head went limp.

Kate freed an arm and shook his shoulder. He thrashed and grunted. His stomach sloshed. It took all her strength to squeeze her way out from under him. She crawled out of the car, clutching the T-shirt. She would leave the panties so Sandy could find them. If he was really doing Doris Iris, a glimpse of white cotton stuffed under the console as he jotted his mileage on the suction-stuck notepad might give him pause. But it would only take a glance at the label—the Japanese Weekend maternity underwear that she still slept in—and he'd know he was off the hook.

*T*hursday morning Kate dressed appropriately for her visit to Axel Staperfene: strappy black leather jacket with violent silver zipper; fitted aubergine blouse; cigarette jeans; and don't-fuck-with-me black boots. The only problem with her image was that she had both children with her: as Consuelo was sick, Barry and Virginia had gone to Carmel for the day, and Sandy was on duty (she hoped too miserably hung-over to master the required fireman games).

She intended to slide an envelope under Axel's door and end their relationship. There was no way he'd be in at seven in the morning.

As she started to push the envelope under Axel's door, she heard chains rattling. Before she could grab the children and run, Axel stood in front of her, rubbing the back of his neck and squinting. He wore a black cotton nightshirt; his feet were bare and hairless, and his buzzed hairdo looked longer and electrified.

"Come on in, Kate," he said, holding open the door as if he expected her, which annoyed her.

Kate thrust the envelope at his chest.

He held the index finger out—perhaps daintily? She hadn't noticed the band on his ring finger. It was ornate silver or platinum with an embedded marquee emerald. Was there really a wife? Or was this a Don't-fuck-with-me ring?

Gus swooped in behind Kate, holding up his fire truck—

"Vrrmmm—Varoom!"

"Can I see what you've got there?" Axel crouched down, holding out the palm of his hand, his black nightshirt tight over his knees. Camille toddled over to him and slapped him a high five.

Gus stopped—the fire truck suspended in mid-air.

"This is a good one," Axel said, spinning the wheels. Camille was trying to climb him.

"I've got a big airplane model inside," he said, rubbing Camille's back as she lay draped across his knees.

Kate bristled. "We need to get going."

"You got any videos?" Gus asked. "You got *Simba's Pride?*"

No way he has *Simba's Pride,* Kate thought, watching Axel squirm. A hundred bucks says he's never heard of it.

"I've got a video on African Pygmies."

"African pygmies, yea!"

"You changed your clothes," Axel said. "Do the street girls out front intimidate you?"

"No. I just—"

"Wanted to look sexier. You see yourself as the quiet, homely type?"

"No." Why was she defending herself? Out of the corner of her eye she saw Axel curl and un-curl his bare toes.

"Why don't you let the kids watch the Pygmies and you can lie down on my sofa?" Axel said. "We can talk some more."

The sofa thing again. Still, though he was the most expensive shrink she'd ever heard of, he seemed to be concerned about her. If she didn't know better, she would have thought that he cared.

"Where's Sandy this morning?"

"At the firehouse." Kate tightened her grip on Camille.

"Why, do you think?"

Kate was still breathing hard. "He's not all that crazy about me."

"How do you know?"

"We're out of here," Kate said, stepping over to Gus. "You're paid off."

Axel's Pygmies—the little Sirens that they were—had

170

transfixed Gus. When Kate tugged on his arm, he stumbled, stiff as if he might crumble into clods of earth.

"Let's get some dates on the books," Axel said. "How 'bout this evening at seven. And noon next Saturday. I must tell you though that my price has gone up to $165 an hour."

"Whatever," Kate said, steering the bleary-eyed Gus to the door. "We're through."

Axel called after her: "Remember I have a 24-hour cancellation policy. After that it's going to cost you."

Kate had no doubt.

Outside Axel's door, Gus was coming to life. "Can we come back here on Wednesday, Mommy?" He was starting to learn the days of the week and had no idea when Wednesday was, but only that it was soon.

Kate, with Camille on her numb hip, held Gus's hand as they navigated the stairs. The numbness was spreading to other parts of her body, sometimes staying all day. She would have to go back to the doctor. Something had to be wrong. "Why do you like him?"

"Because he loves me," Gus said, without thinking. Then he spotted a vending machine at the bottom of the stairs. "Can I get some juice?"

Kate thought: Why is it that children can sense when someone cares? They were like dogs in that way. When you got to be a grown-up, you were constantly checking under carpets for dirt and stealing into medicine cabinets for the ways you might be deceived. Prozac and tampons left over from someone else could cost you a relationship.

Get his bank statements and health records, Kate had commanded her mother, who had known Barry just six weeks and had decided that she loved him. And she was a family lawyer who had seen disillusionment. But maybe hers was an obvious love, the kind children could spot. What children knew of love was someone paying the closest attention.

*T*hat night at six Kate's friend Nadine came over while Barry and Virginia were at a movie. Kate had gone to business school at Berkeley with Nadine's ex-boyfriend. He'd been ex for several months, but Nadine was still hungry for any details about the enigmatic investment banker.

"I ran into him last week at the gym," Kate said. They were sitting around the kitchen table—Gus on top of the Yellow Pages as a booster and Camille in her high chair. The frozen Tater-Tots gave off a burned smell as they baked in the oven. The children were eating fish sticks, while Kate and Nadine drank goblets of Pinot Grigio. It was a makeshift family meal, Kate thought. At least the adults were seated with the children. In a perfect world, everyone would be eating the same thing off plates symmetrical with each food group. The next best scenario was that everyone was eating something the same color—the fish sticks were a muddy yellow, the Pinot more jaundiced. Kate hoped that in a three-year-old's mind there was little difference.

Nadine tossed her curly henna-black hair and cupped her white hand around the bowl of the goblet. Her skin was translucent white, her oval fingernails painted coconut. "Did he look available?" she asked. She pouted and touched the spit curl in the middle of her forehead.

To Kate, Roger Forese always looked available. Nice pull-ups, he'd said to her as she stepped off the cheating machine. Girl pull-ups. Why couldn't she have done a real one?

"He was in a hurry." The guy was permanently in a hurry, Kate thought. You'd run into him at a party and he'd be looking over your shoulder for his next conquest.

Nadine helped Camille pull apart her fish sticks. She had no children, but she had such an easy way with them.

"What was he wearing?"

Kate gulped her wine. "Shorts."

The refrigerator coughed—it had been broken for months. The house was in disrepair. She would have to start taking charge of Sandy's chores—light bulbs and garbage and fleas and the exploding population of mice. At one point the mice had been a crusade for him. He set traps baited with Gruyère behind the water cooler and in the dark corners of their living room, keeping the fire stoked throughout the summer. Don't be afraid, he told her as they watched videos in the living room, mice are afraid of the flames. She remembered him telling her that his father used to stalk mice in the basement with a Smith & Wesson.

Gus tapped Kate on the arm. "I'm going to eat one fish stick, then I'm going to be excused."

Kate thought she saw a mouse leap under the butcher block, but it could have been the floaters doing laps around her brain. "You will eat two fish sticks, or you'll go into the living room and pick up Legos." She liked to give the children choices. With Sandy she'd given him choices—don't leave me or I don't know what I'll do. But here she was, living with the mice, her duffel-bag-husband no longer stoking the fire—the fire that was supposed to make her less afraid.

"I can't believe it's been four months since we broke up," Nadine said, chewing on a piece of fish stick off Camille's tray. "He dumped me September 15th. We'd only started dating March 3rd. He introduced me to his parents on April 30th."

Kate went to the refrigerator and brought the bottle of wine to the table. "How do you remember all these dates? It seems to me it would be better to forget them."

"My analyst tells me that's the way I'm working through this. I'm tagging events, cataloging them, and putting them away."

Kate thought that it seemed an ideal time to bring up her own situation with Axel Staperfene. The wine was creating a warm glow up through her arms, thawing the numbness. "I tried going to an analyst," she said. "He's into leather and always wants to talk about masturbation." She mouthed the word *masturbation,* so Gus wouldn't promptly add it to his vocabulary. "Then he wants me to lie on his squeaky couch with this lilac bean bag over my eyes. He sits behind me on a stool."

Nadine pointed at Kate with the fish stick. "You know what he's doing, don't you?" she said, Nadine, the authority on psychoanalysts. "He's sitting behind you, masturbating."

*T*he next morning Kate pounded on the office door. She still had no key. Heidi, the receptionist, buzzed her in, nodding as if she were on an important call. She'd cut her hair short; the fringes jetted out around her head phones. For all Kate knew she could be listening to Nine Inch Nails. The answering machine caught the calls too often. Heidi's skirts were getting shorter, and her body piercing denser. But, since they turned over receptionists at such an alarming rate at Sports Financial, Kate was letting her slide. Peter had mentioned to the receptionist before James that he liked her leather vest and she had run crying from the office. If you'd heard it from Jennifer Popkins, he'd told her that her vest looked like a wet suit. Then he'd suggested to Kate that they "get a loquacious young lovely" to replace her. All this Kate had documented in his personnel file.

Today, something about Heidi caught Kate's eye. She was wearing a lacy black camisole, the type that would show your bra, or lack thereof, if you unbuttoned your jacket. Kate paused at the reception station.

Heidi pulled off her head phones, her hair standing on end. "Do you want your phone messages, Kate?" She was snapping her gum. Kate ignored this.

"Not yet. I like your shirt."

Heidi dropped her jaw, revealing a wad of pink gum. "Thanks—I wouldn't have thought it was your style."

Kate set her briefcase on the floor and leaned against the reception station. "What is my style?"

Heidi shrugged. "Like, you know, that newswoman Katie Couric or something."

The phone rang. "Katie?" Kate stared at her. "But she's older than me. My hair's longer. I wouldn't have thought—"

"I know, sorry, but it's just my perception." Heidi grabbed the phone. "Good morning, Sports Shop."

Sports Shop! Kate wanted to yank the baseball danglies out of Heidi's ears. Enough was enough.

Heidi hung up. "Wrong number."

Kate jabbed the counter with a pen. "Of course they think it's the wrong number when you answer the phone like that. What happened to 'It's a great day at Sports Financial?'"

"I'm sorry, I thought this was catchy."

Kate breathed again. "So where'd you get it?"

"I just thought it up."

"No, the shirt. Where'd you get the shirt?"

"Oh." She gave her a conspiring smile. "Versace," she mouthed. "Downstairs."

"Really?" It was somehow disturbing that their 21-year-old

receptionist could afford to shop at Versace. The jeans there cost more than she'd paid for her first car. She studied the shirt. The fabric was a fine, delicate lace.

"My break's at ten," Heidi said. "Want me to go with?"

Kate picked up her briefcase and fingered her lip. Shopping with the receptionist was wildly inappropriate. She needed to be fired immediately. Everyone there needed to be fired. Kate turned to her office. "Buzz me when you're ready."

"I will, and, oh, Kate, don't let me forget: Axel Staperfene called to say you missed another session—"

Session?

"—and Pedro Araguz called to invite you to have dinner at his house after the game. He said to wear black."

As in black stockings? She was breathing hard again, her toes were ice. How would she explain it to Sandy?

Heidi put on her headphones again and gave her a slumber-party wink. "Don't worry, Kate. There's lots of black at Versace."

The Versace saleswomen were from another time zone. They were dark and thin as tea leaves with pouty red lips and pants like broom sticks. They stared at her like scarecrows in a corn field and, without moving their mouths, made quick biting comments that she didn't understand.

"That black isn't tonal with her pale skin," the one with the widow's peak said when Kate slid in her stocking feet from the dressing room into the full-length mirror.

Kate smoothed her hands along the rubbery fabric on her hips and was shocked and pleased by the way it grabbed her.

"Let me get the crêpe," said the one with the hair-bun-too-tight.

"She'll need the shoe then," the widow's peak said.

Kate escaped into her dressing room.

Heidi sat on the bench, swinging her feet. After trying on twelve dresses, Kate was no longer uncomfortable being naked in front of the receptionist.

"You look amazing in that dress," Heidi said, unzipping her. "I didn't think you had such a wide range. You look like a rock star."

Kate shook her hair in front of the mirror, feeling that she could, of course, be a rock star. Why had she taken the CPA exam when there'd been such other possibilities?

Obviously, she'd been holding back. If she was going to work out seven days a week, she was going to make sure that somebody noticed her. She pulled down her work skirt off the hanger and stared at the drab charcoal suit coat, with its man-fabric, still swinging like a pendulum on a hanger.

"Which rock star?"

Heidi bobbed her head back and forth as if to music, her danglies swinging. "Pat Benatar. A redheaded Pat Benatar, if I had to pick one, though I don't think you're limited to that."

Kate picked up the dress and held it up to the light.

"How we doing in there?" somebody called sweetly, thrusting another black dress through the gap in the curtain.

They stared at it. Heidi shook her head. "You know, Kate, I'm thinking that Pedro might like you better in some color."

"Like butter?" Kate asked, thinking of Ms. Towne's yellow nip dress—the one that Kate could wear backwards.

*K*ate reached for a pencil. All six #2s were sharpened to a point; it was the one task that Jennifer Popkins performed for her without hesitation, apparently taking some grim satisfaction in it.

Kate's fingers felt too numb to pick up the pencil. She had hot prickles on the tips of her thumbs. She shook out her hand.

Jennifer appeared in her doorway wearing a tight fuchsia sweater and matching stretchy pants pulled snug over her long legs. It looked like a ski outfit. "It's an Axel Staperfene calling collect." She clicked her tongue and swished her pale blond hair. "I just accepted the charges."

Collect?

Kate picked up the phone. She could hear traffic in the background. "Do you always come with a price tag?"

"I'm sorry, Kate," Axel said, in his voice of liquid understanding. "I ran out of change. I didn't like the way our conversation ended."

Kate's phone cord had wound into a tight coil and she yanked it apart. "You're calling me from a pay phone?" Probably in a bullet-riddled booth with gutted phone books on a street with neon hookers and shards of broken glass. Next he'd be calling her from prison—"It's an Axel Staperfene, collect from West Oakland Correctional"—and she'd pick up the phone! The situation was getting seedier and seedier.

"I want you to think about something for me," Axel went on over the cars honking. "I want you to think about your ideal situation. What are the things you're looking for in a relationship? Will you just think about it?"

How could she not think about it once the question was presented? Kate, who followed up on business cards left on her windshield? "We're not doing this anymore," she whispered. Jennifer still stood in her doorway. She leaned on the doorjamb, twisting the toe of her pink pump into the carpet.

"Just think about it," Axel said. He hung up.

Jennifer folded her arms over her encapsulated breasts. "Can't break up with him, huh?" she said.

"It's not a matter of breaking up with him. It's just that—" What was she doing explaining herself? "I'm married."

Jennifer cocked her head and twanged her bottom lip with her pointy finger.

"He's a shrink! O.K.?"

"Didn't take my advice about getting the kid out of your bed, did you?"

"I need a contract drawn up for Pedro Araguz," Kate said firmly, searching her desk for her phone book.

"Peter won't be coming in today," Jennifer replied, pulling a wad of paper out of the front pocket of her ski pants. "He said to remind you about what you talked about." She was reading from a green phone message pad as she scooted back to her desk. "He said you'd understand."

It was time to come clean about Peter, Kate thought. Kingsley was out for the day, resting his vocal cords for the big day on Sunday. All week he'd been sipping warm milk with honey and gargling a salt concoction. J.P. was out, too—no doubt trolling for boys. There wasn't much time left in the bonus race. Where was Deek?

"When can I have my contract?" Kate asked.

"I'm really backed up today," Jennifer said.

"I need it now!"

"It's true, you have some symptoms, but not all the symptoms," Dr. Epman said to her. His gray beard was bushier than last time. Kate was in his winter-white examination room again, naked under a tissue-paper gown. She sat stiffly on his examination table, her toes resting on a cold metal bar below her. The pointy instruments on the counter looked shiny and ready, but were not for her. "No doctor can tell you if you have MS," Dr. Epman said. "I've seen symptoms come and go. You just have to wait and see."

"Wait and see?" Kate said. When she moved, the paper gown thrashed. "There's no test?"

Dr. Epman shook his head.

Leave it to me to find the disease with no test, Kate thought. Just wait and see if I become crippled? Wait and see if I was good enough? Look back at the end of my life and see if I had any fun? Enough love?

Of course, I'm delighted to see you," Father Leo said, though Kate knew he was surprised. Friday night, he was on his way out, smelling of some manly cologne, wearing trendy pants that looked like they were made from shower curtains and a silvery V-neck sweater without the collar. His head was bald and bright as a light bulb, and there she was blocking his narrow doorway. She had a thought: probably when the church was built in the 1800s, women weren't allowed in the priest's office—the doors were built narrow so their bustle skirts wouldn't fit through the doorway.

His steeple office smelled musty, of damp curtains, dyed carnations, and smuggled wine. She'd hiked the three flights of crooked creaking steps to get there, the oil paintings of Christ weeping as she climbed. From the small turret window she glimpsed the Creamsicle sunset over the Mission.

"Shouldn't we use the booth?" Kate asked, digging her fingers into the doorjamb. The office trembled as the church bells rang out for Father Juanito's seven o'clock mass.

"Would you like a booth?" Father Leo asked as casually as a maître d'. He eased back in his thinning-velvet serpent-style chair. He looked to be at the head of a castle dinner table. Kate would sit at the opposite end and make small talk about the weather—a walk to first base just to pass the potatoes.

"I think it's too late for the booth," Kate said.

"That's good," he said, folding his muscular arms, "because we don't have one. You're thinking of the Catholics again. Have a seat." He gestured toward the chair opposite him, palms out, fingers pointing down.

"Oh," Kate said, reddening, but touched and a little grateful he'd remembered their brief conversation. "I haven't seen you at church in a while," he'd said the last time she was there.

"I thought you said Episcopalians were just like Catholics without the guilt."

"I did say that indeed," he'd said, laughing until his wide mouth made no sound. "The only guilt here is what you put on yourself."

Now Kate slipped into the low-back guest chair. "So this is the way you do it—face to face?"

"Do I need my collar for this?" he asked, opening his top desk drawer.

She didn't want to commit. Did her thoughts—only her thoughts—need to be confessed? Or did she want him to stop her?

"What's on your mind, Kate?" He had time for her; his date was probably waiting outside the church in an itty-bitty Miata, but he'd never let on.

Kate couldn't look at him. She studied the parallel grooves in his manicured fingernails. Outside, a noise sounded like firecrackers.

"Something between you and your husband? Or work?"

"Both," she said quietly. "You know I work for a sports firm with professional athletes. I feel...."

He was smiling with pursed chapped lips, nodding his head. "The entertainment industry pumps out so many temptations," he said. "It's all geared to get people to buy—"

"What if I know him?"

Father Leo raised an eyebrow and glanced around his littered desk, layers of papers and cobwebs, stacked Styrofoam cups, and old Lotto tickets. He was looking for a bible; she knew it.

"Not know him in the biblical sense," Kate said quickly.

Father Leo relaxed, his shoulders dropping. "You've fallen in love with another man," he said brightly as if this were an easy fix, as if he didn't want to talk sin. Resist it, resist it, she could hear him saying.

"What's happened to your marriage?"

Kate shook her head, trying not to cry. The room was hot, suffocating, her body was numb from her waist to her knees. "He's gone."

From outside on the front lawn, a coarse voice shouted. "We gotta gang-banger dying down here, folks. Quick, somebody, get the priest!"

Father Leo was on his feet, fastening his collar around his neck. "The apartment manager next door hasn't figured out that there's two of us. Unfortunately, Juanito's doing mass. We'll get this figured out, Kate." He threw the robe over his head and wrestled it on.

Was forgiveness what she'd really come for—three Hail Marys and a time-out in the corner? "Do you ever feel that no one's there for you?" Kate asked him.

"I have God," he said, from underneath the robe. "I'm never alone."

"It's nice," she said, "to have that faith."

*T*his time the door to Room 430 was open when Kate reached the top of the stairs; French music drifted out—she could almost see brush strokes in the dusty air, edgy quarter-notes guarded by a somber treble clef—and she wandered inside.

"I was just having a snack," Axel said. He was sprawled in the leather wing chair wearing another blouse, eating smoked oysters from a can with a toothpick. "Would you like to join me?"

He eats, Kate thought, with some relief. The hell-for-leather drive from the church still had her heart pounding. "No, thank you," she said, sinking into the couch.

"Maybe you'd like a glass of sherry?"

"O.K."

Axel left the room still eating from the can of oysters. He returned with two crystal sherry glasses.

Kate took a sip. "How've you been?" she asked him.

He stared at her, down to what seemed her very bones, at least to her underwear, and she looked away. She recalled her second visit to Dr. Fuller, that initial awkward moment which Kate promptly filled with her How-bout-those-Niners chit-chat, like Cheetos appetizers, and Dr. Fuller had not been pleased.

"Why do you want to talk about me?" Axel asked, but not until after Kate had counted all 16 leather bolts in his leather window treatments. She decided she preferred the lying-on-the couch position, his black eyes on her errant hair, her crotch exposed.

"Do you think it's because you don't want to talk about yourself?"

"I have no problem talking about me."

"Why does that make you feel like crying?"

Kate sniffled. "It doesn't." Seven o'clock. It was getting late, Consuelo would have to get ready for Friday night clubbing, the kids would be hungry. "I'm going to have to leave to go nurse."

"Why are you still doing that?"

"The American Pediatric Society—"

"Do you do everything people tell you?"

Kate shook her head and the couch squeaked. She felt a hot trickle down her cheek.

"How do you feel about your breasts?" She heard him cross and uncross his legs.

"They're O.K."

"Too small?"

"They're not all that small now." Why was she defending herself again? What did it matter if Axel Staperfene thought that her breasts were too small?

"Because of the nursing," he said.

"That is not why I nurse," Kate said. "If you'd let me finish...."

"Does Sandy ever touch them? Caress them?"

"Not often."

"Does it arouse you?"

Kate shook her head again, no, but maybe she was lying. She could picture Axel's view of her hair falling off the black couch. Sandy wanted to touch her breasts, but she'd shut him down; there were places she wouldn't let him go.

"How's this other guy going to be different?" Axel asked. "What are your fantasies about what he'll do to you?"

Kate couldn't breathe.

"Or is it the things you'll be free to do?"

Sandy was off to on-duty training. "A bread-and-water weekend," were his last words as he went through the front door Friday night wearing only an undershirt beneath his leather jacket and a duffel bag over his shoulder. He'd pecked her on the mouth while she heated Spaghetti-Os for the children. Her mother and Barry had gone to 24th Street for take-out Chinese.

When the children were asleep, she searched for Pedro's home number in her purse. She wrapped her rose-stenciled velour bathrobe tighter around herself and tucked the phone under her chin. "I hope I didn't wake you up."

"Look, if you want me to sign, bring the contract over after the game. Say five o'clock at my place. I'll be beat—I'm avoiding the press. We can have dinner here."

Kate was silent. She would get the bonus. Sandy would be thrilled. She realized that in the back of her mind she'd been hoping to tell him that she'd lost the contract—she couldn't do this job—and he'd understand then how sad she really was. That had been the last, best hope for them.

"Kate? You still there?"

"Yeah."

"I thought you'd be happy."

"Happy?"

"So—you coming over? If it's uncomfortable, I'll swing by your office next week."

A lot could happen by next week, J.P. might sweet-talk him, or, worse, he could change his mind. "I'd like to come over," Kate said.

"*W*here are you going in that dress?" Virginia asked Kate. It was ten minutes to four. They were all seated at the kitchen table—Barry, Gus, Camille, and Virginia—eating Barry's turkey tettrazini for an early dinner. Her mother claimed to never let food past her lips after 6 p.m. Barry had discovered Kate's turkey in the fridge—so far no one had discovered the salmon in the back of her car.

"I have a meeting," Kate said, grabbing a plate. She was so tense, she had no feeling in her wrists and the plate crashed on the glass table top.

"Mommy," Gus said. "I can't eat with the fly."

Kate looked to where Gus was pointing. A fat fly buzzed around the platter of turkey tettrazini.

"He's O.K.," Kate said, trying the plate again. "Flies are our friends."

"But I don't like him," Gus said, his lower lip quivering. Kate knew: he would not eat until the fly was removed from the room.

As she scanned the room for a newspaper, her heart pounded. In a rush of strength and dexterity, not unlike a mother lifting a car off the trapped arm of her child, Kate reached for the fly and snapped her hand closed around it.

Gus stared at her wide-eyed.

She was really hyperventilating now. "Is there anything else I can do for you?" she asked, looking around the room wildly.

"Don't kill him!" He covered his eyes.

Gus was at her heels as she went to the kitchen window with the fly in her hand. She opened the window and tossed it out into the even more dangerous street.

"Mommy!"

"When did you stop wearing a bra?" asked Virginia, braless herself in a halter top with feather tassels over her belly.

"Ms. Towne said to lose it," Kate said. She spooned some of Barry's beet-and-carrot casserole (the casserole she'd dissed) onto her plate. Pedro had mentioned dinner, but Kate was starved. On her second date with Sandy he'd told her she was the only woman he'd ever taken to dinner who'd cleaned her plate, and this alarmed her. So what if women nibbled before dates to suppress their dainty appetites, just as men jacked off. Was she now thinking of it as a date?

"Your mother doesn't need a bra," Barry offered.

"But I need support hose," Virginia said, wagging her fork. "After the honeymoon I'm having my varicose veins stripped."

"I won't allow it," Barry said, spearing a chunk of turkey.

It could be worse, Kate thought, Sudden Tan foreplay and a selfless high regard. Was this the set of problems that her mother had traded for? Kate tasted the shredded beets. *Mmmm, buttery.*

Virginia peeked at Kate from across the table, around the box of Potato Buds. Kate knew her mother suspected. Kate swallowed a Valium with a slug of chardonnay.

"You know," Kate said, struck with an urge, "I'm not cut out for this job."

She expected a pep talk—a "Not you, Kate McCabe—look at what you've accomplished—you're a gawddamn CPA or CFA, for crying out loud," but her mother looked at her, her hair in soft wisps around her heart-shaped face, her make-up faded—a dash of honest freckles so rarely seen. Kate had never seen her so beautiful. She looked at Kate as if Kate was off to perform some vigilante act she was too late to stop.

"I used to feel that way about my job at Planned Parenthood," Virginia said, twisting the stem of her wine glass. "The stories were too sad. I was so tired, going out every night."

"Why'd you do it, then?" Kate asked. *Why were you gone?* They both knew the real question.

"I needed to," she said. "Your mother subscribes to the trickle-down theory. What's good for mother will be good for daughter, too."

Kate thought she might live with that.

"If nothing else," her mother went on, "I wanted to teach you that you can be happy."

Kate wouldn't call herself happy, but she could say for sure that her mother was finally happy, and this came as a relief. The Valium began to take hold. "Sometimes I feel I can't keep it together."

Her mother hugged her, her soft cheek pressed against Kate's, not judging, not scolding, just holding her. "I know it, baby. I think I've always known."

On her way to Pedro's, Kate spotted a fire engine parked in front of the Donuts & Chinese shop at 24th and Mission. She wondered if it was Sandy eating with his associates. She pulled over in a red zone and ran to the truck, her strappy heels flexing near to the breaking point as she crossed the street. She was hoping Sandy would tell her to forget about Pedro—we don't need the money—but he wouldn't say that, she knew, and they did need the money.

But it was only a forty-something fireman in the cabin eating donuts out of a paper bag.

"Excuse me," Kate said, rapping on the window with her knuckles. "You from the Mission firehouse?"

"Nope. 5th and Bryant. The bear claws are better over here."

Kate declined the donut he offered, thanking him. He seemed to sense her disappointment. "Want a tour of the engine?"

"Not today." She started to go, but changed her mind. "Say," she said looking at the back of the truck, "what do you call that swing seat in the back? I bet somebody once."

His mustache was full of powdered sugar, and he patted it with a greasy, wadded napkin. "That's the tiller," he said. "Hey, you wanna see the longest hose in the city?"

"Not today."

Next door at the LuLu Cantina Sidewalk Café, a scrappy crowd was watching the post-game wrap-up. The Niners had beaten Green Bay, 22-6.

A woman stood bullshitting with the young surfer-bartender through the open window. From the lipoed-cranberry Spandex and billowing marshmallow blouse, Kate knew it was the illustrious Kim Novak. It was like running into a movie star in your own dumpy bar. "Jumbo bratwurst with chili and onions," Kate heard her order. She wore Kate's black leather jacket—an exact replica—tied around her waist. It was time to make her pay up and stop the onslaught of debt. She would grab Kim's dimpled arm and make a citizen's arrest.

It was 4:55. Pedro's house was just around the corner. She needed the perfect moment to confront Kim. The air was velvety with spices—cumin, Tabasco, ginger, tobacco. Kate, standing with her hands on her hips, her legs slightly spread, her nip dress clinging to her legs with an electrical charge she'd picked up off the firetruck, sneezed. Both Kim Novak and the bartender turned. "God bless you," he said, swishing heavy blond bangs. "Can I getcha a beer for that?"

Kim Novak took her bratwurst and dressed it with gobs of catsup and relish. Any second now she would slip back into the crowd. It was time to act. Kim's mouth was full of bratwurst. Another moment passed. "You look pretty," Kim said to Kate. "Looks like you're going on a date."

Kate eyed Kim's bratwurst. While nursing, there was never a peckish hunger—you needed a steak.

With less indecision than it took her to select her pencil for the Monday morning investment meeting, she ordered from the bartender, "A jumbo bratwurst with chili and onions. To go."

*P*edro answered the door to his renovated Victorian barefoot in a white terry-cloth robe. "Kate, I'm so sorry," he said, taking a step back to let her in. "Traffic was bad. I'm just getting in the shower."

"No problem."

The maple floors were polished to gold. A carved staircase rose out in front of her—up to the master bedroom, she thought. She recalled that these old places rarely had bathrooms on the main floor. She would have to hold it. "And congratulations," she said. She should have brought wine, flowers, something. All she had was the contract in her purse; it was her reason for being there and she felt for it as he kissed her on the cheek.

Pedro touched her on the waist. "I was picturing black," he said, "but I could be buried in this." As he bolted the door, she caught a whiff of his raw sweat, not masked with fancy deodorants—hard-earned sweat—ten-million-dollar sweat. It wasn't unpleasant.

If this wasn't a date, it was starting out like a date. For a greedy moment she wanted it to be a date. It was what she missed about dates, the niceties, the unexpecteds. Fresh strawberries and the whale-shaped soap she might find in the bathroom. The thing she hated about dates (if she could remember back that far) was when a guy appeared buck naked as you exited the powder room.

Pedro led her down a long hall, tightening the belt on his robe. "Before I forget," he said. "Pinto wants a date with your sister."

It took her a moment—Virginia Anne, up to her old tricks.

"She's getting married Monday."

"Huh," Pedro said, "she never let on."

The kitchen was before them in its stainless steel glory. The stove didn't even looked used. The refrigerator was covered with letters and photos—fan mail, Kate thought. She could smell the lavender stationery, see the curly script—the *i*s and exclamation points dotted with fancy stars. On the granite counter Pedro had slapped some slabs of beef (filets, ribeyes—Kate had no idea) spinach tortellini, pints of whipping cream, a Medusa head of basil, and balls of fresh mozzarella. Looney Tunes statues were everywhere. Tweety Pie held a tray of salted almonds in a ramekin, Bugs Bunny the size of a ten-year-old had his hands to his mouth as if calling to her, and Pepé la Pew held a tray with a bottle of Cabernet that was open and breathing next to two goblets the size of fish bowls.

"I thought you wouldn't mind whipping something up while I'm in the shower."

Kate reached for her glass. Was he screening for wives? It felt like a typing test.

"You're an angel," he said, heading for the staircase. A few moments later Dave Matthews's music filled the kitchen like a flash flood. It was coming from everywhere, from jawbreaker-sized speakers that Kate knew were hidden in plants and velcroed behind picture frames.

Kate spent the next five minutes trying to figure out the Wolf range. She was right: it had never been used; it still had heavy-duty plastic wrap in the ovens. Just when she thought she had it working, Pedro was back. He'd quickly combed his damp hair, but the wavy ends were getting away from him. He was still barefoot, but he wore trim khakis, his steadfast chain falling under his collar where his chest was almost smooth.

"I hope you know I was joking about dinner," he said, unwrapping one of the filets. "We'll work on it together."

Kate thought: How much do I really know about this guy?

"But first," he said, holding out his hand, "let's have a dance."

Kate looked at the hand. There was no excuse for a dance. They weren't at a night club where even Kingsley might jitterbug with the wives of the athletes, where even Kate might humor Georgie Porshay. There was no band, no Sandy to tap Pedro on his shoulder to cut in, just Pedro with his outstretched hand.

"Just one," he said. "I promise." At that moment Bugs started blowing pink fluorescent bubbles from his mouth. The bubbles surrounded them, shimmering and dancing to the ceiling.

Kate giggled, it was so corny, but corny like a hundred bouquets of red roses delivered to her office. Pedro held her close, his hands firm on her lower back.

When the song ended, Pedro did not take his arms off her back, and the new song began. "I keep thinking about you that night at the church," he said. "I tell myself, she came—she came to see me."

"Have you gone back?"

"No," he said. "I promised my mother I'd go to mass Christmas Eve, but it bothers me—the church taking money from poor people."

"You don't believe?"

"I guess I don't know what to believe."

The bubbles were getting dense. They were no longer fairytale bubbles to complete the fantasy—just Bugs Bunny spewing detergent suds. It suddenly seemed so obvious what they were doing—they were standing in the middle of his dining room, groping each other. Pressed up against him, she breathed his soap scent. The metallic chain—the crucifix she imagined he wore close to his heart—could be his locker key at 3Com. She thought about digging her hand under his collar and yanking it out, putting everything on the table.

Pedro's sense of duty to a family a half a world away and God who had been so heavy in the air in that small church had given her a comfort that was now fleeting.

What are you looking for in a relationship? Axel Staperfene had asked her. She would have answered, *this fantasy* (if she hadn't been so annoyed)—Pedro chipping away at her armor with his questions, so certain about her; seductions with bubbles and dances, candlelit dinners; a man so secure in his faith, a faith that things might be O.K., a faith that might rub off on her.

But Sandy was the one who knew that she got stomach aches when she was home with the kids, that she was hard on books and hard on shoes. He was the one (as pissed off as it made her) who had told her she needed a good dose of faith. But he wasn't crazy about her. She needed crazy about her. She needed crazy (not insanity like Peter the Red), but crazy enough not to want to move in with the boys.

The song ended. *How do you know?* Axel's voice echoed off. Were all affairs about things you wanted and weren't getting, but maybe hadn't asked for?

Kate glanced at the bloody meat on the counter, then at her hand smudged with blood where Pedro had touched her in his haste to move things along.

"Did Peter tell you the news?" he asked as he dipped her. "I signed with you guys."

"You signed with Peter?" She was upside down.

"You look so crushed," he said, pulling her up. Upside-down wasn't her best angle. He rolled his knuckles softly along her cheek. "You're all the same firm."

"No, it's great," Kate said, her throat tight. "You'll do very well." She wasn't surprised, not really. She also wasn't surprised that there was no reason for her to be here, other than to wreck her life.

Pedro hugged her; she stiffened. She would leave through the front door if he let her. She would live with the children and the dog and the mice; she wouldn't trade one set of problems for another.

"You should have told me," Pedro said. "You thought it would affect us, right? There's so many things I don't know about you."

"It's fine, Pedro. You know, it's getting really smoky in here."

"The stove!" Pedro turned. The Wolf was lit like a torch; the flames were licking at the fan mail on the refrigerator.

The fire alarm whooped then bleated. Kate had noticed the fancy alarm box. The SFFD would be there in seconds.

"I've got a fire extinguisher here somewhere," Pedro said, scrambling for the sink; the flames were spreading down the counter, torching the paper grocery bag. Orange flames leapt into the dining room, igniting a paisley dining room chair.

Kate whacked at the chair with a damp dish rag, but the flames engulfed it. The room quickly filled with smoke; her eyes burned.

"Let's get out of here, Pedro!"

He was still rummaging under the sink. The fire was making a horseshoe around the kitchen, trapping them. She grabbed his arm and he backed out from under the sink.

"My chair!" he screamed, as Kate pulled him. Something coughed overhead, then the sprinklers blasted them.

Then she heard pounding at the door, the splintering of wood.

Eight firefighters dressed in full gear emerged through the smoke. The first one in, a tall woman, trained a hose on the flaming chair. The next one held an axe slivered with wood from Pedro's mahogany front door. Kate knew the hold on that axe before she saw Sandy's determined face under the black-and-yellow hat.

He didn't see her and she hid next to Pedro in the hallway as Sandy stormed the kitchen in full view of their dinner preparations—disfigured candles, torched basil, and charred meats. She folded her arms across her now soaking, transparent dress, unsteady in her extreme shoes that no human should wear.

As they finished putting out the fire, a cold wind whistled through the house. Kate was drenched and shivering—spaghetti straps fell off her shoulders. She pictured the rivulets of mascara down her cheeks. "Hope you got that insurance we talked about," she said.

Pedro kicked at the floorboard with his bare feet.

"All clear!" Sandy yelled.

He believes in this job, Kate thought, with its hard-earned moments of exhilaration.

Sandy finished winding up a hose. He moved amongst Pedro's incinerated furniture with the ease of someone who'd never had a desk job. His eyes were lit, the two-day growth of his beard a little sexy this time. Then he saw her. He lifted off his hat and placed it over his heart and walked a straight line toward her. Kate caught a glimpse of the shiny question mark-shaped scar under his jaw.

Of course, it was him.

"Who's this guy?" Pedro asked.

"My husband."

Sandy stepped up to Kate, not with the blind jealous rage she'd hoped for, but a blindness to anyone but her. "I'm off work now," he said. "Are you coming home?"

Kate took his hand.

"I'm sorry, sir," Sandy said to Pedro, "you'll have to leave now."

Sandy led Kate outside, past Pedro's Corvette in the driveway, to the hook-and-ladder at the curb.

He picked her up and carried her over a moat of puddles that had formed around the truck.

"We've got a Christmas tree at home that's a fire hazard, sir, and needs your attention," Kate said.

Across the Mission, in the eaves of the craggy church steeples, the orange sunset had burned down into embers. □